THE
DEVIL
OF
ECHO LAKE

By
Douglas Wynne

JournalStone
San Francisco

JournalStone books may be ordered through booksellers or by contacting:

JournalStone
199 State Street
San Mateo, CA 94401
www.journalstone.com

ISBN: 978-1-936564-53-8   (sc)
ISBN: 978-1-936564-59-0   (hc)
ISBN: 978-1-936564-60-6   (ebook)

Library of Congress Control Number: 2012941729

Printed in the United States of America
JournalStone rev. date: October 19, 2012

Cover Design and Artwork: Jeff Miller

Edited By: Dr. Michael R. Collings

ENDORSEMENTS

"Ancient gods, haunted forests, the Devil, and Rock & Roll. What more do you need for a great story? *The Devil of Echo Lake* is a beautifully crafted book that puts a unique spin on the classic tale of Robert Johnson and the crossroads. In the first few pages, Douglas Wynne grabs hold and never lets go. You can't miss with this fantastic debut." — Brett J. Talley, author of Bram Stoker Award™ finalist *That Which Should Not Be* and *The Void*.

"*The Devil of Echo Lake* delves into the oh-so-thin interface between reality and the supernatural. Douglas Wynne handles complex issues deftly in this novel. His characters, real and otherwise, ring true. His writing is strong and appropriate to his subjects—temptation, acceptance, realization, and ultimately redemption." — Dr. Michael R. Collings, Author of *The Slab*, *The House Beyond the Hill*, and other tales of wonder and fear.

"Doug delivers the quiet, atmospheric horror that pervades the story with the deft touch of an experienced writer. I may not have heard of Douglas Wynne before I started reading *The Devil of Echo Lake*, but now that I have finished this excellent debut novel, I can honestly say that I'll be looking for more of his work in the future." — Joseph Nassise, bestselling author of the *Templar Chronicles* and the *Great Undead War series*.

"This book sings a dark, dark song -- it's got a grim rhythm that even rock-and-roll has forgotten. If you're standing at the crossroads and you don't know where to go, take the road that leads you to this book." — Chuck Wendig, Author *of Blackbirds* and *Mockingbird*.

ACKNOWLEDGEMENTS

I'm very grateful to my early readers for their insightful critiques throughout the drafting process: Jeff Miller, Phil O'Flaherty, Chuck Killorin, Melissa Corliss-DeLorenzo, Sue Little, Jen Salt, Glyn Forster, Stacia Decker, and Jill Sweeney-Bosa. Thanks also to Carol Kutz for making a lifelong reader out of me in the sixth grade, to my grandmother—to whom this book is dedicated—for typing up my first horror stories without batting an eye, to my parents for always supporting my creative endeavors, to Jeff for rocking the cover, to the gnomes who pluck weeds in the story garden at AQ Connect, to Christopher C. Payne and his team at JournalStone for being allies and angels just when I most needed them, to Brett J. Talley for helping me to see the forest for the trees, and most of all to my amazing wife Jen for believing.

For Barbara Whitehouse
1927 - 2012
I'll be looking at the moon, but I'll be seeing you.

11/7/12

For Ed,
Thanks for reading!
Best,
Douglas Wynne

PART I
BIG IN JAPAN

"In the middle of the journey of life, I came to myself in a dark wood, where the direct way was lost."
Dante

ONE

Billy Moon didn't know exactly when he had sold his soul. There had been no pact penned in blood, no dusty crossroads. Maybe it happened that night on the bridge, the night he met Trevor Rail. Maybe his soul was tucked away in one of those paragraphs of legalese he had skimmed over hungrily in his mid-twenties—his eternal spirit leveraged against mechanical royalties and recoupable advances in a five-point font. *I sold my soul,* he thought, and it fit. Like a perfect chorus summing up the verses of his life, it rhymed with the rest of him.

* * *

On the last day of the *Lunatic* tour, Billy received a harmless-looking fax that felt like a death sentence. It was from his manager, Danielle Del Vecchio. She had left Japan two days earlier, confident that the final show at the Tokyo Bay NK Hall would go off without a hitch. Billy took the envelope from the bellhop and mumbled, "Domo." He'd given up trying to tip them, but it still felt weird not to. As the suite door glided shut, he collapsed into a stuffed leather chair. He shook the page free of the envelope, which he tried to fling across the room like a Frisbee, although it disappointed him by flying like a bat.

Billy,

Trevor just called to inform us that he has you booked at Echo Lake Studios in upstate NY for the next 2 months. I know it's short notice, but Gravitas doesn't mind paying for you to write in the studio this time. It's a residential studio out in the woods, so you'll be free of distractions. We'll fly to NY on 10/30. You're doing the MTV Halloween show on 10/31, and then I'll have a limo take you up to the studio on 11/2. Would have just called, but now you have your schedule in writing so you won't forget. Break a leg tonight!
xoxo

Danielle

Billy let the page flutter to the floor. He took a cigarette from the pack on the coffee table and lit up. The afternoon sun warmed his face and hurt his eyes. He could see his reflection on the dull gray surface of the TV screen: tangled, unwashed hair, black kimono, belly hanging over the waistband of his underwear. He didn't like the image so he exhaled, banishing it with a breath of smoke.

Why couldn't she call him on the phone like she had every other day for the past ten months? So he'd have it in writing? No, she had to *fax* to tell him he'd be spending the next two months hunting songs for the third album in the woods with Trevor Rail because she knew he was having reservations about Rail. It was just like Danielle to drop the bomb from a safe distance. *Just* got a phone call from Trevor, my ass. But then, if honesty was to be the word of the day, he had to admit that "reservations" was an understatement. What he felt about Rail was more like pure, undiluted dread.

He hadn't talked to her about that in any depth, but if he had, she would have just told him to stop smoking so much pot because it was making him paranoid. And she'd probably be right. Still, could she blame him for being paranoid when he had to divine his fate from some fax while everyone with the decision-making power in his life was on the other side of the world?

Billy looked at the heavy oak door and remembered where he was. Someone was knocking, and he wasn't sure how long they'd been at it. The knocking started up again, but now it was deeper. Someone had switched to pounding on the door with the side of a fist.

"Billy, you better be getting laid 'cause if you're passed out drunk, I'm gonna have to beat your ass."

Flint.

Billy opened the door. The pressure that had been building in his head over the fax dissipated at the sight of Flint's mischievous grin—missing tooth, scruffy dimpled cheek, and all.

The guitarist scanned him from top to bottom and back again, from behind a pair of sunglasses that looked like welders' goggles. It was a wonder he could see anything at all through them, but he must have because he said, "Christ, Billy, don't you even dress yourself when Danielle's not around? Come on, we gotta be at sound check in half an hour. Don't want to blow it on the last night, do we?"

Billy gave a half-hearted smile. "No. After all, we're finally big in Japan."

On the way to the limo with Flint, Billy was called over to the front desk by the concierge who had a small package waiting for him, delivered by a local shop. Billy unwrapped it in the back of the car, finding under the brown paper a dragon-themed red and gold silk brocade box with silver clasps.

"Sexy," Flint said beside him, looking at what lay on the gold silk lining.

"A knife," Billy said, stating the obvious.

"Not just a knife, bro. That's an authentic Japanese *tanto*."

Billy picked it up gingerly and turned it over in his hands. The handle was scarlet silk wrapped in a diamond pattern over some black textured material. The silver end-cap on the hilt was engraved with a cherry blossom. Three more flowers in mother-of-pearl adorned the black-lacquered wooden sheath. It was stunning, exuding a graceful, evil beauty.

"What's a *tanto*?" he asked, staring at it.

"That's one of the three blades a samurai would carry. My old roommate was way into this shit. Samurai movies every other night. Dude had some replicas too, but nothing like this. That's real stingray skin on the handle."

Billy drew the blade from the sheath and examined it—nine inches of tapered steel that looked sharper than anything he had ever handled in his life.

"*Whoa*, dude. Put it away before we hit a bump. That thing is sick. Who's it from?"

There was a small envelope in the box. It contained the knife's registration with the Japanese Ministry of Education and a second card with a sword-smith's insignia and a typed message:

Dear Billy,

A small token to celebrate your recent success on the Japanese charts. Please bring it with you to our sessions. I think it would be brilliant to get some photos of you with it for the cover art. Looking forward to working together again.

Yours,

Trevor

"It's from Trevor. He wants pictures of me with it."

"Cool."

"Samurai blade, huh? I thought they carried big swords."

"They had three different blades for different jobs. The katana would be for the battlefield—that's the long one. Then there was a medium size one for close combat, a waki-something-or-other, I forget. And this one here for ritual suicide if they were captured or disgraced."

Billy laughed without humor. "I've barely even written anything for the next album, and he already knows he wants me posing with a Japanese suicide knife in the artwork."

"See that's what makes ol' Third Rail a marketing genius. He's already thinking about how to bridge your new Asian audience with your crazy goth chicks, who like to cut themselves. The crafty fucker."

* * *

They closed the show that night with "I Like to Watch," a

techno-metal song *Rolling Stone* had called, "a scathing high-decibel diatribe against the vampiristic nature of the news media." Billy staggered out of a foggy wash of blue lasers as he struck the final chord on his blood-red Les Paul, then slammed his fist down on top of his amplifier, making the spring reverb inside it rattle and shudder in what became a series of explosions echoing throughout the hall. Only when the sound had almost faded did the applause swell up and break over the stage. Exhausted and bathed in sweat, Billy was once again impressed by how intently Japanese audiences listened. In America there was always some drunk guy yelling during a quiet section, but that never happened here.

He handed the guitar off to Phil, his tech, bowed low to the crowd, and ran down the metal stairs beside the drum riser. A second set of boot heels echoed in the narrow corridor, and he cast a glance over his shoulder at Flint. Looking ahead again, Billy threw his arm out behind him, pointing at the floor somewhere in front of Flint, then swept it forward to point at the double doors at the end of the corridor and the security guard stationed in front of them. He passed the dressing room and heard the guitarist's steps falter.

"Where are you going?" Flint called.

"Out. Come on."

"The street? What are you, tripping? You'll be caught in an autograph mob."

"Not if you hurry up. Most of them are still wondering if that was the last encore."

"No they're not. I saw the house lights come up."

"Then we really better move."

Billy and Flint shoved their shoulders into the doors and pushed through into a clear night sparkling with city lights.

A small group of Japanese goths flocked up the steps to the exit with CDs and permanent markers held aloft.

"Billy, I don't see the car," Flint said. "I don't think we're on the right street."

"Don't worry about it. I just want to get some air."

"That's the last thing you'll get if we hang around here."

Billy looked around at the kids. There were five of them, who had probably skipped the last song to stake out this particular exit. *Well, they got lucky.*

"Hey, are you all together? Did you come to the show together?" Billy asked as he scribbled a black squiggle across the front of a jewel case.

They all started talking at once, and he couldn't make out a coherent sentence, so he said, "Who has a car?"

A muscular kid wearing a wife-beater and a small silver cross on a chain said, "I have a van."

Billy noticed that this kid was the only rocker among the goths, with their black clothes, makeup and dyed hair. This one looked like most of the Japanese rock fans he'd seen, a walking advertisement for American corporations: Converse sneakers, Levi's jeans, pack of Marlboros poking out of the pocket of a plaid shirt, unbuttoned to reveal the beater and the cross. Totally Americanized from his smokes to his personal savior.

"Where's it parked? I want to get out of here."

One of the goth girls started jumping up and down, tugging at the bottom of her sweater. The kid with the van smiled. He looked at Flint, "You coming too?"

Flint glanced at Billy. "This is not a good idea, bro. It's Tokyo, for fuck's sake. I couldn't read a train map if I had to."

"You're such an old lady," Billy said. Then to the rocker kid, "It's our last night here. Take us some place interesting. Show us something we can't see at home."

"Where's home?" the kid asked. He seemed way too cool for the situation. Billy decided he must not be a fan, just a ride for some of these other kids. When the jumping girl settled down and clasped her arms around the rocker's bicep, Billy decided she was probably his sister. There was a resemblance.

"Good question. Flint, where is home? New York? I have a house in San Francisco. Fuck, I don't know. I think the Hilton is home."

The kid laughed and said, "Man, this place want to *be* New York, and you have shit in California you won't find here, but I can definitely show you something you don't see at Hilton."

"Well then I guess it's not anything sexual. I'm game. Flint?"

"Man, you're in a dangerous mood."

Billy just grinned.

"Yeah, I'm game." Flint sighed.

"Kiyoi," the kid said over his shoulder. "Tell your friends they have to take the train home."

"Why can't they come too?" she whined.

"Not enough room. And your idol want to see something exotic. I'm not taking a bunch of kids."

"Where we taking them?"

To Billy it sounded like the kid said, "Tosainnuring."

The girl gasped. "That's so cool. Guys, you have to go home." This was met with groans of complaint. "Give me your CDs. Maybe they sign them in the van. Come, come on, give them to me. I'll call you guys tomorrow. I promise."

The rocker, who said his name was Munetaka, trotted across the street and unlocked a white van. Billy, Flint, and Kiyoi followed.

The city dwindled behind them until a few faint stars could be seen twinkling through a veil of smog over Mount Fuji. Billy had feared the drive might be one of those regrettable private moments with a fan in which he was deluged with questions, but Kiyoi was deadly silent after he and Flint signed the stack of CDs. Her English was good, but she appeared to be too afraid of saying something stupid to venture any conversation at all. Billy considered breaking the ice just to put her at ease, but after singing for two hours, his voice was hoarse and he was content not to use it if he didn't have to.

When the van stopped, Flint pulled the door open. They found themselves in a pockmarked, muddy lot in front of a warehouse with blacked out windows, somewhere south of the city. A couple of orange sodium lights poured their jaundiced glow over the lot, illuminating cars whose riders' muted voices could be faintly heard from somewhere inside the cinder-block building. Shouting and cheering seeped through the cracks in the walls, mingling in the cool, quiet night with the ringing in Billy's ears.

Munetaka rapped his knuckles on a door Billy hadn't noticed. It opened to reveal a lean Japanese man in mechanic's overalls. Munetaka rolled up the sleeve of his flannel shirt and flashed a tattoo Billy couldn't quite make out. It might have been a stylized animal mask like the ones on totem poles. The doorman waved them in.

They descended a flight of stairs lit by a series of red neon tubes and stepped into the back of a crowd. The men at the front were yelling, their shouts the only sounds in the room. Whatever they were here to witness, it didn't involve music, and although there was plenty of alcohol being passed around among the revelers, the quiet put Billy on guard. It was unsettling to be in a crowd of drinkers without so much as a rave beat. Even sex shows had a beat. What kind of party was this, anyway?

Flint leaned into Billy's loose, black curls and said, "What do you think, bondage show?"

Billy studied his friend for signs of fear. "I don't know. It smells strange in here. Some of that Jap porn is pretty foul."

He felt a skinny arm encircle his waist, and Kiyoi slid around him as if he were a pole in a strip club. She had her mouth open, and he saw a little round tablet on the flat of her tongue. In the red light, he couldn't tell what color the tab was, but what difference did it make? Whatever it was, she'd apparently had one already and it must have loosened her up. He bent down and allowed her to push the pill into his mouth on her soft tongue. Her kiss tasted like cinnamon, medicine, and sweat.

Billy swallowed the pill.

"What is this place?" he asked her.

"Come on," she said, tugging on his arm, pulling him away from Flint and into the crowd. A moment later they spilled into a space where there were no more bodies to buffer them, and Billy fell to his knees on the concrete floor. It was shit—that was what he had smelled. He felt his heart hammering hard in his ribcage.

At first he thought he was seeing a six-legged crimson beast spinning toward him. Then he realized it was two dogs, entangled, tearing at each other's throats, blood pouring down the swaying dewlap of the one on the bottom, mixing with its fawn coat and the red neon light to form an image of homogenous murky gore. The dogs went about the work of mauling each other in eerie silence. Billy had grown up with dogs, was anything but afraid of them, yet here on his hands and knees just a few feet away from the vicious melee, he felt a short burst of piss escape him before he could stop it.

He clutched at Kiyoi's long black skirt and looked pleadingly up at her, "What did you give me?"

"Shabu."

"What?"

"Speed."

He tried to stand, but his boot slipped out from under him in a puddle of dog blood. His chin hit the concrete floor, and as he bit his tongue on impact, he tasted his own blood. Kiyoi squeezed his jacket in fistfuls at the shoulders and tried to pull him up, but she had only succeeded in getting him back on his knees again when the dogs broke apart, the loser slumping to the floor in a heap of mangy fur and disjointed bones. The crowd roared with equal parts triumph and outrage.

A shaven-headed handler with a sharp black goatee stepped into the ring and slipped a wire loop over the winner's head, but the dog had already made eye contact with Billy. It lunged at him, flashing its frothy red jaws in a quick, chattering rhythm that spattered droplets of blood and saliva across Billy's cheek and forehead. Later he would wonder if the dog had reacted to his prone position, his submissive stature at the moment it had noticed him, fresh from the kill. Or did it smell his urine and the scent of fear radiating from his pores as the speed was transmuted into sweat? But in that space of three deafening heartbeats, when the dog's eyes locked in on him, all he could think of was Trevor Rail and a fragment of an old, old song playing to the beat of his heart.

Got to keep movin, blues fallin down like hail

Got to keep movin, hellhounds on my trail

Billy felt his fingers and toes going numb as fear surged inward, closing off his senses. Pink video noise swarmed from the neon tubes in his peripheral vision, narrowing the tunnel through which he viewed the dog's thick neck, bloody muzzle, and flashing fangs. The rush of blood roaring in his ears drowned out the foreign voices. He imagined the pressure with which it would jet across the room if the dog bit him. His throat constricted, but he soon realized that this wasn't another symptom of his terror; someone was pulling on the collar of his leather jacket. Someone stronger than the girl was hauling him to his feet, wrenching him back from the mouth of the monster and into the crowd.

* * *

Danielle Del Vecchio flipped her cell phone open, dropped it on the tile floor and exclaimed, "Shit!" through her sea kelp mask. Flavio, her manicurist, picked it up and placed it back in her left hand, then resumed his work on her right. She reclined again and said, "Yes?" It was Donnie Lamar at Gravitas.

"He's fine," she said. "Don, get a hold of yourself. I said he's fine.... What? No, it wasn't a pit bull.... Uh-Huh. A Tosa Inu.... I don't know. It's some kind of Japanese mastiff. I *guess* it looks like a pit bull. I don't know. Who cares? It didn't bite him.... It scared the living hell out of him, but he's fine now.... Yes, his hands are *fine*, not a scratch. Stop being so hysterical, okay? He'll probably get a song out of it.... Mmm hmm. Yeah, I'll tell him. Flint was there. He's okay too.... Don, can you hang on a sec? I have another call coming in. It might be Billy.

"Hello? This is she.... Evan Malhoney? The fireman. Billy's told me so much about you. What can I do for you, Evan? Billy's on his way home from Tokyo today. He gets into LAX at nine ten tonight.... What?" She sat up straight and wiped the kelp strips off her face, yanking her hand back from Flavio so fast she cut her finger on the edge of his emery board.

"Pen, pen!" she whispered. Flavio shot out of the room and returned before the door could finish swinging shut, bearing a ballpoint and a pad with the salon letterhead.

"What's the best number to reach you at? Give it to me anyway.... Okay. Sunday, Pearce and Sons Funeral Home, Port Jefferson," she said, scribbling. When she had finished writing, she closed her eyes and listened. She said, "Evan, I'm so very sorry." She looked at the phone, took a breath and pressed a button.

"Donnie? That was Billy's brother. His father just died of a heart attack. He's going to New York sooner than he thinks."

* * *

Billy Moon, his band, and crew landed in L.A. on Friday night in the rain. Danielle was waiting for him in Arrivals. Billy knew someone was dead before she even touched his arm and searched in vain for a place to sit him down in the empty corridor. She wasn't wearing any makeup, and her face was so solemn and pale that he almost didn't recognize her at first. If he trusted anyone, he trusted

Danielle, but seeing her face devoid of all pretense was something new. He had learned a long time ago that acting was an essential skill in a rock manager's toolkit. She needed to change faces from mother, to motivational speaker, to mad dog depending on who she encountered around the next corner, or on the next call in the queue. Seeing her standing there in the vast vaulted hall of Terminal 4 with no mask or strategy in her eyes both embarrassed and scared him.

She took his hands in hers. Travelers rushed past with their coffee cups and paperbacks, rolling their luggage to the exits and taxi stands. A soothing female voice made some echoing announcement. Then Billy was taking a fist full of Kleenex from Danielle, marveling at how quickly his eyes had filled with too much water to see anything but splintered light and how much sniffling he had to do all of a sudden to keep the mucus from dangling down into his lap in this crowded place where someone might recognize him.

He caught himself resenting her for exposing him to this unexpected grief in public. But then he remembered that he had made a career out of being emotional in public, an observation that made him laugh and cry at the same time, as he wiped his face and tried to breathe. Keith, his bodyguard, stepped in front of him and folded his arms over his broad chest. The foot traffic flowed wide around them, as if the man were a boulder in a stream.

Billy told Danielle to get him on the next plane to New York. After doing her best to convince him to at least spend the night before flying again, she relented and bought him a ticket. By midnight he was back in the air, without so much as a change of clothes, flying over the Great Plains with lawyers and executives whose laptops illuminated the first-class cabin like a video arcade. In their company he looked even more like a vampire than usual. He turned inward, behind his sunglasses and headphones, letting his favorite duo, Jack Daniels and Joni Mitchell, lull him to sleep.

When he woke up, the sun was rising behind New York and the pilot was telling them to fasten their seat belts for the descent into JFK.

On the ground, Billy kept the shades on to avoid eye contact and kept walking when anyone called his name or touched his jacket. As a kid, he'd thought rock stars looked cool in sunglasses. As an aspiring musician in his twenties, he'd found them pretentious. Now he knew them for what they really were—privacy. Eye contact was how they trapped you, the leeches who wanted to rub up against your aura of fame and take the residue of glamour back to their mundane lives. It never seemed to cross their minds that you had mundane bullshit to deal with too. Hunger, grief, a moody girlfriend, a dead father, and maybe some of that was on your mind today as you made your way from here to there on your tired feet like everyone else. Didn't they understand that he had bad days just like they did? If he didn't want to sign his name every fifty yards on a given day, did it really have to mean that he was actually "an asshole in person?" He fixed his eyes on a far-off point on the concourse ceiling and kept walking.

On the street he flashed a wad of cash at a cab driver and climbed in. By midday he was on the north shore of Long Island winding through tree-canopied suburban streets he hadn't seen in years. The cab dropped him at number 14 Huckleberry Lane.

The house he had grown up in no longer resembled the one he remembered. His father had been renovating it for as long as Billy could recall. He suspected the man hadn't even been finished working on it the day he died, but the small transformations it had undergone each year while Billy was away chasing his dream amounted to what looked like a whole new house: a porch where the hedges had been, a bay window where there had been none, new vinyl siding. The old cars had been replaced too and Billy wondered as he walked up the path, if the classic convertible Mustang he had bought the old man when *Eclipse* went platinum was in the garage. The house was still a two-story Cape, but it looked like an impostor sitting among the trees he had climbed before the guitar came into his life.

Then he looked up the cracked cement steps and any feeling he had that this wasn't home evaporated at the sight of his mother in her nightgown behind the storm door, the reflection of red leaves and cotton clouds overlaid on her ghostly silhouette.

TWO

The first leaves were starting to fall when Jake Campbell stepped off the Greyhound bus in Echo Lake, New York. He had started his journey the previous day in Florida with a cup of coffee in one hand and a suitcase in the other. There had been no one to send him off as he boarded the bus in the gunmetal-gray, pre-dawn light. Ally had kissed him good-bye and wished him luck back at their apartment in Winter Park, and she was probably already asleep again by the time he bought his ticket.

As the bus passed through the Carolinas, Jake imagined her cleaning the apartment after the previous night's party and then maybe going to the library to return the books he'd left with her—the apartment where he no longer lived (unless he fucked this up) and the library where he would no longer be a member. It still felt unreal, things had happened so fast.

By the time the bus reached New York, Jake felt unsettled. He tried to tell himself it was just the fast food and the long hours on the road, but when his sneakers hit the sidewalk of Main Street in Echo Lake and the beauty of the Catskill Mountains spread out before him above the rooftops, he had to admit he was nervous as all hell about his ability to do the job.

Jake pulled his suitcase out of the luggage bay and scanned the street for anyone who looked like studio personnel. *How am I supposed to tell?* He had barely formed the thought when a stocky young man with a shaven head, braided beard, and eyebrow ring nodded at him and extended a hand tattooed with a scorpion on the webbing between thumb and forefinger. Jake shook it, surprised by the gentleness of the grip.

"I'm Brent. Are you Jake?"

"How'd you know?"

Brent shrugged, "You look like a college guy."

"Hmm."

"I don't mean anything by it, just nobody else who got off... Come on, car's this way."

Brent led him to the rusted remains of a Buick station wagon and scooped a handful of food wrappers, plastic bottles, and dirty socks out of the hatchback to make room for Jake's suitcase. Another scoop and toss in the front seat cleared a collection of CD jewel cases with fractured covers to make room for Jake's feet. The car shot out onto Main Street with more speed than Jake expected, the dashboard buzzing to the pulse of System of a Down.

Jake was grateful for the deafening music because it absolved him of the need to make conversation while they passed through town. Hopefully the ride would be long enough to hear some of Brent's thoughts about the studio, but for now he just wanted to take it all in. He and Ally had looked at the Echo Lake Chamber of Commerce website, but there hadn't been many photos of the town. Now he had a chance to take quick inventory of what the place had to offer.

It was weird, passing through a small town in a shitbox car doing something just shy of the speed of sound and trying to assess the place as a new home, all to a soundtrack of dark, paranoid heavy metal. There was a Laundromat (essential), supermarket, graveyard, funeral home, Greek restaurant (looked decent), library (big enough for Ally?), never mind—bookstore, head shop, hardware store, ice cream shop, movie theater, and we're out of town watching the trees and farm stands go by. Jake knew there was more to it than what had just flashed by, but he didn't know it would be two weeks before he would have another chance to see it by daylight.

In the middle of nowhere, without so much as slowing down, Brent turned the car off the paved road and into a gap in the trees Jake hadn't even noticed. Clouds of brown dust swirled around the vehicle as it bounced and rocked over potholes, climbing a dirt road through the densely wooded hillside.

"We keep a low profile," Brent said. "It's like the fuckin' Bat

Cave."

Jake glimpsed the occasional barn or cottage through the trees, but when the road became more of a wide, steep trail, he couldn't help musing that maybe it would end in a desolate backwoods clearing where his driver would rape and murder him. A couple of deer looked up from grazing just long enough to take notice of the lumbering car.

Brent downshifted and forced the tired wagon up a final, steep incline. At the top of the hill, the sky opened up and Jake could see the muted purple peaks of the mountains in the distance again, now forming a regal backdrop for the building in the foreground. Tall and sprawling, it was a marvel of cedar planks that fanned out in spirals from its pyramidal peak down to its multi-tiered deck, a cascading series of high windows reflecting the lush pine forest in fractured segments on all sides. Something about it reminded Jake of a galleon out of a pirate movie.

"Here we are," Brent said, "Main Building. Eddie's office, maintenance department and tape library. It's also Studio A. Studio B is—"

"In the barn, right? And Studio C is in an old church."

"Yep, you've done your homework. C'mon, let's see if Eddie's around."

They found Eddie in Studio A, an enormous concrete room with a vaulted ceiling from which a small fleet of semi-cylindrical wooden sound-reflecting baffles hung on strings, resembling rowboats seen from under water. The walls were draped with tapestries and horse blankets for additional absorption, and the vast wood floor was covered here and there with oriental carpets. Eddie was directing a couple of assistants or runners, who were pushing a grand piano into a corner. He bounced a basketball and shouted directions, the sound of each impact of the ball against the floor telling Jake all about the gorgeous reverberation of the place.

Eddie turned and threw the ball at Jake, who caught it partly with his hands, but mostly with his stomach.

"You Jake?"

"Yeah."

"Eddie O'Reilley." He extended a huge hand.

Jake dropped the ball and shook the hand.

"How was your trip?"

"Fine. Took buses all the way from Orlando like Susan said to."

"We'll reimburse you for your ticket. Did you get a receipt?"

"Yes."

"Come on, I'll show you the control room. You won't be out here in the tracking room much on this project—it's a rap session, so it'll be all about samplers in the control room. There's a booth over there for vocals, but that'll probably be the only mic. We're just clearing the live room so they can use it as a basketball court when they're not working."

Jake followed Eddie's blue flannel shirt and shaggy head of white hair into the control room, where the older man sat down in a mesh-and-leather swivel chair. He sent its twin gliding across the floor to Jake. This time Jake caught with just his hands. He sat down and scanned the room, feeling like the first mate on the *Starship Enterprise*. There was a state-of-the-art SSL mixing console spanning the entire length of the room below a wide double-plate window, through which he could see runners wheeling the basketball hoop into place. The console was flanked on both sides by multi-track tape machines— almost relics in the year 1998, but in the other corner, wearing the blue trunks, was the Pro Tools rig that was about to do a smack-down on the mammoth multi-tracks and send them to the Smithsonian.

Eddie ran his hand through his thick hair and Jake noticed a wedding band. His new boss had bags under his eyes and a friendly, disarming smile.

"So this is the room you'll be working in for the next... two weeks, I think. You'll be second engineer to a guy named Rick Delahunt. The producer is Tutenkhamen. Young guy, but he's hot all of a sudden. The artist is Tokin' Negro. They get here on Monday, so you have today and tomorrow to get to know the patch bay and set up some of their gear. The only things I'm sure you'll need a lot of are D.I. boxes and adapter cables. You can borrow some from Studio B, but make sure you check with Brian first. He's the assistant in there this week. They're doing some last minute overdubs on a David Bowie project."

Jake's eyes must have widened at that.

"Yeah, the Duke. You like his stuff?"

Jake nodded.

"Me too. In fact when I was about your age, I was the assistant on a record he tracked in the city."

"Cool."

"We're going to put you up in one of the cottages we keep for clients here on the grounds. You'll have a kitchen, bedroom and bathroom while you're on this project and for a while after it's done, until you have time to look for an apartment. But no housekeeping, so do your own dishes. If you're even there long enough to eat. I doubt you'll see much of the place."

"That's fine. How will I get to work? I'm gonna buy a used car, but for now…?"

"A runner will give you rides for now. Any other questions?"

"Not until I look around."

"Okay, did Susan talk to you about pay?"

"Not yet."

"Bloody Christ. Why can't people do their jobs? It starts at seven an hour. We can talk about a raise if it works out."

Jake nodded. It was what he had expected, but when his father—who had paid for a good chunk of his education—asked about it, he was probably going to present it as an annual figure, pre-tax.

"I know it's low," Eddie said, "but if this is what you want to do for a career, it's about getting experience at this point."

"I know. That's pretty much what my teachers said to expect."

"And you'll find that the cost of living around here is lower than Orlando. Sure is a *lot* lower than Manhattan. You can get a two bedroom with a fireplace for six-fifty a month." Eddie smiled and rose from his chair. "Well, I'll let you get acquainted with the gear."

* * *

Later, on the phone, Ally said, "That's nice, Jake, a fireplace? That'll be really useful if you don't get paid enough to make the heating bill."

"The heat will never be on because I'll never be home," Jake said. "Look, if I started out as a runner, it would take me about a year to even get to this point. They're kind of taking a chance on me."

"Who's your first client?"

"Tokin' Negro. Just got out of prison."

"No shit."

"None whatsoever."

"And how much are they paying for the studio time?"

"Uh, Studio A is twenty-five hundred per day."

"Of which you get seven dollars an hour to basically run the room. You're the cheapest tool they're renting, sweetie. You deserve more than that."

"But think of all my classmates who didn't get a placement, who racked up just as much debt, and now they have to schlep their resumes around L.A.—where I *know* you don't want to live, and neither do I—just so they can get a chance to make six an hour brewing coffee and emptying the trash."

"How can studios get away with that? That's not even minimum wage. Those guys could be making coffee at Starbucks for more than that and they'd be getting tips!"

"Ally, it's a competitive business. Very competitive."

"Well, I don't like it. I'm sorry."

"Maybe you just don't like me going away."

"Yeah."

"Everybody who succeeds goes through this stage. It's where you prove that you want it bad enough to pay your dues, and that you're not going to freak out some rock star who's in a vulnerable creative state by saying some fan-boy bullshit. It's where I prove I know what I'm doing and I'm not going to erase the damned tape. Then they'll pay me more."

"Okay. I *am* happy for you."

"I know."

There was a silence on the line. Jake looked out the back window of the cottage into the dark woods.

"David Bowie's here for a few days."

"Really?"

"Yeah. I don't know if I'll *see* him. He's in Studio B, which is in a barn somewhere. How fucking cool is that?"

"Pretty fucking cool."

"Will you come up and visit when this project is over? We can go apartment hunting together."

"Jake, I haven't decided yet if I'm moving."

"I know, but I have to live somewhere. You might as well like the place."

"Okay, I'll come. How much of the town have you seen?"

"Not much, but I think you'd like it. It's pretty artsy. I saw a coffee-table book lying around that tells how Echo Lake was an artists' community going back to the turn of the century. And Woodstock is close enough that you can still see which houses Jimi Hendrix and Bob Dylan once rented. You can tell it's New York City's backyard. I think you'd feel right at home here."

Silence on the line again.

"Allison?"

"I'll come and see you in a couple of weeks, when you have the time, okay? Just, let's not get ahead of ourselves. You should focus on your job right now. A lot is happening for you."

"I know. I've just been thinking about how you've already ruled out Florida for grad school, right? So why stay there while you're figuring it out?"

"Well, my parents are here, for one thing."

Outside the window something slid out of the trees and bounded across the grass about thirty yards from the cottage. Jake could barely make it out in the dusky light but it looked to be about the size of a deer, only white. The notion that it was a dog crossed his mind, but the way the light danced across its torso made it look like anything but fur. More like pale flesh stretched taut over a ribcage. It seemed to flicker in an odd way, like a projection. Jake squinted, but it had already disappeared into the tree line at the far end of the lawn. He peered into the shadows where it had vanished, then startled when a pair of violet lights flashed back at him, like cat's eyes reflecting passing headlights. The back of his neck prickled, and his stomach churned. But then, of course, he would feel unsettled with the long trip, the job jitters, and the fear of losing her.

"Jake, are you there?"

"Yeah. I'm tired."

"You sound funny. Are you okay?"

"Yup."

"Don't start lying to me now. You never have before. Look, we can talk about it, but I just won't know until I can see the place."

"No, it's okay. I think I'm more tired than I realized. I'm gonna go to bed. I have to get up early to get a handle on the room."

"Okay. Love you."

"I love you, too."

Jake hung up the phone, picked up his bottle of beer, and froze before it reached his lips. Something out there at the edge of the woods had caught his eye again, and he knew that it couldn't be, but it looked like a naked woman walking away.

THREE

There was a wake, with no coffin, just an urn, at a small funeral home. It was held in Port Jefferson, just fifteen miles from Billy's mother's house. *That's what it is now*, he realized, standing in the receiving line, shaking hands, and not hearing a word anyone said to him. *It's my mother's house. Not my parents' house. She lives there alone.* It seemed fundamentally wrong that it should be this way, his mother living by herself, but he couldn't think of anything to do about it.

On Monday evening they drove out to Montauk Point. Evan had a connection, through work, to the captain of the fireboat, and he had arranged to have the immediate family taken out on the boat at sunset to scatter the ashes at sea. It was what the man had wanted.

Billy read a poem by Yeats. Evan poured the ashes into the wind. William Malhoney Sr., hadn't been much for poetry but something about Yeats had resonated with his Irish blood. The old man had even memorized a few fragments just from returning to them over the years. Billy read "Into the Twilight."

Afterward, they went back to Evan and Sandy's house for coffee and pie.

"None for me," the widow said, waving the coffee pot away. "It'll just keep me up."

"Mom, I've made up a bed for you in the baby's room," Sandy said. "Evan and I would like you to stay here tonight. You're not working tomorrow, right?"

"No, my kids will have a substitute for the rest of the week. But Billy can drive me home. I fixed up his old room for him."

Evan stood and cleared the dirty pie plates. "Why don't you both stay here tonight? Billy can sleep on the living room couch; it's a convertible."

"It's fine with me, Mom," Billy said. "Then you can turn in as early as you like and I won't have to wake you just to drive home."

"Alright then, I think I'll go to bed now if we're staying." She rose and kissed her two boys goodnight. After kissing Billy's cheek, she laid her cold fingers against it and said, "Thank you for coming all the way from Japan, Billy. It means a lot to me that you're here."

He smiled faintly and said, "I didn't, Mom."

Sandy led her mother-in-law to the baby's room, leaving Billy and Evan alone at the table.

Evan said, "What? What's that look on your face mean?"

Billy sighed. "I don't know. She makes it sound like I'm a friend of the family. Like there was even a question of whether I'd come from California or Japan or Mars for that matter. She doesn't have to thank me for it. Makes me feel like a creep."

"You're upset because Mom thanked you?"

"No. Just…. Shit, forget it. Forget I said anything."

"You must feel pretty guilty if it ruffles your feathers that Mom's grateful to see you."

"Well, you know, Evan, only the Catholics can make you feel guilty by thanking you."

"Are you still on *that* soapbox?"

"Come on, you know it's true. We grew up in the same house. Hell, Mom used to bitch all the time about the guilt trips her mother laid on her."

"I thought you got all that bile out of your system on your first CD. You do know how to beat a dead horse. At Dad's funeral, no less. Unbelievable."

"Evan, it's just me and you in this kitchen, okay? It's not Dad's funeral. Forget I said anything. I didn't come half way around the world to fight with you."

Evan snorted a short laugh, "So it *is* a big deal: half way around the world. You have to cancel any concerts?"

"No. I didn't mean… I just thought she meant… Let's just drop it."

"Jeez, you're really sensitive."

"Well, Dad just died. I'm supposed to be sensitive, right?"

"You're supposed to be paranoid like that? Somebody says 'thanks for coming' and you read accusation into it? How do you deal with the critics in the paper?"

"I don't read that stuff."

"Well that's good, 'cause I saw some pretty unkind words about your last disc in *People* magazine."

"*People* isn't exactly speaking to my demographic."

"Whatever."

"You're jealous."

"Yeah, Billy, I'm jealous that I don't get to live my life on buses and in rehab clinics."

"It's the money, right?" Billy said. "Like when I bought the car for Dad. You didn't have one nice thing to say about it."

"Well since you brought it up, what the hell *was* that anyway? You don't hardly talk to the guy for five years and then you buy him a car one day? It was like you were sticking it in his face how you were right all along about being able to make a living at music, and as soon as you could do it, you had to prove it to him in his own terms, right? It's not like the car was a gift to thank him for years of support. It was about you having something to prove."

"It was not."

"Well, he knew it was."

"He said that?"

"He knew. You were showing him you could afford the nice things he couldn't afford for himself—because you were right about dropping out of school to get high and play in a band."

"Yeah, you're a real psychoanalyst, Evan. Did Sandy come up with that one? Of all things, I can't believe you're busting my balls about the car. I just wanted to do something nice for him."

"Then you should have called him from the road once in a while."

Billy said nothing. He looked at the ceiling. The silence was punctuated only by the sputtering of the coffee maker. Then he said, "Yeah, I should have."

"Coming home to see them sometimes would have meant more to him than buying them things."

"You were always closer to him. You were so much more like him. You still are. I know I'm a fuck-up, okay? It doesn't mean I like to hear it. I wanted to make him proud. He always told me I'd never make any money at music, and I just thought that when I did, maybe he wouldn't be so damned disappointed. I couldn't rebuild an engine with him like you did and have those hours you had with him, drinking beer in the garage... So I bought him a car. Big deal. Fuck, maybe I did have something to prove. I don't know; it doesn't matter now."

Billy stood up and said, "I'm gonna drive back to Mom's house. I'll pick her up in the morning and take her to breakfast. Tell her, okay?" He threw his jacket over his shoulder.

"Billy. Don't go. We have plenty of room for you. It's actually a really comfortable pull-out."

"I want to sleep in my old room tonight. Tell Sandy I said thanks for the pie." Billy opened the front door and felt in his jacket pocket for his mother's car keys.

"Hey, Billy. Are you gonna be around for at least a few days? For Mom."

"Yeah, I want to look up an old friend."

"Who's that?"

"Johnny Russo."

"What *trench coat* Johnny? Johnny Black Magic? *That* Johnny?"

"Yeah. He has a wife and kids now. Runs a restaurant."

"Okay. Remind me not to eat there."

Billy stepped out into the night and gently pulled the door closed behind him.

* * *

Jake was perched on a stool at the workbench in the shop, soldering dead cables and wondering if he was getting cancer from the lead fumes for seven dollars an hour, when the phone rang. It was Eddie, summoning him up to the office. On his way through the corridors and up the spiral stairs, Jake couldn't help wondering if he was in trouble.

Had the mix engineer at the Hit Factory in Manhattan called to complain that the track sheets didn't match what was on the tapes? Would he have heard it in Eddie's voice? The guy was a little hard to read, and a few words on the phone weren't enough.

Jake nodded at Eddie through the glass door of his office. The manager was sitting behind a cluttered desk in a forest of Post-it notes. He was on the phone, but he waved Jake in and pointed at a seat. Jake sat down and took in the framed album covers on the walls, the black and white photos on the desk.

The pretty lady had to be Eddie's wife. The fat, stately old man with the long, thinning white hair and Stetson must have been the late Charlie Hoffman, famed patriarch of Echo Lake Studios, and in his heyday, the power broker for at least three 1960's rock icons. His widow Lucy now owned the property.

"He's selling the studio in Hawaii?" Eddie said to the phone. "Just the gear? Well what kind of console is it? No, I'm not in the market for an API, but I might be interested in some of his outboard gear. What's he running for mic pre-amps? Uh-huh. Why's he selling?"

A long pause.

Eddie laughed. "It's not about the trends turning against him, it's about song craft. He should turn off the computer and write some decent tunes again.... Yeah.... Yeah.... Nobody listens to dance music outside of clubs anyway. *House* music? Tell him if he wants to write house music he should write another song like 'Horses in the Surf.' You write a song like that, you buy a big fuckin' house. Listen, Marty, I gotta go. Get back to me about those pre's, okay? Right. Talk to you."

Eddie put the phone down, leaned back in his chair, and brushed some pretzel crumbs off his blue denim shirt. He gestured at the bag on his desk, "Pretzel?"

"Thanks, I'm all set." Jake said.

"So how are you settling in? Susan tells me you moved out of the cottage. You find a nice apartment?"

"Yeah. Found a place on Main Street, right at the edge of town, just a few miles from the studio. And my girlfriend is even going to move up and give it a try."

"Good, good. How's the car search going?"

"I should have a beater soon. Maybe sometime next week."

"Okay, well I'm sure you can keep getting rides with the other guys until then."

Jake nodded.

"I have your next assignment. I want you to work on the Billy Moon record in Studio C. Starts on November second—that's next Tuesday." Eddie tossed a copy of the November schedule across the desk and brushed his hands together, sending salt grains onto the carpet.

"Cool. Who's the engineer?"

"Kevin Brickhouse."

"Wow."

"Yeah. It'll be an education. Trevor Rail is the producer. He's a little intense, but you'll do fine. Today I want you to go down there and get familiarized with the Neve board. You have any questions, find Brian. The church is also a residential studio. Sleeps four. I don't know if Moon is bringing a band with him, but we may put some of them up in the surrounding cottages if it's a big entourage. The church hasn't been used for housing in a while, so while you're down there this afternoon, I need you to help out with moving some antique furniture that's cluttering up the place. Call James LeBuff's pager; it's on the directory. Tell him to meet you there with his truck. Buff already knows which pieces have to go."

"Okay."

"You also need to call Brickhouse before Friday to find out which mics he wants to reserve."

"How long is the project scheduled for?"

"It's a big block of time. Moon will be writing in the studio— asinine, but good for us. They have the room until New Year's Day. After that, it's booked to another client. Don't worry; you won't be on that one, so you'll be able to catch up on some sleep before you're re-assigned."

It was a nice day for a long walk. The first thing Jake saw when the gravel road wound around the bend at the bottom of the hill was the belfry poking out above a stand of pines set against a backdrop of purple hills under drifting cloud shadows. It had rained in the morning and the mist was still burning off the trees. When he reached the church, he saw that Buff's pickup truck wasn't there yet. He guessed Charlie Hoffman must have had the trees planted like that to create a privacy screen.

A working church would have needed to stand out on the hillside to draw the locals to its doors, not hide behind a green curtain like this one. But the imported trees were not yet tall enough to conceal the building entirely. Jake expected it would take six or seven more years with heavy rains before the belfry was obscured.

Stepping under the canopy of boughs onto a carpet of brown pine needles and twigs glazed with crystallized sap, he found a weathered white clapboard building. There was a horn under the eaves, no doubt wired to the burglar alarm for which he had a code written on a business card in his wallet. A series of stained-glass windows adorned the side of the building, but he couldn't make out their subjects from his current vantage point. Around the corner, atop a set of concrete steps, he found a pair of high-arched doors with iron bindings.

He fished a crowded key ring out of his pocket and tried two before finding the one that popped the lock. Once the doors were opened, he had one minute to locate the keypad on the support beam where Eddie had said it would be and punch in the code to keep the siren from blaring. He found it and typed the code from memory without taking the card from his wallet.

For a moment he worried he'd punched in the wrong number because a chiming sound continued to ring throughout the church. He had noticed it as soon as he stepped inside but hadn't focused on it until now, dismissed it as the sound of the alarm system counting down the narrow window of deactivation. Now that the sound hadn't shut off, he zeroed in on it, and simultaneously recognized three characteristics: it was not emanating from the keypad box but rather from the loft above and behind him; it was not a chime but a piano note being struck with monotonous repetition; and it was being played with the sustain pedal down so that the decay of each note echoed in the rafters.

He craned his head, but from this angle, he could see nothing up there. Just the purple, green and gold mosaic of a stained-glass rosette depicting the ascending Virgin, high in the wall above the choir loft.

Who the hell was in here, if he had just turned the lock and killed the alarm? It had to be a piano tuner Eddie had neglected to mention. And he or she must have entered through a back door with a key of their own. *If anything, I probably just re-armed the alarm,* he thought, looking at the control box. It appeared to be inert.

Hoping he wouldn't trip the motion detectors, he walked toward the end of the big hall where the altar would have traditionally been situated. A drum riser draped with red Persian carpets occupied that space. No alarm sounded. He peered up at the choir loft again where, from this angle, he could now make out the raised hood of a grand piano, but still no sign of a person.

The monotonous chiming note persisted.

He recalled a mind game he would sometimes play when he heard a musician hitting a single note: testing his ability to identify it. He knew he didn't have the gift of perfect pitch, but that had never prevented him from giving it his best shot. It was a kind of ear training to make the effort, and on the rare occasion when he was correct or even close, it was deeply gratifying.

Piano was his primary instrument, so he also had the advantage of recognizing the timbre of certain keys. Now he guessed E above middle C and made a mental note of it. He would find out if he'd guessed right when he got up there and asked the guy.

Only he wasn't so sure he wanted to go up there. A cloud passed across the sun outside, darkening the stained-glass panes above the piano, and Jake dragged his fingers across the palm of his hand, finding it clammy.

There's no one up there.

But there had to be. Maybe the tuner was kneeling under the piano to put some WD-40 on the sustain pedal, reaching up to strike a key. A plausible scenario. Still, he found he was reluctant to look for the stairs that would take him up to the loft. Was it simply that this place had once been a church? Was that what had him spooked so easily?

Okay, fuck it. Stop working yourself up and go find out. He drew a breath to call out, "Hello?" but before he could get the word out, a metallic clank resounded throughout the room and a shockwave of fear surged through his neck and shoulders. It was the double doors being thrust open. A sandy-haired man wearing a baseball cap, dirty jeans, and a T-shirt stepped into the room. He had pale blue eyes and a graying handlebar mustache.

"James?" Jake asked.

"Call me Buff," came the reply. Their voices reverberated in the empty hall, and in the silence that followed, Jake noticed that the piano note had ceased.

Buff seemed to be trying to read the expression on Jake's face.

Jake stepped toward him, extending his hand, and said, "I'm Jake." Buff shook it, but not without a slight hesitation.

"So where's this furniture we're moving?" Jake asked.

"Upstairs. Follow me."

They climbed another of the spiral staircases the architect of Echo Lake Studios had been so fond of and reached the second level. The piano loft was at one end, a set of small curtained-off bedrooms at the other. A catwalk with a waist-high wooden railing ran the length of the church, connecting the two halves of the second floor.

"How much of this was originally here when it was a church?" Jake asked when they reached the top of the stairs.

"This side was already here. It's where the organ used to be. And the seating for the choir, of course. Organ was a big, old pipe jobbie. That was gone long before Charlie bought the place and turned it into a studio, or he would've kept it. Charlie added the catwalk, the bedrooms, and bathroom up here. Some clients don't like the piano being up here but it's never coming down. Charlie always said this is where it sounds best, up close to the steepled ceiling. And they say it's good for separation."

"Yeah, makes sense that it'd be easier to keep other instruments out of the piano mics if it's way up here. But what about piano players who want eye contact with the rest of the band?"

"There's another one downstairs. Baby grand."

"Oh. That must be the one that's getting tuned."

"I think Eddie'll have 'em both tuned before your project starts. Now that it's getting cold out, he'll probably have Dickie come in and give 'em a tweak every morning, if your client's using them."

"Dick is the piano tuner?"

"Yup. But I don't know for how much longer. His hearing's starting to go. Especially at the upper end of the keyboard. Might be time for him to retire."

Buff was heading across the catwalk now, with Jake in tow.

"I heard him when I came in," Jake said. "He may still be

here."

Buff stopped walking, and Jake almost bumped into him. Jake's first thought was that Buff was regretting making the comment about the old guy's hearing when he was probably right below them and possibly still possessed of a keen enough ear to pick up their conversation. "Heard him, did you?" Buff said.

"When I came in. Tuning the one downstairs, I guess."

Buff turned to look at him. They were standing in the middle of the narrow catwalk between the two lofts. Buff grasped a railing in each hand and shook his head slowly.

"What?" Jake asked, but he thought he already knew.

"You unlock the double doors to let yourself in?"

"Yeah. Is there a back door, off the control room?"

"There is, but it doesn't unlock from the outside because you can't get to the alarm box fast enough from there. Dick uses the front door like everybody else. You didn't hear him, because he ain't here."

"Are you sure?"

"Yeah, I'm sure. He doesn't work on Fridays, anyway. Takes his wife to the physical therapist in Kingston for her back."

"I guess I was mistaken,"

"What exactly did you hear?"

"I dunno. Maybe nothing. Maybe a clanging hot water pipe."

"They don't clang in this room. That would ruin a track, right?"

"Right."

"So you heard someone playing the piano." Buff's mouth curled up in a lupine grin.

"Not *playing*. I thought I heard one note. So it probably wasn't a piano. Hey, does the bell in the tower ever ring from the wind?" Jake's eyes brightened as the idea occurred to him.

"Maybe in a hurricane."

"I don't know then. I don't know what I heard."

Buff leaned against the railing and took a pack of Camels from his pocket. "Man, I always thought it was bullshit, but *you* wouldn't even *know* the story. Now that's something."

"What story?"

Buff poked his unlit cigarette at Jake's shoulder. "Those guys in the shop didn't tell you to put me on about this, did they? Shit, they did, didn't they?"

"I have no idea what you're talking about."

Buff lit his smoke, dragged and exhaled at the rafters, "You heard the ghost, my friend."

Jake smiled. "Ghost?"

"Yup, the ghost of Olivia Heron. I've heard the story since I was a kid, but even working here, I never met anybody who actually heard her play. And I've been doing odd jobs here since I was seventeen. Thought it was bullshit, a folk tale."

"Okay, fill me in already."

Buff savored his cigarette and the moment, nodding his head as if in internal agreement that yup, that was the way to tell it for maximum effect.

Jake drummed his fingertips on the railing. This guy apparently preferred killing time to working. And yet, he couldn't suppress the need to know, even though it was irritating to think that he might have to trade the relief of knowing he could trust his ears for the lousy alternative of not being able to trust reality.

"The way I heard it, she was the church organist back in the late 1800s. They say she was a well-liked member of the congregation until after her husband died. Everyone tried to help her out when that happened, treat her like family and what not, but she became distant and withdrawn. Used to disappear for days at a time in the woods here, by the church. Nobody knew what she did on these little expeditions, if she'd sleep on the moss and pine needles or what, but she'd always be back for the Sunday services to play the hymns.

"Only, the music started getting weird. Just a little at first— some dissonant chords thrown in here and there."

Jake chuckled nervously. "She was a jazz innovator ahead of her time," he said, trying to lighten the dramatic tone Buff was going for.

"That's not what people thought," Buff said. "And the music got a lot more disturbing as time went on."

"Maybe she was expressing her grief through her playing," Jake said.

"Maybe. But people started to connect it up with all the solitary walks in the woods and word got around that she was communing with the Devil out there."

"They thought she was a witch?"

"That's right. And then one night, long after midnight, the reverend found her playing in the nude. Churning the most depraved music out of those towering pipes, riding that mighty Wurlitzer like some infernal beast." Buff grinned from ear to ear now, making Jake think of a cartoon he'd once seen of the Big Bad Wolf.

"That's a hell of an image. Did you just come up with that?"

"Nah. Guy I heard tell it maybe the sixth or seventh time coined that one. Irish fella, this was, over at the Bar-n-Grill one Halloween. But it kinda makes the story, don't it? I had him write it down on a coaster."

"So this really happened?"

"Oh, she was real, alright. It's in the town record. They hung her from a tree right out there in the churchyard. 'N' ever since the day she was hanged, people have heard her playing in the empty church from time to time. It was the organ at first, until they burned that in a big bonfire. Sold the pipes for scrap. But that didn't stop her because now people—like *you*—say they hear her playin' the peeyana. It's the *church* that's haunted—shoulda kept the organ. And I always thought it was a crock of shit until today. She must like you."

Jake didn't feel like laughing anymore. He thought of the pale shape he had seen bounding across the meadow behind his cabin on his first night in Echo Lake, and of the violet eyes glimmering at him from the edge of the woods. He thought of the sweating bottle of beer he'd held in his hand that night as he squinted at the peculiar visage, and wished he could have one now. Or several.

"Where's this furniture we're moving?" he asked, his voice tremulous.

Buff laughed and slapped him on the back. "Over here."

* * *

Allison sang the theme from the *Twilight Zone* after Jake told her the story. They were getting ready to leave the apartment for a night on the town, inspired by a blurb in the local paper that described the annual costume parade followed by fireworks over the cemetery.

A town of artists and alternative health practitioners transplanted from New York City, Echo Lake was serious about its pagan holiday. Jake found this a little ironic considering what their forebears had done to the local witch just a few generations ago, but times had changed—so much so that the church was now a studio.

"He was definitely playing with you," Allison said. "A little Halloween fun at the new guy's expense."

"You'd think," said Jake, "but I really did hear the piano."

"Couldn't there have been someone else there? Like that runner, Brent? Someone sitting under the piano, playing the note you heard, and then laying low while Buff spooked you out."

"I don't think so. There was no place to hide up there."

"Well then, it must have been the naked witch," she said, wide eyed and deadpan. "Didn't that guy Occam say that the sexiest explanation is the most likely?"

* * *

The streets were crawling with children in masks and makeup, and while there were a handful of plastic costumes from the local drug store, the majority were homemade efforts, some profoundly creative. There was a girl draped in black veils through which a network of tiny white Christmas lights twinkled (Look, she's the night sky!) and another who wore a framed canvas replica of *The Scream* by Munch, with a hole cut out for the child's face.

Jake and Allison went in their street clothes as spectators. It was a night that burned itself into Jake's memory like a double-exposed photograph—a strange juxtaposition of impressions. Child ghosts draped in shimmering cloaks of translucent metallic fabric and parents wearing skull and ghoul face paint illuminated for a half a second among the tombstones and oak trees by the green fire of sparks falling slowly to earth through drifting clouds of smoke.

Stop-motion war-zone visions of dime-store zombies running on the dewy grass over the real dead, the smells of gunpowder, lilac, and marijuana on the breeze. And in the midst of this dreamscape, the taste of his girl, here with him, more precious than ever, no longer a partner of convenience in a college town, but starting a life with him in this, their new home.

By the time Jake's head hit the pillow at the end of the night, the ghost of Olivia Heron seemed like one more imaginary specter in a town crawling with them.

FOUR

Billy sat across a table from his high school buddy and ex-drummer Johnny Russo in a smoky corner of Angelica's, Johnny's restaurant in Babylon, home town of WBAB, the classic rock station they used to listen to in Johnny's van in what now seemed like another life. Billy had stopped in just before closing time. The place was empty, except for the kid washing dishes beyond the brick archway with the batwing doors a few feet from their table.

Billy tapped his cigarette into the glass ashtray at his elbow and asked, "How's Angie?"

"She's good. I'll tell her you asked. I'm awful sorry about your Dad, Billy."

"Thanks. We got the flowers you sent. Made me realize I have one true friend."

"You home for a while?"

"No, I have to head upstate tomorrow, to a studio up there. I'm gonna rent a car and take in the fall colors on the way up. Driving helps me clear my head."

"Yeah? How *is* your head? I don't know what it's like to lose a parent so I can't say I know what you're going through, but I imagine it's especially hard when it happens without any time to prepare."

"Yeah. He, uh, had one heart attack before this one—two years ago—and my mom got on his case about what he could eat, but this was out of the blue. I was on tour when it happened. Just finishing, actually. I was scheduled to be in New York this week anyway. Canceled an MTV thing I was supposed to do. I'm in no shape to be in front of a camera."

"That's the right thing to do, slowing down a little. Some

people go full tilt with work when they should be taking time to grieve, you know? But it catches up with you later."

"Well I don't know if I'll really be slowing down much. My contract requires me to deliver another album on the company's schedule. But I feel like a *lot* of things are catching up with me lately. So maybe some time out in the woods won't be such a bad thing."

"How's your mom?"

"She's okay. I mean, she's coping, I guess. She's not talking much. And when she tries to cheer *me* up..." He dragged on the cigarette. "Just makes it worse."

"How do you mean?"

"I don't know... She told me she gave her sixth-graders an essay assignment to write about their hero, and one of the kids wrote about me."

"Little ass kisser," Johnny said with a smile.

Billy laughed. It was a broken sound that turned into a cough. "I don't think the kids know she's my mother. Anyway, Evan's the hero. He's a firefighter. A hero, I am not. I just feel guilty when I'm around them."

"Billy..." Johnny leaned in and waited until Billy stopped stamping out his butt, brushed the hair out of his eyes, and looked up. "What's up? What do you have to feel guilty about? Success? Your father dying? It's not your fault."

Billy said nothing.

"Jesus, Billy. Is that what you think, your father had a heart attack because of you? What, did you make the news for some sex and drugs episode? 'Cause I must have missed it."

"No, nothing like that."

"Then what?"

Billy drummed his fingers on the table and said, "Johnny, can I ask you a weird question? I know it's been a long time since we talked, and you might not want to tell me, so you can just say so."

"Go ahead."

"Remember in high school, you started reading those books about, I don't know, magic, the occult?"

"Yeah?"

"Well, I know we were metal-head kids, and every teenager

wants power, right? Over girls and adults, mostly because you know you have none. I still play with that dark mystique and kids respond to it."

"I know what you mean. There's more to it than that."

"Is there? That's what I'm asking. In your experience, is there something to it?"

Johnny sat back and took a deep breath. "I was probably drawn to the occult for the reasons you mentioned. But it led me to other things. That dark taboo claptrap eventually leads to deeper books, if you're serious about finding the real deal. For me it led to studying Hebrew Kabalah."

Billy smiled. "Who knew heavy metal album art could be a gateway to harder stuff—Jewish mysticism. That would have given the PMRC pause for thought."

"I doubt it."

"You still into it?"

"Not so much anymore. It's just techniques for altering your consciousness at will, getting in touch with God or enlightened mind or whatever you want to call it. Like yoga. But when Angie and I got married and opened the restaurant, I didn't have as much time for spirituality. We wanted to start a family. I stopped playing, too, but that was more of a career choice. I knew if I was living in a van, I'd end up divorced."

"A lot of people I know in L.A. are into witchcraft and Kabalah. I never took it that seriously myself, but some people I respect do. Still, it's L.A. Tom Cruise and John Travolta seem like they have their shit together, but they're into Scientology. Anyway, what I wanted to ask is: do you believe in... spiritual entities?"

"I do."

"Like angels and demons?"

"For lack of better terms, sure."

"Do you believe in the Devil?"

Johnny laughed. "No. I don't think there's any such thing, exactly."

Billy shook another cigarette out of the pack. He twirled it in his long, thin fingers without lighting it.

"So are you going to tell me your story?" Johnny asked.

"What do you mean?"

"Come on, people don't usually ask the kind of questions you're asking unless something weird happened to them."

Billy lit the cigarette. Until now he had been carrying around a vague notion, but he hadn't articulated even to himself exactly what he thought had happened. He said, "The night my father died, I had a really good scare."

"Did you have a dream about his death? I've heard of that happening."

"No. It was a dog. Not in a dream, a real dog almost attacked me, scared me pretty bad. But here's the weird part: the thing I was most aware of at the time was my heart pounding."

"And you think that through some... invisible connection, you may have caused your father's heart attack. Half a world away."

"Is it possible? I mean, he's my father. I've heard stories about mothers who can sense when their kids are in danger."

"Billy, you probably need to unplug for a while and get some rest. I think you're a lot more stressed and burned-out than you realize."

"But don't you believe in psychic connections, mind acting on matter over a distance, something like that. Is that possible?"

"Okay. I think it is, but I don't think it applies here. If you really think about what you're saying, it's kind of narcissistic."

"What?"

"You think you're responsible for everything. For your father's *second* heart attack, which had nothing to do with you. Think about it, instead of wondering about his health and his eating habits, you're thinking about what was happening to *you* at the time. Your emotions are so powerful they can kill someone? That is what you're suggesting, right?"

"But you just said—"

"It's not your fault. Stardom is doing a number on your head, but listen to me man, *it was not your fault.*"

"Wait a minute..."

"Seriously, Billy, you are not the cause of everything. Why do you think I have those little heart icons next to certain dishes on the menu? Men your dad's age have heart attacks sometimes. Your dog story is a coincidence. A synchronicity at best."

"Isn't that a Police song?"

"Yeah, and a book by Jung. It means an acausal connection. No cause and effect, just a remarkable meaningful coincidence. How did you get attacked by a dog, anyway? Don't you have a bodyguard?"

"I was being stupid. But it seemed more ominous than a coincidence at the time. And ever since, I can't get that Robert Johnson song out of my head, 'Hellhound Blues.' They said he sold his soul to the Devil."

"That's just because white guys were jealous of him getting so much pussy."

"I think he must have believed it, or he wouldn't have written those songs about it."

"You said it yourself. It's a mystique. Look, Billy, your father just died. You need to take a break and get some perspective."

"Too much fucking perspective," Billy said in a perfectly convincing English accent.

"Spinal Tap?"

"The immortal words of Nigel Tufnel."

Johnny laughed. "It's good to know some things don't change. It's good to see you, man. You should come home more often."

"Yeah, that's what I hear."

"So you think you've got hellhounds on your trail, huh? I get the feeling there's more you're not telling me."

"If you have some booze in this joint, I've got a story that just might change your mind about the Devil."

* * *

Echo

By the time his voice cracked on the high note at the climax of "Crucifixation," Billy Moon had decided that tonight was the night he would kill himself. No point in doing it on stage, though—the bar was empty.

It was a Tuesday night in January of 1994 and Purple Jesus was playing a gig at O'Niells, a dank little dive a few blocks from the Mystic River. The barroom was set apart from the room with the foot-high, beer-stained stage by a half wall over which the silhouettes of a few regulars could be seen nursing pints and watching the Bruins game. Even the house soundman had ducked in there to drink and watch the game, leaving Billy's mic to whistle and howl with feedback the guy pretended not to hear.

Billy knew he should be angry about it, but all he could feel was the black shroud of depression winding around him as he sang, making it hard to draw enough breath to deliver the last line when the final distorted chord receded. He didn't even bother singing it, didn't look at his mates, just stomped on a footswitch and fiddled with his tuning. As if it mattered whether or not the instruments were in tune tonight.

A few weeks earlier, Billy had stopped taking his Zoloft. The drug kept the black shroud down around his knees, but Billy knew it was doing so by suppressing the very emotions that he considered his stock in trade. To write, he needed to feel something. But the only song idea the un-medicated muse had granted him so far was a clunky title, 'Hope Prolongs Misery.' And that wasn't even original, he had to admit, dressed up in a new melody or not.

The phrase had been with him since high school when Kim McLane, the first punk chick he'd ever had a crush on, had felt him staring at the nape of her neck in Sociology class and, turning to lean over her fiberglass seat, had whispered the words in his ear. *Hope prolongs misery.* It was the inverse of the American Dream.

For a little while, there had been Friday and Saturday night gigs. Club owners seemed satisfied that their little crowd drank like a big one, but somehow, the moment when a small following might have grown had passed and they were back to Tuesday nights and the slapback echo of bodiless spaces.

Jim Cassman, the bassist and default bandleader talked the guys into playing a few more songs and treating the empty gig like a rehearsal, but by that time, Billy already knew there was nothing to rehearse for. When Jim finally laid his bass in its case, and Andy crossed his sticks on the snare drum, Billy didn't hang around to help load the van. He picked up his own guitar case without a word and walked out the back door while his bandmates called for their complimentary pitcher of Bud.

Outside, the sky was a luminous battleship gray, infused with urban light pollution, snowflakes swirling around in the streetlights like ash. He walked toward the river, the wet slushy snow saturating his combat boots until his feet started to go numb. Passing under the green girders of the Tobin Bridge, he saw the sign they had posted for jumpers: DESPERATE? DEPRESSED? HOPE PROLONGS MISERY. He wasn't sure what that last part really said. Probably some 800 number.

The Tobin Bridge does not provide a scenic view of a romantic city skyline, just smoke stacks with pulsing red lights and flickering strobes, towering over vast paved lots scattered with forklifts, the crumbling asphalt somewhere giving way to the ice floes migrating down the black river. Not much to remind you of what you have to live for.

He reached the halfway point, sat down on the railing and took his guitar out of the case. He would play one last encore for the night, and then exit stage left. It felt impossibly important that the last song he and the boys had half-heartedly trudged through not be the last thing he ever sang. The last song of a lifetime should be something with heart. *One more time, with feeling. Take it from the bridge.* He laughed. A broken sound that seemed to come from someone else.

For a moment, he couldn't decide what to play, couldn't even make his fingers move properly to find a few chords and stumble upon an idea of what made sense, and he knew it wasn't just because they were cold. He was scared. Scared, but also sure, in a peculiar, distant way. Finally, he dug in and tore through a ragged version of a ballad called "Wrestling with Aphrodite."

A couple of cars went by. No one stopped. He was getting colder by the minute and by the end of the song, the fear had gone down to a murmur. He took a pen from his pocket, and scribbled on the back of the night's set list: *FOR JIM.* He put the note in the pick compartment, laid the guitar back in the case and snapped it shut. He would leave it on the bridge for someone to find. There was a luggage tag on the case, so if whoever found it didn't just steal it, maybe it would be connected to him when his body washed up.

He felt a pang of regret about leaving the guitar on the bridge in the freezing cold for God only knew how long, snow piling up on it. It was a Gibson, and he knew that if the guitar ended up in Jim's care, like he wanted it to, his friend didn't have the money to repair a warped neck.

But that guitar still had a few more Billy Moon songs in it because of what happened next.

* * *

He stood there on the edge watching the snow spiral down into the icy black water. He reminded himself of the likelihood that if he left this bridge with his feet on the ground, he would end up as assistant manager of the pharmacy where he worked as a stock boy—overweight, using his store discount to keep a small arsenal of foot-care products in the medicine cabinet of his crappy apartment, and taking his acoustic out of the closet once a year to play it when he's drunk enough. He stepped out with one combat boot pointing toward oblivion, as light splashed over the scuffed toe.

He couldn't help it. He looked up at the oncoming car. The light moved too slowly. It was coming to a stop.

He heard a door open, but he couldn't make out what kind of car it was or who just got out, not with the glare of the headlights in his eyes. Then he heard a voice coming from the light: a lazy melodious voice with a British accent. It spoke his name. He was trying to make sense of what he'd just heard, but his brain flat out rejected the idea that someone had called him by name—nobody in this city knew his name. That was why he was hanging off this bridge.

Certainly no one who drove a car knew his name. All his friends rode the T. The idea it was his boss flitted through his mind, but not with an accent like that. *Is someone from work fucking with me?* Had it been his boss, it would have only strengthened his resolve to throw his weight forward and end it. Only that felt wrong, too, because he had been interrupted.

Playing his encore and putting the guitar to bed in its plush velvet case felt right. It kept him in his suicide trance. But he couldn't have the last thing he ever heard be his boss offering to give him a lift, in his best Nigel Tufnel impersonation. The suicide trance felt a lot like his songwriting trance, but the perfect rhyme he could feel forming on the dark periphery of his short life turned out to be a clunker that he just couldn't bring himself to end the third verse with. It was all wrong.

The man called Billy's name again. *It must be a cop who tracked me down for something, but I haven't done anything,* he thought. There was something deeply unsettling in the taunting singsong quality of the voice and as was the way he was so exposed in the headlights, like being on stage where everyone looking at you is a faceless silhouette beyond those blinding, hot aluminum cans. How could someone feel threatened by anything when in the act of offing himself? But he did.

He stepped toward the car to put a girder between his face and the light and could see a black limousine with a driver in a cap. One of the back doors was open, allowing a pool of red light to spill out onto the road like a fever. The man behind the seductive voice stood at the edge of that pool of sickly scarlet aura, grinning at him, wearing a tan suit, no tie, and sporting slicked-back black hair. Scruffy, in a rich sort of way, like a musician. Or a drug dealer.

That almost makes sense. He wondered, *Who did I fuck over? Did the band sell some pot on this guy's turf and now he's going to make an example of me?* And the fear threw his petty vanity into stark relief.

The snowflakes blowing across his face in the high wind started to melt a little faster on his flushed skin. He understood in that moment that even though he would have gone through with it, his suicide wouldn't have been motivated by pure despair and self-loathing. It would have been his last shot at infamy in the absence of fame. Now the prospect of getting whacked by a drug lord and making the papers as a dim-witted, small-time pot peddler scared the hell out of him. It was a pitiful fifteen minutes. Jumping from the bridge, a guitar left behind, would have put a stamp of authenticity on his death. Suffering Artist: Exhibit A.

Billy approached the car, and the stranger smiled. He swept his hand toward the soft red interior in a grand theatrical gesture ending in a slight bow.

Billy found his voice, hoarse and ragged. "How do you know my name?"

"I'm a fan. Good show tonight. I can tell you weren't at your best, but I have a knack for spotting potential."

"You were at the bar? I didn't see you."

"I saw you."

"Who are you?"

"Trevor Rail. I'm a producer. Grab your guitar. Let's take a drive."

FIVE

The air inside the limousine was redolent of rich leather and fine tobacco. A red lava lamp on a low table between the backseat, where Billy sat rubbing his cold hands together, and the rear-facing seat where Trevor Rail settled in was the only source of light in the cabin. It must have been on for a while, because the lava was surging and writhing as if trying to break free of the glass. Rail cracked a window, withdrew a slim metal case adorned with elaborate scrollwork from his inner breast pocket, and offered Billy a cigarillo. Billy shook his head. Rail took one for himself and lit it with a silver Zippo, also engraved, possibly depicting a rooster with snakes for legs, but Billy only caught a glimpse.

The producer didn't say anything for the first few drags, just sat there, appraising Billy wreathed in scarlet-tinged smoke. Billy had the feeling the guy was taking inventory of his assets. Tallying points for cheekbones, subtracting for the understated chin, adding a few for hair. Of Trevor Rail's own features, Billy could see now how handsome he was: slightly hooded lambent blue eyes coming across as a disquieting shade of pale here in the lurid light of the cabin, salt and pepper goatee tapered to sharp sideburns, teeth that would have been white as alabaster in clear light, here taking on the appearance of scintillating rubies when at last the man smiled and asked, "Do you write most of the material?" There was a hunger in the question.

Looking at those teeth, Billy felt that his hands might never be warm again, but he found his voice and said, "Some. All of the lyrics, some of the music." He shifted in the luxurious seat and cast his gaze down at the guitar case resting at his feet. "Jim's good at connecting parts and coming up with arrangements."

"How about that one, 'I Like to Watch.' You write that?"

"Yeah. That's one of mine."

"First piece of valuable advice: dump them."

"Huh?"

"Your mates. Dump them."

"Why?"

"Because you won't need them where you're going."

"And where's that?"

"If you listen to me, the zenith, my boy."

"What do you mean?"

"Let me guess. The band considers itself a democracy. Everyone tosses his spare cash in a jar; everyone contributes something to the overall *sound*, eh? Even the drummer gets a writing credit on your CD because you're the Four Musketeers. Brothers-in-Arms. Am I right?"

"Something like that."

"Do you know what constitutes a song by the definition of the United States Copyright Office? Lyrics and melody. That's you. Lyrics and melody. You can't copyright a drum part, a chord progression or a guitar sound. So when you write a hit song that could do well enough to buy a nice house, why should you have to give a quarter of a million dollars to some bass player who happened to be in the room when inspiration struck? It's your melody someone hums when it's stuck in their head, your words they remember. Perhaps even your pain that gave it life." There was something harrowing in the way Rail pronounced the word *pain*, some resonant overtone that vibrated in the air between them like a rope snapping taut. Billy felt a hollowness in his stomach, a tightness in his throat.

"I haven't written any hit songs."

"Sure you have."

Rail turned to the mini-bar, took out a bottle of Bacardi and poured two shots. He pressed a switch with his right forefinger. The nail was long for a man's, but immaculately manicured. The little window behind him slid down and he told the driver to take them back to Manhattan. The way he said the word made it sound like an enchanted island kingdom. Then he raised his glass to "catastrophic success."

Billy didn't know what to say, so he drank.

He wondered if Rail was for real, or if he was some kind of moneyed pervert, willing to drop some cash on whatever props would help him to seduce young men he'd taken notice of. With a little homework, a smooth talker could play on your hopes and dreams long enough to get you off your guard. And the guy sure could talk. He talked about who he knew at each of the majors and how much money Billy could expect in a bidding war.

He went on about the psychology of A&R men and how they were like hot women who expected the talent to grovel at their feet because they held the keys to the kingdom, but in reality, behind that power dynamic, they really only ever wanted someone if they thought they couldn't have him.

Ever in fear of losing their jobs, they made most of their decisions by looking at what the competition seemed interested in. He knew who had engineered all of Billy's favorite records and what those guys were working on now, and who was in rehab, and which *Rolling Stone* writer would favor you if you let him blow you. The guy was for real.

Billy hadn't eaten anything in about six hours, and the Bacardi went straight to his head. By the time the limo passed through Hartford, he was sold. His ship had come in. By almost diverting his destiny, had he somehow forced God's hand? His ego bloomed, watered by alcohol and ambition. He couldn't wait to tell Kate.

At the thought of her, he sobered a little. "Wait, why are we going to New York?"

Rail laughed. "To pluck you out of the brackish backwaters of the industry, for starters."

"But nobody knows where I am. When I don't show up at two in the morning with the other guys, my girlfriend will be worried."

Rail's mouth twisted, trembled on the verge of laughter. Billy asked him what was so funny.

Shaking his head, Rail poured more rum. The grin melted back into his handsome face as he handed Billy the glass. Billy took it, but didn't drink, just stared at Rail, waiting for him to answer the question until, unable to hold the man's unblinking gaze any longer, he had to look away at the first thing his eyes could focus on—the bat logo on the bottle. The silence spun out. When Billy glanced up again, Rail was still staring at him like a dog establishing dominance, the red lava undulating in his black pupils.

Trevor Rail spoke softly. Billy had to lean in to make out the words over the hum of the engine. "Don't kid yourself, Billy. You weren't concerned about Kate an hour ago, when I found you on the bridge. That's when I knew you were ready."

"Ready for what?"

"To leave them all in your wake. Everyone who's been holding you back."

"Kate's not holding me back. Wait, how do you know her name?"

Rail's mouth twitched, a flicker of that sardonic grin. Before it could form, his face morphed into a mask of overwrought sorrow. "Oh, Billy," he said, "don't be ashamed of your selfishness. You're an artist. It's your nature to be self-absorbed. It's practically your duty. You can't help that that's the way you're wired. And now, for the first time in your life, you're facing it: being honest about it. You were prepared to jump tonight, to let go of all your attachments, to let everyone you love mourn you. That requires a deep well of selfishness. To let your own pain trump everyone else's. You need to learn to use that. Let that impulse focus and guide you, and it will take you all the way."

He paused, giving Billy time to absorb his dark logic.

"*Then* you will be ready to give something to others, to the *world*, because you were true to yourself, not consumed by what other people want you to be. But it begins with severing the ties that bind you."

"Maybe I don't want to."

"Don't lie to yourself."

"I don't see why it's a big deal to let her know I'm alright. Do you have a cell phone? I'll still go to New York with you."

Rail cocked his head and spoke over the lowered glass at the driver. "Stop the car." The driver pulled over. As soon as the car stopped, Rail reached past Billy and opened the door. "Get the fuck out."

"Why? What did I do?"

"I thought you were serious, but you're clearly not ready. My mistake. Get out."

"Whoa, hold up. You can't just dump me in the middle of Connecticut."

"The hell I can't. Out." Rail pointed a finger at the hot top.

Billy cradled his guitar case to his breast and climbed out of the car. The door slammed shut. The limo crawled forward toward the stream of cars and trucks flying past on I-84, the left blinker flashing as the car picked up speed.

Before he knew he was doing it, Billy took a deep breath and let out a roaring scream, pushing his voice from the diaphragm as if he were on stage with a dead monitor and the band louder than bombs.

"WAIT!"

The brake lights lit, the car slowed, but the amber blinker continued to flash. Billy ran beside the gleaming black limousine. The tinted rear window glided down, and Rail gazed obliquely at Billy with a contempt that made him feel like he was a bum shaking some coins around in the coffee dregs at the bottom of a Styrofoam cup.

"Okay, I'll do it," Billy said.

"Do what?"

"Anything. Whatever it takes."

Rail laughed. A word from the sign on the bridge flashed in Billy's mind. DESPERATE? The car stopped rolling.

"You really pissed me off for a minute there, Billy."

"I'm sorry. I am serious. I am."

"Don't offend me like that again. I offered to make you a *rock star*. More beloved and influential than most presidents. Longer term too, if you play your cards right. More pussy than an Arabian prince. And you start talking about your *girlfriend*? Have some respect for the magnitude of what I'm offering you."

The door opened. Billy climbed in.

As they closed the distance to New York, the January moon kept pace with the car, and Trevor Rail spoke the truth of Billy's situation. He said he *expected* Billy to be an egotist. He would have no use for him if he wasn't. He had seen artists lose faith and question their own value. He had seen performers sabotage their own success because deep down they didn't feel they deserved it. You had to be an egomaniac to survive in the long run. Some singers reconciled this predicament by seeing themselves as saints, using their influence to save the world. Rail scoffed at the folly. "I prefer proud sinners. I can lay the world before you like a dish, Billy. But only if you're willing to make sacrifices."

Rail poured Billy another drink. He went on in that smooth, droning British lilt. War stories, jokes, little insights into Billy's childhood. Billy laughed, wept and watched the limo cabin fracture into a stained glass mosaic through the tears.

And then there was New York, all lit up and glittering like ice chips in the black fur of some beast under the moon. Billy wondered if the rum was spiked with something. It didn't matter anymore. He felt good. The road was broken at intervals by sections of steel plates that made the car bounce on its shocks. Soon, taxicabs flocked around the limo like a swarm of bees.

Rail's driver was aggressive enough to run with the best New York engine jockeys, maneuvering the unwieldy vehicle with precision, if not grace. Billy was thrown into the air above his seat a few times, hitting his head on the plush ceiling, feeling the steel frame through the fabric.

Rail stowed the empty glasses and laid a sheaf of legal-size papers on the little table beside the lava lamp. Densely printed small type.

"What's this?" Billy asked. He had to raise his voice to cut through the noise of the engine, now working harder, and the background cacophony of taxi horns and hydraulic truck brakes compressed by the channel of tall buildings they were moving through.

Rail leaned in, close to his ear. When he spoke, Billy could feel hot breath in his hair. "It's a production contract. It grants me the privilege of recording your first album. If I secure a deal for you, I retain points on the record and a modest percentage of the publishing. You will find it's quite fair." He drew a black felt tipped pen from his breast pocket, uncapped it and moistened the tip by placing it on his tongue for just a second—a quick gesture that was at once predatory and erotic.

Two conflicting voices arose within Billy simultaneously. One was a piece of advice he'd heard from several sources over the years: *Don't ever give up your publishing rights.* The other was just a victory cry. *I'm getting signed! I'm finally getting signed!* His heart pounded so hard that he looked down to see if his shirt was moving. He took the pen in his clammy hand and unconsciously placed the cap in his teeth, clamping down on it like a nipple as he scanned the blocks of obscure legalese in the wavering bloody light. The car continued to rock and sway through the urban canyons of Manhattan.

In a flash, Billy saw the walls of the car disappear around him, the profusion of sparkling lights from the skyscraper windows replaced by stars above a dark sea. There was no land in sight. He was riding the back of a mammoth black wave from towering crest to bottomless trough, his stomach left somewhere high above and behind him in the plunge. Trevor Rail still sat across from him, not in the jostling white leather cabin of a limo now, but in a mouldering rowboat, holding the dripping oars above the water, teeth flashing like rubies from deep within a black hood. The image was vividly present, but gone in an instant.

Billy looked down at the papers and tried to focus. It was hard to read—the motion of the car, the alcohol, and his ignorance all conspiring against comprehension. He remembered how quickly he'd been kicked to the curb in Hartford for asking to call Kate. What was he going to do now, ask to call a lawyer?

I'm getting signed. The words were an incantation against all misery. They would have a powerful effect on everyone in Billy's life. He imagined how their faces would look when he told them the news—his father, his boss, his band mates. Everyone who had ever politely encouraged him while privately scorning his chances. He would be vindicated. For every time he'd taken a song to the band that they had turned down, he would be vindicated.

But he could see Jim's face a little too clearly. Could he really look Jim in the eye and admit that he had signed away *any* rights to the songs they'd written together? Could he really walk out on the band?

A new voice arose in his crowded mind, dressed in the tone and inflections of the man seated before him. *At midnight, you were ready to throw your life away, your flesh and blood, and now you're worried about a few percentage points on some money you haven't even earned yet.* That was enough to silence his guilt and doubt. Trevor Rail had found Billy Moon at the bottom, in his darkest hour. He had nothing to lose and the world to gain.

He put the pen to the paper and signed his name after the X.

* * *

The limo crawled up a narrow alley and stopped in front of a dumpster. Rats scampered over the lip and shot off into the dark. The driver got out first and opened the rear door. Billy climbed out with Rail on his heels.

"Where are we?" Billy asked.

"I'm going to show you what you have to live for."

"In a piss-stinking back alley? This ought to be good."

"In there," Rail said, pointing his long fingernail at a reinforced steel door. The only indication of what lay beyond was a piece of gray driftwood hanging from a black iron scroll arm above the entrance. Painted on the wood in gold leaf in an archaic script were the words: CARNIVORE'S CARNIVALE

Rail knocked. The hinges shrieked and the door opened to reveal a bald-headed black man with a gold ring the size of a small doorknocker hanging from his nose. Rail inclined his head ever so slightly and said, "Good evening, Peter."

"Evening, Mr. Rail."

Peter reached out with a muscle-ripped arm and pulled on a heavy metal bar, like a gambler spinning a slot machine. A second, inner door opened like an air lock, releasing a wash of industrial voodoo drums and chainsaw guitars.

The space inside was packed with the sort of New York revelers who look like they've just stepped out of the six pages of cologne-drenched fashion ads one has to flip through to find the table of contents in *Vanity Fair*: bare-chested omni-sexual golden boys in Armani vests and emaciated girls in rawhide-laced slit skirts, thick black eyeliner, electric blue hair. The air was tinged with hashish smoke and pheromones and underneath it all, a bass note of charred flesh and iron.

The room, which at first sight had appeared vast, soon resolved itself into a claustrophobic box when Billy noticed that the purple and yellow robo-lights were reflecting back at him off mirrored walls. A tall, thin girl with a pallid complexion, dressed in a sequined leotard completed by a top hat and baton, stretched like taffy as she danced. It took Billy a few seconds to decide that he was not, in fact, tripping. They were funhouse mirrors.

A path opened through the crowd when Rail walked across the room. Even those whose backs were turned to him, or who danced with their eyes closed, stepped aside instinctively at his approach. When he and Billy reached the other side of the dance floor, they passed under an archway of heavy wooden scrollwork painted with cracked gold. The volume of the pounding music dropped down enough in this new space—more tunnel than hallway—to allow conversation as they passed through.

"What is this place?" Billy asked, touching the silky sleeve of Rail's jacket.

"It's a private club," Rail said. "The finest fresh flesh in New York."

The music receded behind them, and now Billy could make out another sound coming from somewhere ahead, growing louder. It was a drip-drop splashing sound, echoing through the tunnel. He looked down and saw that they were walking through a thin layer of water he hadn't noticed before. The passageway was long; the only light the purple and yellow flicker on the ceiling far behind them at the mouth, and a dim blue glow up ahead.

Billy hesitated, thought of turning back. Who was this guy, anyway? His survival instincts were being triggered with each step they took away from the crowd. Billy stopped walking. Rail seized his wrist and pulled him forward with enough force to make him slip on the wet floor. As he tumbled toward it, throwing his hands out and bracing for impact, he felt his leather jacket tighten around him. Rail had caught him with one hand. In both the tug and the catch, Rail had revealed surprising strength. He steadied Billy and released him.

There was a scraping sound of flint and steel—a lighter sparking a flame. Rail's shadow-painted face floated in the darkness, drawing on a cigarillo. The producer held the flame aloft, raised an eyebrow at Billy, and exhaled pungent smoke through his nostrils. He tilted his head toward the floor. It was hard to tell for sure by the wavering orange light, but before Rail capped the lighter, Billy thought he could discern a thickness in the consistency of the liquid running down the grated gutter at the margin of the tunnel. Not dirty water. Blood. The smell of iron in the air suddenly made sense.

Rail said, "Watch your step."

Billy froze in place. Was it *human* blood?

As if reading his mind, Rail said, "It's not exactly legal or kosher, but trust, me it's the best steak on the hoof you'll ever try. They have fresh oysters, too. Keeps you young, consuming things that still have life force in them."

They walked on and came into the blue-lit room where a waiter was parading a drugged bull before a table of sharp dressed, clean-cut young men seated with an older woman whose place at the head of the table gave Billy the idea that they worked for her in some capacity. Rail nodded at her as they passed through the room. Billy couldn't tell if she smiled at him, or if her face was permanently rigged with Botox injections.

"Don't stare," Rail muttered. "It's not polite." He put his hand on Billy's shoulder and guided him to a tread-plate spiral staircase that descended from a corner of the floor.

The last thing Billy saw before the floor eclipsed his view was the waiter drawing a long, thin blade from his sleeve, and dipping it down his throat like a sword swallower at a circus. The sight of the docile bull made Billy think of the rum Rail had given him on the ride down from Boston. Was he drugged? He couldn't tell. He felt light-headed, only half in his body. The alcohol, the drive, this dreadful place, the hypnotic voice of his guide—all of it was extinguishing lucidity.

At the bottom of the stairs, Billy found a black velvet curtain with a heavy, silver silk rope. He tugged on it. The curtain parted in the middle, and from behind him, Rail said, "I called ahead and ordered for you."

Billy laughed as he took in the view. It was a harem. The room was made to resemble a large tent. Tapestries were draped from the ceiling and walls. Big, square velvet pillows covered the floor atop several layers of overlapping Persian rugs. The only light came from a star-shaped tin lantern hanging from a silver chain in the center of the room, its myriad pinprick holes emitting the golden rays of a candle burning within.

Six naked young women lay sprawled around the room on the pillows. Billy's laughter tapered off when he noticed that the reason they were all so immediately, strikingly beautiful to him was because they all looked like Kate. Even by the uneven candle light, he could tell that none of them looked exactly like her twin, but they all shared her basic body type, her height, her mane of loose, curly red hair, her breasts. One had her eyes—another, her hands—on a third, the lips were just right. The illusion was good enough to cause a tightening of his black jeans. The girl with the perfect hair relieved that discomfort by unbuttoning and unzipping them.

She led him with a gentle grip into the center of the room where he fell to his knees on the pillows, just below the star lantern and another dangling silk rope. Now the Kates were stripping him of his jacket, shirt and everything else down to his socks with astonishing efficiency. He wondered if they were so well coordinated in everything they did.

They were.

Two tongues fluttered at his earlobes while two more did the same at his nipples. Then the mouths at his ears moved down to his nipples to replace the other pair, which in turn brushed across his hips and met at last in a long slow kiss around the part of him that was one. A fifth Kate was kissing his lips while the sixth embraced him from behind and sucked on the nape of his neck.

The configuration continued to evolve in perfect speechless synchrony.

When they had brought him to the brink for the third time and he was groaning between great heaving breaths, sweat stinging his eyes, pelvis vibrating with tremors of impending orgasm, they suddenly ceased their adorations as if in response to some silent cue.

Billy cast about trying to set his eyes on Rail. A flame revealed the man's face in the corner when he lit a cigarillo, holding it between the ring finger and pinky of his right hand and sucking the smoke through the tunnel of his fist, an effect that made his hand appear to be kindled from within.

Rail spoke in smoke, his voice oily and resonant. "This token will be a reminder to you. The consummation of our contract." He reached into the pocket of his slacks and withdrew a shining platinum ring. One of the Kates pried Billy's clutching right hand from a pillow and held it out to Rail. Billy felt the metal mouth devour the knuckle of his ring finger.

Rail said, "From this night forward, you are married to the music, Billy Moon. Serve the music first and all else is yours for the taking." Billy closed his fist. The ring felt heavy and cold. Trevor Rail raised his voice in mockery of a priest orating a Latin mass and intoned, "In the name of the riches, bitches, and fame everlasting, amen."

The Kates resumed their rhythmic work as if they had never stopped, like a funk band kicking back in after a false ending.

"Oh, God," Billy said.

"Not quite," said Rail, pulling the silk rope that dangled over Billy's chest.

Blood sprayed from the pinprick holes in the tin star lantern. The candle sizzled and sputtered out.

SIX

"Looking back, I think I sold my soul."

"To the Devil," Johnny said.

Billy set his jaw and made a tic that was almost a nod.

"That is one fucked-up tale, my friend. And your producer has probably taken you for a ride in more ways than one, but does he have to be the Devil incarnate?"

"He showed up in my darkest hour and made me a star. Played every hole in my heart like a flute."

"And now you feel like payback time is nigh?"

"I do."

"Okay, even if I accept the possibility of a Devil, you still didn't make a deal for your soul as far as I can see based on what you've told me. Did that happen later?"

"That's what I can't figure out. I think it was subtle, like I was supposed to recognize the moment and what it meant, but I didn't. I didn't see anything about a soul in the contract. Sometimes he seems to talk in symbolism. As a songwriter, I hate to admit I don't always get it. But I never raised my left hand and made an oath. I never signed a piece of parchment in blood." Billy chuckled nervously at how hokey that sounded. "Maybe just telling him I would do whatever it took... Maybe letting him put this ring on my finger." Billy rotated the platinum band on his right hand with the thumb and forefinger of his left, a wheel turning on an axle.

Johnny smiled. It was a kind smile, not condescending. He said, "Well I think you're alright, bro. It doesn't sound like you made a pact. But you're going up to that studio in a couple of days. Is that to work with this same producer? Satan himself?"

"Yeah."

"If you want my advice, you should call it off. Just cancel and take some time to step away from all the head games."

"I can't. I'm under contract. Last disc didn't do so hot, and now they say they'll drop me if I don't play nice with the King Midas who produced my one hit."

"Well then, at least get some rest before you drive up. You look like shit."

"Thanks, Johnny. You always know how to make me feel better."

PART II
PRIVATE DEVILS

"For where God built a church,
there the Devil would also build a chapel."
Martin Luther

SEVEN

Billy Moon came to Echo Lake on the second of November, a perfect fall day. Jake arrived at the church at eleven in the morning, one hour before the session start time. He parked his newly purchased, rusty Pontiac under the stand of pines, unlocked the double doors, and set the heavy black flight case he was carrying on the floor. The vast room was silent from the waxed floorboards and threadbare Persian rugs to the cobwebbed rafters. A hint of Pine Sol and the stronger aroma of fresh brewed coffee hung in the air. He had passed Rita, the head housekeeper, on the road from the main building.

Jake poured himself a paper cup of coffee in the kitchenette. He put a CD on in the control room and patched it through to the monitor speakers in the big room so he could listen while he set up. It was Peter Gabriel's *Passion* soundtrack, a record that had kindled his interest in engineering in the first place.

He looked over his notes while the coffee and music sparked his brain into work mode. Kevin Brickhouse had requested a pretty standard assortment of microphones for the drum kit, and Jake had them all in the flight case. On the phone, Brickhouse had put Jake at ease with his friendly tone, but he also sounded tired. He had even joked that he would be leaning pretty hard on Jake if he didn't get some sleep before leaving the Hit Factory, where he was finishing up a Ska record before making the trip up I-87 to Echo Lake on his Harley. "Thank God for Peruvian rocket powder, eh kid?"

As second engineer, Jake's first priority was to keep the session moving without a hitch, hovering in the background like a good waiter, never voicing his own opinions on musical matters unless they were asked for, and then as diplomatically as possible. If everything went smoothly, he should be seldom noticed and take no credit for the session's success.

But if things went awry, if equipment failed, as it invariably did in every project, or if the engineer made a mistake in front of the producer, it was his job to step in and remedy the situation, bypassing or replacing the faulty gear so fast no one noticed, or (in the case of operator error) taking the blame to save face for the guy making ten times the pay he was.

In a room lined wall-to-wall with buttons, knobs, and LCD screens, he was expected to be able to patch a sound through any combination of processors in any order without hesitation at two in the morning, in the dark, after three weeks of fourteen-hour days, catering to the whims of ego maniacs and drug addicts.

For this he could reasonably expect to earn rent and gas money and his name in microscopic print somewhere in the CD booklet. That was the apprenticeship his teachers had told him to expect. It was worth it, they said, because if you persisted and made a good impression, the day would come when an artist or producer would ask you to engineer the next one. Or, if you were very lucky, the engineer you were assisting would get sick and put you in the driver's seat, so make sure you order his Chinese food from the worst joint in town.

It wasn't rocket science, but there were producers who acted like it was open-heart surgery. One mistake could cost you your career. There was the legend about the assistant who had walked off in the night, never to be seen again, after realizing he'd accidentally erased a Steely Dan master tape, or the one about how Paul Simon had vomited upon learning an assistant had erased one of his vocal tracks.

It reminded him of that children's game Operation where you tried to remove plastic bones from the patient with a pair of metal tweezers, and a buzzer went off if you touched the sides. You were trying to get something out of the artist without damaging it—probing the heart without jolting the nerves. Recording music was a craft that existed somewhere on the borderland between art and science. Terrain that Trevor Rail and Kevin Brickhouse were reputedly very good at navigating.

Brickhouse made a loud entrance shortly after noon. Jake heard the Harley coming long before it pulled up in front of the church. He had once seen a picture of Brickhouse in *Mix* magazine, but the man's appearance had changed since then. He no longer had hair, for one thing, and judging by the cinnamon and salt stubble that framed his face, Jake could tell he had taken the skinhead option as a rock fashion solution to the receding hairline he'd already had in that magazine shot.

He wore a black t-shirt that said *guttermonkey* in a lowercase logo, under an unbuttoned blue denim work shirt and blue jeans smeared with oil from the hog. An open bracelet made from a metal rod with a ball bearing on each end adorned his left wrist while an athletic wristwatch as thick as a double-stuffed Oreo squeezed the other above the hand that was swinging his Captain America motorcycle helmet by its leather strap.

He smiled at Jake with eyes that were friendly but sunken. Something about that look made Jake think of concentration camps.

"You Jake?"

"Yes. Kevin, it's good to meet you."

"I don't think you were here the last time I was."

"I'm new here."

"Brian still work here?"

"Yes."

"Cool. I'll have to drag him out for a beer one of these nights. So, I see the drums made it. We won't set up any mics for them until they bring a drummer in—probably not until next week at the earliest. To start, I think we'll just be rolling tape while Billy plays around on the guitar and the computer. Just documenting song ideas, but we have to be prepared to use it as a master if he gets anything good down, so I want you to start by printing code on track twenty-four for the first few reels. That way we can lock in with his laptop and even automate some rough mixes later on."

Jake got to work immediately. He was almost finished prepping the tapes when Trevor Rail arrived. His first look at the legendary producer eased some of the low-grade anxiety that had been plaguing his stomach ever since Eddie had assigned him to the project. Rail had cemented a reputation as a mean bastard, but Jake had been lacking a mental image to attach to the noxious persona.

Steve, one of the other assistants who had worked with Rail in the city before coming to Echo Lake, had done his best impersonation for Jake while they sat in the shop doing busywork. Steve's English accent needed work, but he had sworn that the content of such priceless one liners as "Talk while I'm listening to playback one more time and I'll do a razor edit on your windpipe" were taken verbatim from old "Third Rail."

With a build-up like that, Jake was taken aback when the Trevor Rail he met on November second greeted him with a disarming smile that offset the seriousness of the man's white-frosted black goatee and widow's peak. Rail's nose and sideburns were sharp and angular, but his posture and clothes telegraphed the kind of laconic ease that Jake associated with wealth. When he introduced himself, his voice was gentle and courteous, his accent soft and attractive. It was difficult to imagine that voice rising in anger. *What was I expecting*, Jake wondered, *a tail?*

But when Trevor Rail curled his fingers around Jake's eagerly extended hand and squeezed it firmly in his own, everything changed. There was a low, droning malevolence transmitted by that hand, and Jake recoiled from it as if he had just opened a kitchen drawer in someone else's house, searching for a butter knife, only to find a handgun instead.

Rail ambled around the big room, chatting with Brickhouse about where he wanted Billy Moon's workstation set up. More road cases had been delivered by Rock-It Cargo since Jake had opened the building, and Rail said he didn't expect to get any further than setting up and maybe tracking the skeleton of a song tonight, if Billy was up for it.

"Does he have some strong material this time?" Brickhouse asked.

"I don't know if he has *any* material. We're going to write. Together, maybe."

"No kidding. I didn't know you wrote music."

"Well, let's say I have ideas. I'm more of a concept man. A catalyst," Rail said.

"So it's going to be a concept album?"

"God, no. Not like what they used to mean by that. But all of the best rock records have some kind of concept behind them, and Billy is at a point in his career where he could use one. Even Kurt Cobain, who despised all of that pompous seventies crap, had concepts."

"So what is it? What's the concept for this record that has no songs yet?"

"Maybe… Love and Death? What has great music or poetry ever been about, but those twin forces that undo a man?"

"Anyone ever tell you, you can be more pretentious than your artists?" Brickhouse said with a smile.

"I won't deny high ambition. I want to make an immortal record."

"Immortal, huh? Sure you don't want to just stick with making *immoral* records? You're good at it."

"Kevin, I want to produce something that will still be on the charts in twenty years. A record that will outlive modern rock."

"I'd say that was grandiose, but these days, it shouldn't be too difficult. Just make a hip-hop record and it'll outlive rock-and-roll. Rock is gonna be marginalized just like jazz and blues were. Whatever rock is—guitar music—it's gonna be the soundtrack for nursing homes when the boomers retire. It won't be cool anymore. That's why I'm working like a mad motherfucker while I can."

"You may be wrong, my friend. A new generation is discovering the first Doors album. They're buying *Imagine* and *Electric Ladyland*, and in twenty years, new kids will still be buying *Nevermind*."

"All of those albums outlived their creators because the artists died young."

"There is something romantic about it, don't you think? It adds to the mythos."

"Worked for Elvis."

"Elvis, you see? His myth outlived the rock-and-roll of his time. He and Bob Marley are on par with Jesus. They're more than rock stars; they're spiritual icons. That's what I want to do: shape a legend." Rail plucked a red pen from a coffee cup and twirled it in his long fingers.

"But you can't plan that. You just have to be in the right place at the right time. Those artists are freaks of nature. And who can say why the world was ready for a certain voice?"

"I think some voices would reach an audience in any time. Styles come and go, but a voice that's telling the truth about sex and death, a voice that's been shaped by those energies, saturated by them... That's magnetic. And it's the magic of this business to capture that genie in a bottle and sell it."

Jake had given up even pretending to organize cables within earshot of the conversation and had drifted closer, fascinated.

"Maybe you can capture that," Brickhouse said, "but you can't create it or contrive it. Why do you think all these A&R sluts are always getting laid off and bouncing from one label to another? Those guys can't do it either. You can't manufacture gods. You can't calculate genius."

"Genius is overrated."

"Well, the magazines sure do wear the word out. But Lennon, Morrison and Hendrix... Those guys were in a feedback loop with a cultural zeitgeist. Not likely to happen again in this jaded age, if you want my opinion. And that messiah thing? I don't think that's genius, exactly. More like a combination of beauty and tragedy."

"There you have it: Sex and Death."

"I thought your concept was Love and Death."

"Love is elusive. Sex can be inspired with far greater precision."

"And how do you inspire death?"

"I suspect it has something to do with putting the artist in the right place... at the right time."

Rail lit a cigarillo and cast his gaze around the church in silence, taking it all in before heading back to his black BMW and disappearing up the dirt road toward the main building.

* * *

Jake was busy setting up equipment for the rest of the day while the pale light drained out of the sky. At seven-thirty Rail called the control room to ask if Moon had arrived.

"No sign of the artiste yet, eh, Jake? Alright, then. Take a dinner break and call me when you see the Moon," Rail said and hung up.

Brickhouse sighed and drummed his hands on the Neve console's leather palm rest. "So now we're starting at what? Eight, nine, or ten? Man, I don't know if I'll be awake by then."

"There are a few beds upstairs," Jake said. "You could take a nap, and I'll wake you up if Billy shows."

"That's tempting. But I've been up for almost seventy-two hours already. If I go to sleep now, I won't be worth shit in two hours. I'll just feel worse." He rubbed his eyes with thumb and forefinger. "Do you know if I'm bunking here anyway?"

"Eddie said Billy wants to sleep here so if he gets an idea in the middle of the night, he can just come down and grab a guitar. You have the house across the road to yourself. It's the old church rectory. Rail's up the hill in the mountain house."

"Well, if I'm staying right across the road, I may as well go unpack my saddle bags. Be back in a bit."

Jake took the cordless phone with him and went upstairs to watch TV and wait for Billy.

When he came back down after an hour of back-to-back sitcoms, he found Brickhouse in one of the isolation booths using a tape-splicing razor blade to cut lines of cocaine on the metal surface of an empty tape flange. He watched as the engineer snorted up through a plastic straw, shook his head with a little shiver and glanced up at Jake through the window. Brickhouse pointed down at the little pile of coke with raised eyebrows. Jake held up his hand and silently mouthed the words, "No, thanks."

Jake busied himself with filling in the hourly log on the work order for the day's session, which so far didn't entail much. He walked back into the big room to brew another pot of coffee, heard a couple of piano notes cascading down from the loft and froze in his tracks. He looked up, expecting to see no one, and instead saw a thin figure in a black T-shirt and tight black jeans hunched over the keys, face obscured by a mass of wavy black hair, cut straight at the chin. Jake let out a little plosive breath that was equal parts laugh and sigh.

He turned on his heel, went back into the control room, and dialed the mountain-house extension on the phone. "Billy Moon is here."

Trevor Rail entered the church ten minutes later. Jake was threading a fresh tape onto the multi-track, Brickhouse was scrolling through the LCD screen of a signal processor, and Moon was still poking around with an arpeggiated chord progression on the grand piano up in the shadowy loft above the hanging lamps that cast pools of yellow light on the scratched and tape-marked wood floor of the big room.

The piano playing stopped when the double doors closed behind Rail. Jake watched through the control room glass as Billy Moon slowly floated down the spiral staircase and leaned against the banister near the bottom, staring at the producer. Jake could read the tentative body language, but not the expression on Moon's face—there was more light in the control room than out there and Jake's own reflection was superimposed over the reunion scene as Rail approached and then embraced his artist, cupping Billy's head in his large hand, then looking him in the eyes with their foreheads pressed together like lovers about to kiss. Rail was saying something. Moon was nodding a little. Jake wished the talkback mic was on out there.

A moment later the pair came into the control room, and Moon gave a pat on the arm to Brickhouse, who slapped the singer's shoulder, completing an awkward maneuver that was not quite half a hug, accompanied by a mutual, "Good to see you, man."

Jake introduced himself with a quick handshake before withdrawing to his place at the back of the room to await instructions. Billy looked relieved. He sat down heavily into one of the ergonomically perfect swivel chairs, rolled backward, put his Doc Martens up on the cushioned lip of the console and lit a cigarette. Rail leaned against the wall beside the cedar-framed glass doors through which a stone path could be seen winding away among the moonlit dead leaves down to a rushing stream.

Rail put his hands in his pockets and crossed his legs, the tip of one oiled, snakeskin boot pointing at the floor. His voice sounded lazy and indifferent when he spoke. "So, Billy, what would you like to do?"

Billy took a slow drag on his cigarette.

"D'you have any songs you'd like to play for me? Your rig is all set up out there. Of course, if you're tired, we can start fresh tomorrow," Rail said.

Billy took his time stamping the butt out in the ashtray Jake had set beside him on top of a rack of vintage pre-amps, then said, "Yeah, I've got something I could play you. Been writing on the computer in hotels a little bit. Keep in mind, it's just a rough sketch at this stage."

Things started happening fast after that. Billy powered up his laptop and sat down at the workstation Jake had arranged on a red Persian carpet in the middle of the big room following a diagram Danielle Del Vecchio had faxed him. Spinning knobs on a little desktop mixer and an array of synth modules, Billy conjured up a groove—sparse at first, just a heavy, deliberate drumbeat, which gradually built in volume and intricacy as he added pulsating bass lines and scratchy bursts of sampled guitar noise.

Brickhouse quickly identified each musical element and assigned them to tracks on the tape machine. Jake wrote the names— KICK, SNARE, HAT, SYNBASS, GTR1, GTR2— with a Sharpie in neat block letters on a strip of white masking tape under the console faders. Brickhouse called out orders to Jake for various compressors and reverbs, giving him just enough time to grab a pair of cables from a hook on the wall and stab them into jacks in the matrix for each device before calling out the next configuration. "Give me that bass line through the LA-2A on insert four, and patch aux two to the 480L, pre-fader, return on channel twenty-six."

The groove looped over and over. Eventually it stopped mutating, and Jake looked up at Billy through the glass, just in time to see him grab the cheap talkback mic from the boom stand over his keyboard and pull it closer. Brickhouse was looking down at the console when Jake reached over his shoulder and pressed a tiny button the size of a Tic Tac in the vast field of controls.

Brickhouse saw what Jake had done and completed the idea by shooting his right hand out and slapping the PLAY and RECORD keys on the multi-track remote control pad beside his chair. There was a sound of mechanical tension arms locking into place and tape began to roll just a half a beat before Billy started singing.

Do you bite your lip?
Do you twirl your hair?
Do you swing your hips?

Do you even care?
Do you raise your voice, drop your pants,
Do you even have a choice, did you ever have a chance?
In a dirty phone booth
Do you swear to tell the truth?
How do you speak the language of love?

As below, so above
As the serpent, so the dove
The world is whispering the language of love
You can hear it in the calm
In the space between the bombs
The world is whispering the language of love

Do you pierce your lip?
Do you paint your nails?
Do you start to strip
When all else fails?
Do you crack your whip, empty your clip
Sing and dance on a sinking ship
For love

Billy stopped singing and slapped the space bar on the laptop. The groove stopped short, the last beat echoing through the reverb processors in the control room. "My voice is shit tonight, but you get the idea."

Rail pushed open the glass plate doors that separated the control room from the big room, took a long slow breath, and said, "I smell money. Simply fantastic, Billy. The ragged voice even sort of suits it. Have you been chain smoking since your father's death?"

"Yeah."

"Well, keep it up, mate. It adds character. What do you say we go into town for a drink? We'll pick it up in the morning." Without waiting for a reply, he called out, "Kevin, come have a drink with us," and to Jake, "We'll pick it up tomorrow at eleven sharp."

The three men put their jackets on. Brickhouse lingered a moment in the control room before following them out to Rail's car.

"Good job catching that vocal on the fly. 'Night, Jake."

When the sound of Rail's car had receded into the night, Jake spun the tape off the take-up reel, packed it into its box and finished documenting the equipment settings. He picked up his black nylon bag and slung it over his shoulder as he walked through the live room toward the front door. Moon would be going upstairs to sleep when he got back from the bar, so Jake left most of the lights on, darkening only the control room, which continued to sparkle and pulse with the perpetual activity of flashing LEDs.

He was halfway across the floor toward the ironbound oak doors when he heard the piano in the loft sound a solitary note. He froze in place, awash with dread, ears pricked.

It came again, like a bell.

He thought of bolting across the remaining distance to the door, but he knew that to do so would only lend credence to the notion that something real and awful was happening here. He resisted the urge. What if he was imagining the sound? It was certainly not difficult to vividly imagine a single note being struck on the instrument he had played since childhood. It wasn't as if he were hearing a fully fleshed-out, two-handed piece of music. Surely his mind could evoke a single repetitive note in such detail that it seemed real to his tired brain.

So why not climb the stairs and see?

Would the note grow louder as he ascended to the loft? Would he see the key moving, like on a player piano, driven by some invisible hand? He felt the pressing need to urinate, but not here; it could wait until he got home.

The note rang out again. Tension iced his shoulders and he let out a short cry. He wondered if it was a black key or a white.

He looked at the other piano under its canvas cover in the kitchen area. Walking to it felt like walking through the shallow end of a pool. The solitary note from the loft resounded again as Jake lifted the cover and raised the keyboard lid. It was a high note, something in the octave above middle C.

He struck the E in that octave. As it faded, the phantom note came again, clashing horribly with the diminishing tail of the note he had played. That meant he had been very close in his guess. But the fact that a note he had actually played could vibrate with such dissonance in relation to what he wanted to believe was an aural hallucination caused the hair on his arms to rise as if lightning were about to strike nearby.

The note from above sounded again.

He struck the next key down from the E he had tried and that was it. That was the one: unison. It was D, an octave above middle C.

As if pleased with his discovery, the grand piano in the loft played four notes this time: a short melody starting on the D, moving up, then down low, then up again, like a doorbell chime.

Now there was a beat to accompany the melody. It was his heart.

EIGHT

Billy staggered out of Trevor Rail's ink-black BMW and up the church steps. He dug the key the runner had given him on arrival out of his jeans pocket and unlocked the big doors. Inside, the studio was dimly lit and quiet. He found the spiral stairs and climbed them singing to himself as he went, "There's a lady who's sure, all that glitters is gold... hmm... hmm... hmm... hmm...."

At the top, he passed the grand piano and headed across the catwalk to the other side. The loft over here was divided into two areas, the catwalk running down the middle. Long white curtains hung from thick dowels to create private spaces, not quite separate bedrooms. The curtained-off area on the right side had two twin beds, the one on the left a queen and a closet-sized bathroom. Each room was furnished with antique dressers, night tables and lamps with handmade paper shades.

The air smelled of cedar and lemon, and it all added up to a cozy summer camp vibe that reminded Billy of a cabin he had stayed in with Evan and their parents one long-ago summer when they had been vacationing farther upstate in the western lakes region. The memory brought with it another scent—the smell of charred toast cooked on a portable propane grill. His father had called it Camp Toast. Billy pushed the memory down and focused on his surroundings.

His Martin acoustic guitar lay on an upholstered chair in the corner. He picked it up and sat at the edge of the bed, hoping that fatigue and the light buzz of alcohol might conjoin to jimmy the door between the hemispheres of his brain and let his muse slip through. But as his fingers roamed, he found nothing new forming on the fretboard, just the chords of the Zeppelin song he still had stuck in his head from Trevor's car stereo. It was one of the first songs he had ever learned to play. He still remembered the very first.

Billy had learned the three chords that unlocked rock-and-roll's secret language like the Rosetta Stone from his uncle the summer of his tenth birthday. Uncle Tim had dropped in for a couple of weeks that turned into a couple of months on his way to find God. The timing was auspicious because Billy had just discovered his mother's box of Beatles records in the attic while digging out his snowsuit that winter.

By the time Uncle Tim arrived with a guitar and not much else, the last of the snow had melted, and Mom's tulip shoots had found their way out of the dirt and into the light again, and a scratched and dusty copy of *Rubber Soul* had been flipped over on the record player in Billy's room at least a hundred times, but it still had secrets to reveal. Like the sitar Uncle Tim pointed out on "Norwegian Wood."

"Why are you going to India, Tim?" Billy asked on a sunny August afternoon as they sat on the deck, rocking gently back and forth on the big wooden swing seat, listening to the chiming sound of ice cubes knocking against the sides of their glasses of lemonade. "What's there?"

"Yogis, young Will."

Billy wrinkled his nose. "What's a Yogee?"

"A very wise man. Some of them can even do miracles."

"Like walk on water?"

Uncle Tim nodded, "Mmm hmm."

"And fly?"

"Maybe. In a way."

"I don't believe you."

"That's okay. You don't have to. That's why I'm going, to see for myself. I'll let you know if it's true."

"What else can they do?" Billy asked, knowing that believe him or not, indulging Uncle Tim was always more entertaining than dropping a subject.

"Oh, all kinds of wondrous deeds."

"Like?"

Uncle Tim leaned forward, turned the palm of his hand up at the sky and wagged his index finger back and forth. Billy leaned in closer.

"I saw a picture of one of these fellows balancing the weight of his entire body on the tip of his dick."

Billy sprayed lemonade out of his nose and bounced up and down on the swing, laughing until his eyes watered. Uncle Tim raised the calloused, nicotine-stained finger in front of his mouth like the big hand of a clock pointing at midnight. Billy could see the indentation of a guitar string running a dirty gray groove across the tip of that finger.

"Don't tell your mother I said that."

While Billy caught his breath, Tim put his glass down on one of the wooden deck planks at their feet. Perspiration spread a dark stain through the sun-bleached wood in an instant.

Tim took his acoustic guitar from its case and strummed a chord.

"So you've been listening to the Beatles, kiddo?"

"You bet."

"You know that song 'Falling?'"

Billy shook his head.

"Sure you do. You know, 'Falling'." Billy's expression turned serious, almost reverent as Tim sang the lines and struck the chords, but his eyes also lit with a measure of joy.

"That's 'I've Just Seen a Face,'" Billy said.

"Yeah, 'Falling.'"

"You can play that?"

"Sure."

"The whole thing?"

"Yup."

Billy looked uncomfortable for a moment, as if searching for the words or the courage to ask his uncle for the keys to his rusted Camaro. Then he raised his eyebrow and said, "Can you teach me?"

Tim laughed, "Fuck yes, kemosabe. I mean, yeah, I can teach you, just—"

"Don't tell my mother you said that. Got it."

That late-summer day on the deck swing had been an unexpected awakening. His idea of what he could become instantly expanded. Through all of the chaos and trials that would follow in the years spent becoming, there would be so little of the easy clarity of that one afternoon when all of his life's ambition was handed to him in the shape of wood and steel. That had been the real beginning of his 'overnight' climb to stardom. But when had he started falling? Where was the beginning of that?

He laid the guitar back on the chair, undressed and slid into the queen bed, surprised and pleased by the softness of the sheets. He lay there for some time but sleep did not take him. Even after the long trip out of the city and into the mountains, the recording, and drinking, he felt restless. God knew he was tired and half in the bag, but despite the comforts of this place, he remained unsettled. Something was most definitely wrong. He rolled over and lay there listening to the memory of the groove they had demoed, looping round and around in his head. It was mixed with a strange droning sound that he recognized, when he focused on it, as a symphony of crickets or cicadas. He tuned into the texture of their sawing rhythm. And then he knew what was disturbing him. The insect drone was the *only* sound he could hear at all. No cars, no planes, no people on the other side of the wall fucking, no urban techno chatter. No voices on the street. This was the quietest place he had been in at least a year.

He rolled back over, stared up at the shadows in the high wooden beams and fell into sleep.

He was going down the spiral stairs, but now there were many more of them. He kept going down and around in the darkness. On and on. He had to get to the ground floor to answer the door. Someone was ringing a bell. It was a chime, a chime-sequence doorbell, like the one his mother had at the house where she now lived alone. Four notes, a common pattern for a doorbell but something about it was strange, a little odd, a little dissonant for a doorbell, not very welcoming. What uninvited guest did that melody herald? Down he went and around. The bell chimed.

It was dark—very late or very early. Was there a faint light growing in the stained glass windows above? He couldn't be sure. Maybe it was moonlight. Who could be calling at this hour? He stepped down and down, his shinbones aching, and at last he came to the bottom. Behind him were the oak doors. He went to them, grasped the handle of the one on the right, clicked the catch with his thumb and pulled it open. The dark air was cool and still. Even the insects had quit for the night. There was no one there.

The doorbell chimed again.

Closing the door, he turned and walked across the room. His computer equipment was gone from the floor along with the oriental rugs. Where the cables and rack cases had been there were now rows of pews. He walked past them down the aisle, up the few steps to the drum riser, where now there was an altar. Purple and yellow flowers spilled over its white-linen draped surface. Beyond it, the glass doors of the control room were gone. In their place, he found red curtains covering a little alcove with a floor made of flat paving stones. At the back of this space, a crumbling brick-and-mortar stair led down… to what? The answer floated up from nowhere: a *root cellar*.

The bell chimed. Could it be coming from down there? He listened. There was a slapping sound like a bare foot or a fish jumping in a puddle of water. Again the doorbell. Someone wanted in. Someone was persistent. But it was dark down there in the stairwell. He thought of lighting his Zippo, but it was upstairs in his jacket pocket with his smokes. He urgently wanted one now.

Billy stepped down the stairs. There were only five, and at the bottom he stepped into a shallow puddle. The smell of dusty earth filled his nose and mouth. And something else underneath. The something else reminded him of the time his father had recruited him to help take the bathroom sink apart because the drainpipe needed replacing. He had been fourteen at the time, and his father had decided he would make a good enough flashlight holder. The stench that flooded his sinuses when the sink trap was opened had been a putrid brew wafting up from black muck bound in tangled hair and clotted mucous. His father said the clog had probably been building up for forty years or more. Now that smell was here in this earth cellar, just below the cleaner scent of dirt.

Unable to stop it, he watched his hand floating out before him into the murky darkness. He expected to touch a tumorous façade of dirt, roots, and cobwebs. Instead, he felt wood under his fingertips. Sliding his fingers down the surface, he felt the grooves of spaces between the planks and at last, a cold metal latch that hooked down in an L-shape, pointing at the floor. It felt rough and rusty in his hand and he could picture orange residue staining his palm.

The chimes rang again. He lifted the handle and the latch popped open. The door swung toward him on shrieking hinges, a muted blue-gray light flooding the space around him. Somehow this was no cellar but a door to the outside. It was almost dawn beyond the threshold and the light delineated the figure of a man just a few feet in front of him. The brackish odor was overpowering now, and Billy wondered if it came from the figure in the doorframe or from the puddle at their feet—the puddle that encircled both his own Doc Martens and the black and tan sneakers on the other side of the threshold.

He knew those sneakers, had seen them toe to toe with his boots like this on more than a few plywood stages in Boston, amid stomp boxes and battered floor monitors.

Billy swept his gaze up the shadowy body over the dark brown corduroy jeans, feminine hands, red-and-white plaid shirt unbuttoned to reveal a faded KISS concert T. A shirt worn so often that it had become speckled with little holes in the thin fabric, the black cotton bleached to light brown here and there from too much cheap Laundromat powder. Jim had loved that shirt; Billy had hated when he wore it to gigs—and emerging from the ratty collar, the head of a dog, a Japanese fighting breed, its fawn-colored dewlap soaked with dark, syrupy blood, its muzzle dripping thick loops of saliva, ears pricked forward, lips curled back to reveal long, red-stained, incisors.

The dog-man cocked his head to one side and sniffed Billy's neck.

Billy's flesh crawled, and his testicles tried to climb up inside of him. Then the sound of a piano lid slamming down jolted him awake.

Moonlight illuminated the long white curtain beside his bed. The church was silent. What had woken Billy? A piano lid? Were there mice in this old building scampering over the equipment at night? Or had it been a car door?

He rolled out of bed, fully alert now, and looked at the small, unstained window at the end of the loft through which the moonlight cast a milky square on the floor. He went to the window and looked down at the needle-covered ground where studio staff parked their cars. The lot was empty. He scanned the landscape—the brook, the dark line of the woods beyond, and in the other direction, the dirt road running up the hill to the main building.

A figure stood at the edge of the road.

Fear flushed through his chest like ice water when he registered the shape as a human form. Someone was standing down there, gazing up at his window, motionless. How long had the figure been there watching and waiting? Everything was painted shades of indistinct gray in the thin moonlight, but Billy knew the posture and stature of this man, the cut of his clothes and hair, well enough to identify him without the details. It was Trevor Rail.

Billy didn't know if his own face was visible in the window, but he took a small step back, his eyes trained on the watcher the way a deer might focus on a wolf.

Rail slowly raised his left hand to chest level, palm up, as if weighing an invisible fruit. Fire bloomed in the palm of that hand, a ball of searing flame tumbling skyward and vanishing in the cool air. Billy took another step back. Rail mirrored the move, merging into the ground mist and shadows. Gone.

* * *

Jake was maneuvering his car around a series of potholes filled with coffee-colored mud a quarter of a mile from the church when he heard the first gunshot. He wasn't sure of what it was until the second report crackled through the woods. He wondered if it was deer season. The morning was cold and bright beneath the brilliant blue dome of the sky. Jake parked under the pine stand and got out.

He was just setting his foot down on the second step up to the studio doors when another shot made him jump, this one so loud and close that he looked down to make sure he wasn't hit. Scanning the tree line, he saw Trevor Rail perched on a large boulder at the edge of the forest, aiming a pistol into the dense foliage. Rail pivoted in a smooth sweeping arc, holding the gun with both hands. Jake didn't know the first thing about marksmanship, but based on what he'd seen on TV, Rail's form looked perfect.

Jake pushed his glasses up on the bridge of his nose and tried to glimpse what the producer was aiming at. He couldn't see any animals in the trees but that didn't mean they weren't there. He hoped Rail was just shooting wood.

Rail fired again and this time Jake saw a mist of blood floating between the trees for a second in a little clearing on the other side of the gurgling brook. It almost blended in with the autumn colors of the leaves. A buck with a full rack of antlers leapt into view and bounded off into the heart of the forest.

Rail swiveled, apparently keeping a bead on it for another seven seconds or so, but he didn't fire again. When the sound of the buck's retreat across the dry leaves had ceased, Rail examined his gun for a second, the first time he had taken his eyes off the woods since Jake's arrival. After this brief moment of admiration, he slipped the weapon into the pocket of his black wool overcoat and jumped down from the lichen-speckled boulder onto a litter of skeletal leaves.

"What the hell was that?" Jake said.

"Do you like venison, Jake?"

"*What?* You can't just shoot deer around here."

"I asked you a question. Do you like venison?"

"I've never tried it."

"Oh, but you simply must. You've no idea what you're missing."

"I don't see a hunting permit on the bumper of your Beemer."

"Touche'." Rail nodded at the church steps and waited for Jake to precede him. When Jake took the cue and stepped up, he half expected to feel the muzzle of the gun in the small of his back. His inner voice had almost refuted the irrational expectation when a fresh wave of fear surged over him in response to an altogether different stimulus.

As he opened the door, Jake heard the little melody that had come from the playerless piano the previous night.

Except now it didn't sound like a piano. It was the same phrase, no doubt, but it was being played on some sort of bells—big, dark bells, like Malaysian temple gongs. He imagined heavy discs of hammered bronze, dirty and ancient. The flesh on his arms prickled, and he almost expected to smell ozone in the air as he stepped into the big room. Then he saw Billy, seated at his Kurzweil synthesizer, playing the phrase over and over again on the plastic keyboard.

"What's that?" Rail asked.

Billy seemed not to have heard the question. He continued playing the little melody, slowly, meditatively. Rail stood beside him, hands buried in the pockets of his coat, eyes fixed on the keyboard and Billy's fingers, one of which bore a plain platinum band.

Billy stopped playing, letting the last note die out in a long wash of reverb through the room monitors. He looked at Rail and said, "Just a little scrap I heard in a dream." His eyes remained fixed on Rail's face, which Jake couldn't read as he walked to the control room, as slowly as possible, listening to the two men.

"Maybe it will become something," Rail said.

"I don't know. It's a little dull. Sounds like an out-of-tune doorbell. Don't you think?"

"Yes, but it's all about context. We may find a place for it, if only in a bridge or an intro."

In the control room, Jake threaded last night's master tape onto the multi-track and wound it back to the beginning. By the time he had his notes and coffee ready, Brickhouse had appeared and was asking Jake to fetch him a cup, too. When Jake returned from the kitchenette, Rail was giving Brickhouse the game plan for the day.

"We're going to re-track 'Language of Love.' Burn over the version from last night—the vocals were useless anyway. This time we'll get the whole song down, beginning to end. I imagine we'll add live drums later. For now, I want to work fast and get Billy's ideas down while they're fresh."

The session went according to plan. The only snag came during Billy's guitar overdubs. He had done three tracks of different riff ideas on his Les Paul, through a cranked amp, when he got frustrated during an attempt to double an exact performance of the third riff to fatten it up. Rail, who had suggested the double-track, finally told Billy to forget about it. They could go back and nail it on another day. It didn't matter at this early stage anyway. But it was too late; by the time they moved on to vocals, Billy was already in a bad mood.

"Do you smoke when you sing?" Jake asked him while positioning the mic.

The rock star glowered at him before answering, "No. Why?"

"Never mind. If you'd said 'yes,' I would have asked you not to blow smoke on the U47. My boss would have my head if you did, that's all."

"Well you can relax. I can get through a whole take without a drag, okay?"

The vocals surprised Jake. He had been expecting Billy's defeatist attitude after the guitar tracks to carry over into less than stellar singing, but in fact the reverse was happening. Billy sounded much better than he had the previous night. His voice was husky and sexy and oozing with sarcasm.

"Put a star on the track sheet," Rail told Jake. "It's a pretty special first take. He probably won't be able to do as well once he starts thinking about it."

"Like the guitar track," Brickhouse said. "Too much thinking."

"Not quite," Rail replied. When Brickhouse looked up from the meters with a furrowed brow, Rail elaborated. "I wanted him to bang his head up against that one for a while. Billy sucks at doubling guitar parts, he always has. He's too sloppy and spontaneous a player. If we need a good double, we'll chop one together in the computer. But *trying* to get one pissed him off. And Billy sings best when he's pissed off."

* * *

At eight o'clock, Rail called for a dinner break and told Jake to get the Wurlitzer electric piano from Studio A and set it up for an overdub while he, Billy, and Kevin went into town for a bite.

Jake did as he was told and had just finished when the trio

returned. His stomach was growling by the time they resumed work, tracking a little three-chord pattern that Billy played on the Wurlitzer during the choruses. It didn't take long. After that, the session started to devolve into hanging out, and Jake could sense that Trevor and Billy were out of fresh ideas for the day. Maybe he would get something to eat before midnight after all. He kept busy tidying cables and organizing track sheets, but his curiosity was piqued when Trevor asked Billy, "Did you get the gift I sent you in Tokyo?"

Billy's lax body language subtly tensed under his tight black clothes. "Yeah," he said. "Thanks."

"May I see it?" Trevor asked. "You did bring it along as I asked?"

Billy nodded, hesitated, then got to his feet and sauntered out to the stairs. When he returned from the loft, he carried a fancy silk brocade box, which he placed atop an equipment cabinet.

Rail took a languid drag on his cigarillo. The heavy smoke cascading from his nostrils made him look like a dragon as he lifted the lid of the box. Jake almost sighed audibly at the sight of a short, scarlet-and-black handled knife on a bed of gold silk. Flowers glinted on the black scabbard in mother of pearl, like the inlays on an expensive guitar.

Brickhouse breathed a low whistle of appreciation.

Trevor Rail drew the blade and turned it this way and that, admiring its lethal beauty, light flaring off the razored edge.

Billy said, "It's cool and all, but I'm not so sure about using it in the artwork."

"Why not?" Rail asked absently, his eye still on the keen edge.

Billy seemed to search himself for a reason. "Well, the flower theme, for one thing. It's kind of feminine, don't you think?"

Breaking out of his hypnotic examination of the play of light on steel, Rail met Billy's eyes and said, "The samurai revered the cherry blossom because it doesn't wither on the branch but falls at the pinnacle of its beauty, in full bloom. To them it represented a noble death, embraced without fear at the peak of a man's powers. *Better to burn out than to fade away*, and all that. So you see, it's a very rock-and-roll symbol."

Billy just nodded. The knife went back into the scabbard with the decisive snap of well-oiled, snug-fitting hardware, and then disappeared into the box to the clicking of clasps. End of exhibit. End of discussion.

The night wrapped up with a rough mix of the song, and just when Jake thought he was done for the day at ten past midnight, Rail called over his shoulder on his way out of the control room, sliding into his wool overcoat. "Jake, dub three copies of that DAT onto CDRs for me. Tomorrow morning we'll have a runner FedEx two of them to the bassist and drummer. Goodnight."

Brickhouse shot Jake a *Sorry, kid, but that's the job* look before pulling on his own jacket and following Rail out the door. Billy grabbed a beer from the fridge in the kitchenette and climbed the stairs to the loft where Jake heard him turn on the TV. Alone in the control room, he tore the shrink-wrap from the first CD blank and set about dubbing and writing labels.

He wore headphones while making the dubs, listening for any digital glitches or flaws. He was also still memorizing the lyrics and song structure to make the job of navigating the master tape a task he could perform without pausing to think.

When he took the headphones off, the sound of the TV was absent. Maybe Billy had gone to bed. Jake put the master tape away, turned off the lights and walked across the big room, touching the pocket of his L.L. Bean field coat on the way to make sure he had his car keys. Crossing the room, he noticed a tightening of his breathing and realized he was bracing himself to hear the piano. When the sound came, he wasn't startled, but he still felt his stomach drop.

He almost quickened his stride, but then he remembered that Billy was here, possibly sleeping or possibly also hearing the phantom melody. Clearly, he had heard it last night, if only in his sleep. He had regurgitated it this morning. If it woke him now, would he think Jake was playing it? For a split second, the idea scared him more than the notion of a ghost in the church. If Billy complained to Eddie or Susan that Jake woke him up in the middle of the night, playing the piano across the loft from his bedroom… But what if Billy heard it and saw the piano bench empty?

Jake took a deep breath and climbed the stairs.

At the top, he saw that the most obvious explanation was the one that had evaded his tired brain. Billy was seated at the piano, hammering out those four uninspired notes, over and over. Jake turned on his heel and put his foot back down on the top step as quietly as he could, but Billy spoke, "I don't usually dream melodies."

Jake didn't know what to say.

"I think the only reason I'm stuck on this one is *because* it came from a dream. It's pretty unoriginal, don't you think?"

Jake refrained from telling Billy exactly how unoriginal it really was. Instead, he said, "I guess Rail's right about it depending on the context." He took two steps toward the piano, looking over Billy's shoulder to see what note he was starting on.

Billy played the four quarter notes again: C, D, G, C.

Jake said, "Maybe you'd like it better as a guitar riff, if you messed around with the rhythm. Or maybe on piano but in a different key."

Billy asked, "Do you play?"

"Yeah, a little. Piano was my instrument at school."

There was silence between them for some time, except for the piano. Billy played the monotonous sequence. Jake watched him play it. Finally, Jake said, "Try it up a whole step, in D."

Billy's fingers climbed up the keyboard and played the same intervals a step higher. It didn't sound that different at all. Then he stopped playing and sat staring at the keys without blinking. The church was totally silent now. Billy's lips parted but he didn't speak. Jake felt a small pain in the palm of his hand and found that he was clenching his fists, digging his nails in as he waited for the D key to play itself right under Billy's nose. It didn't.

Billy looked at Jake, eyes wide, and said, "That's a funny melody."

Jake raised an eyebrow.

Billy played it again, this time singing the note names as he played them. His tired voice crackled, "Dee, Eee, Aay, Dee… Dead. It spells dead." He stood up from the bench, picked up his beer bottle and drained it into his mouth. "I'm going to bed, Jake."

"Okay."

Billy closed the lid on the keyboard. He walked across the catwalk, leaving Jake standing alone beside the piano, trying to find his feet.

Billy parted the canvas curtain, hesitated, then said, "You were right; it's much more interesting in that key."

NINE

Two weeks into the project, Billy Moon had demo versions of six new songs completed, and Trevor Rail decided it was time to start laying the foundations for master recordings with a live rhythm section. The drummer was Steve VanHausen from Cradle of Fire, the bassist Jeff Cabenieri from Diamond Head. The two had never played together before, but their bands had toured with Billy on Lollapalooza the previous summer. By the end of the first take of a song called "Black Curtain," the chemistry in the room was palpable.

But it wasn't good enough for Trevor Rail, who might as well have been pacing the control room with a cat o' nine tails. The producer wanted to splice together the best performance of each section culled from three or four takes of each song. In the computer, the edits would have been fast and easy, but Rail insisted they be done on the analog master tape with a razor blade, resulting in a grueling series of late nights for the engineers.

After the fourth night of edits wrapping up around four in the morning, Kevin Brickhouse was starting to feel like a zombie. The mirrors on the handlebars of his Indian had told him he was looking like one too, but his assistant, Jake, wasn't looking so hot either, and Jake didn't use rocket powder. Brickhouse knew he looked like shit, but as long as the kid looked like shit too, he didn't have to worry about it. It wasn't his lifestyle that was killing him; it was just the job. Good.

He looked out of the control room window at the rectory across the field. It was just a little farmhouse with crosses cut into the doors, but damn, the bed was comfortable. The place had a country charm that made him wonder what it would be like to finally settle down someplace quiet, maybe even get married again. Probably boring as all hell. He wondered if maybe it wasn't such a good thing that this studio had windows—in Manhattan they were as rare as truly great songs—because knowing that dawn had crept up again and being able to see the house where his bed waited was probably only making him more aware of how tired he was. Better to have no sense of place beyond the studio walls and no concept of time beyond the number of beats in the bridge.

He pressed PLAY and listened to the edit again, trying to relax and not focus on it. This time he only paid attention to his tapping foot as the music went by. If the splice was too early, it should catch his attention when his foot felt awkward. But it was smooth; he kept right on tapping into the third chorus. He looked at Jake and raised his eyebrows.

"Sounds good," Jake said. "Undetectable."

"Hopefully it'll still sound good when we're awake."

In the gray murk outside, a slouching shadow moved past the window, toward the front door of the church.

"Here comes Gribbens to drag your sorry ass across another sunrise," Jake said with a hint of mirth in his otherwise tired voice.

"Aw, shit."

"Why don't you just tell him you're going to sleep?"

"I should. He might have something for me, though."

Ron Gribbens was a runner who had been flirting with the transition to assistant engineer for over a year. Apparently Eddie didn't trust him enough yet to promote him outright, but he was often assigned to help out with setup or mixdown sessions that required extra hands. Brickhouse had met him on a session he'd done in Studio A the previous winter. A low-fi indie band called Upchuck. Their producer had been stuck on the asinine idea of tracking the entire band live in the big room with stage monitor speakers instead of headphones, resulting in feedback and bleed-through problems that required extra hands to sort out.

Gribbens had done a competent job and had charmed the band enough to stay on for a few days after the extra help was justified. Then Eddie O'Reiley asked him what the fuck he was doing chalking up overtime if the monitor problem was solved and put him back on deli runs. But the band, and Kevin, had been sorry to see him go. Even if everyone knew Gribbens was something of a liability—a well-meaning kid who would probably unplug the right wire at the wrong time if allowed to hang around long enough—he more than made up for it with personality. His jokes had a way of diffusing the tension that so often arose from musicians taking themselves too seriously. Brickhouse figured if the kid's musical timing was as good as his comedic timing, he would probably rise to engineer before some of his more technically gifted peers.

When Gribbens got wind that Brickhouse was back at Echo Lake for the Billy Moon project, he had started dropping by after sessions with a six-pack, a bottle of Stoli, or a bag of weed. At first Brickhouse had been happy to partake of these gifts, and tired as he was, he did enjoy the kid's company. They would hang out in the little living room of the rectory watching some rare video—a bootleg of Jeff Beck at the House of Blues, or four hours of Spinal Tap outtakes—and getting drunk.

But as the late night editing sessions grew longer, the kid's charm was thinning. The only problem was—so was Brickhouse's personal supply of Peruvian Rocket Powder. And Ron Gribbens was probably the only person he knew in this town who could score for him.

Gribbens opened the glass doors and poked his head into the control room. "Hey, can I come in? Are you guys still working?"

"We just finished," Brickhouse said, leaning back in the leather chair and stretching his arms until his shoulders popped. "But keep it down while the door's open. Billy's sleeping upstairs."

"Right, sorry." Gribbens closed the doors behind him and leaned in over the console, his eyes wider and brighter than they had a right to be at this hour of night, or morning, or whatever it was. Brickhouse didn't think stimulants were responsible for that, though. Ron Gribbens always seemed to be running on a higher voltage than everyone around him.

"Hey, Kev," Gribbens said, "how can you tell there's a rock singer on your doorstep?" He paused. "He can't find the key and he never knows when to come in."

Brickhouse slammed his head into the console's leather wrist rest three times in slow motion, then looked up and asked, "How long have you been working on that one? Do you ever stop?"

Jake sidled past Gribbens and slung his bag over his shoulder. "See you later."

When Jake was gone, Brickhouse said, "I don't suppose you have any coke you could loan me?"

For the briefest instant, Gribbens looked serious. He said, "No, but I may be able to get you some. Do you need it right away?"

"For tonight's session. I've been awake for I don't know how many days. Even if I catch a few hours this morning, there's no way I'll be able to do another session. Not without getting sloppy and making mistakes."

Gribbens nodded and said, "Did you know that after a few days without sleep, the DMT in your brain kicks in? Are you tripping right now?"

"No."

"Damn. Let me know if you start tripping. I always wanted to know if that's true. I heard that you dream while you're awake if you go long enough."

"Listen to me, Ron. I'm not looking to trip right now, okay? I need to stay awake to work today. Can you score?"

"Pretty sure, pretty sure, man. But do you have cash? I would need cabbage up front. I know a guy."

"Cool." Brickhouse pulled a wallet on a chain out of his back pocket and peeked into the fold. "Shit, I used the last of my per diem for take-out. Can you front me until tonight? I *have* to go to bed now, but I can hit an ATM in town before the session starts."

"Kev, how long has it been since you held my job? You think I have coke money? Man, I practically work for free. I can't even fix the alternator on my ride right now."

"Sorry. How can you be a runner without a car?"

"Susan, the assistant manager's letting me use hers for the errands in the daytime for now."

"Oh. Well, fuck it then. I'll go to the ATM right now."

"Are you taking the Harley?"

"That's my only ride, if you don't have one."

"Cool, can I ride on back? You can drop me at home on the way back from town."

"I guess. But I only have one helmet."

"So?"

"So there's a helmet law."

"What are you, Ralph Nader? It's four-thirty in the morning and we're going to get coke money. You're worried about the *helmet law*?"

"I could fall asleep on the bike. Seriously, it's not out of the question."

"Come on, that's lame. You're not gonna fall asleep. Do you want to score or not?"

"Okay, but *you're* wearing my helmet."

"The Captain America Bucket? Fuck yeah, baby!"

Brickhouse picked up the helmet by the strap and tossed it at Gribbens. They walked down the front steps of the church and climbed onto the bike. Brickhouse turned the key and kicked the Indian to life. He revved the engine with the fringe-draped accelerator and felt the kid's arms wrap around his waist.

The bike jolted out from under the trees onto the dirt road, spitting up gravel and pine needles. The sky over the field was still dark except for a few shreds of pink cotton. Even that nascent light disappeared when they left the clearing behind and wound down the hill into the thick shadows of the woods. Brickhouse switched on the headlamp. Ground mist swirled around the bike in slow churning eddies.

"Faster!" Gribbens shouted over the engine.

Brickhouse leaned over the handlebars and gave it a little more juice. Gribbens's laughter was snatched from his mouth by the wind. Brickhouse shifted his weight and eased up on the throttle as they came around a bend in the road toward the bottom of the hill. He was about to gun it again when he saw twin points of light in the tunnel of trees up ahead, low down near the ground in the mist. His first thought was, *animal eyes*. He knew what the reflections of the bike's headlamp in a pair of cat, skunk, or possum eyes looked like, but these were larger, and stacked vertically. Half a second later, they were close enough for him to understand what he was seeing: it was a buck lying in the road, head tilted at a bad angle, antlers throwing stark shadows across the ground.

What Kevin Brickhouse saw next, he would not understand for

the rest of his life, which was now the length of a song.

A gray shape was draped over the carcass. Impossibly, it appeared to be a naked woman, her hips voluptuous, her face concealed by a veil of long, dark hair. Was she wrapped around the dead animal in a futile effort to help it? A crazy woman, out here naked in the freezing night? She turned her head toward him with a slow, strained resistance, and he could see she was ripping a red tangle of gut out of the deer's belly with her teeth.

Unconcerned with the roaring machine that was now bearing down upon her, she had only turned her face toward the motorcycle to stretch the bloody cords in her mouth. Her eyes, unlike the deer's, did not reflect the light of the bike's headlamp. They were vacant black tunnels at first, but in the fraction of a second it took Brickhouse to register the scene, they kindled from within, emitting a dim blue phosphorescence, apparently fueled by tendrils of blue mist rising from the carcass and wafting into the woman's nostrils.

He had time to think that it was strange how there was no blood on her face, considering what she was doing. It looked like she was trying to eat the raw flesh but was made of something too subtle to really connect with it, her only real sustenance the blue vapor.

He released the throttle, slowing as much as he could without breaking and skidding on dead leaves, but the bike was moving too fast. The woman's face raced toward him in the shuddering beam of the headlamp, which only made the image somehow thinner. Brickhouse jerked the handlebars too sharply to the right—a reflex sparked by pure aversion, un-tempered by thought. The bike spilled, became a spinning hulk of blue chrome and black leather.

Ron Gribbens screamed. Gravel shredded his jeans and dug trenches into his thighs, the bike pinning him to the ground and dragging him forward.

Brickhouse was thrown off before the bike had completed one rotation. He landed on the buck's antler rack, the pitted spires piercing leather and flesh, impaling him through his rib cage and the hollow of his right shoulder. Pain blasted out all of his senses like a wash of white noise, but only for an instant. He coughed out a spray of blood, and when his vision cleared, he saw the wraith woman again, now mere inches from his face. Her head floated over his broken body, as if she was smelling him, inhaling the etheric emissions of warm plasma.

The red glow of the day's first light spilled over the ground, and the woman faded even more than she had in the glare of the headlamp. It was a small mercy. Simultaneously, his vision swarmed with red specks, the combination producing an effect not unlike a pixilated digital video image from a worn out camcorder tape. He coughed up a string of pink saliva. *This is it*, he thought, *this is where it all ends.*

Through the distorted vision, narrowing to a tunnel, his gaze settled on the last thing he would ever see: a chunk of regurgitated deer liver. He could feel his broken guts trying to vomit, but then the life force required to jettison it drained out of him.

* * *

When Eddie O'Reiley came around the bend in his dust-covered Jeep Cherokee on the way to the main building, he nearly drove off the road at the sight of Ron Gribbens pinned under a motorcycle, sobbing, the broken body of Kevin Brickhouse twisted around a deer. The stars and bars helmet that looked like the one worn by Peter Fonda in *Easy Rider* lay on the ground between them.

Eddie called 911 on his mobile phone. He could see that the Harley was only pinning Ron's leg, and since the kid didn't appear to be losing blood, he picked it up by the handlebars and pushed it over to the nearest tree he could lean it on. It was almost too heavy for him, but he managed.

"Don't try to get up," he said. "I called for an ambulance. Did you hit your head?"

"No. I just got dragged. I had his helmet on. Oh God... Oh fuck..."

"Who was driving?"

"He was."

"Can you feel your toes if you try to wiggle them?"

"Ah! Yeah. But it *hurts*."

"Okay, don't move. Your leg's probably broken, but I think you were lucky."

"*He* wasn't. Is he dead?"

Eddie looked Gribbens in the eye for a few seconds. He

nodded.

"Oh God, oh man, this is so fucked. It's my fault."

"Was he on something?"

"No. I don't think so. I don't know. He just finished working. I asked him for a ride 'cause he was going to the seven-eleven."

"Why is it your fault?"

"I was telling him to go faster."

"And he did?"

"Yeah."

"Gribbens, what the hell is the matter with you? Why do you think we put signs up? It's a winding dirt road. There are deer everywhere. Blind curves. The fucking speed limit is fifteen for a reason."

"I'm sorry."

"A man is dead. You're lucky to be alive."

Gribbens sobbed. "Eddie, I'm sorry. I'm so sorry."

"How am I going to explain this to Lucy?"

"Isn't she in Belize?"

"Yeah, but I'm gonna have to tell her a client died on her property. Kevin Fucking Brickhouse, no less. Fuck me. I'm not even at the office yet and this is how the day starts."

Eddie turned his back on Gribbens and forced himself to take a closer look at Brickhouse. What a mess. He couldn't look away. He had assisted Brickhouse himself a couple of times when he was getting started in L.A. in the seventies. The man had been one of the best. By the time Eddie moved back to New York, he was considered a capable engineer himself, but he already knew he would never be in the same league as Brickhouse. He was okay with that; he had also already seen that the lifestyle came with a price.

Maybe taking the management gig at Echo Lake had saved him from driving into a tree some sleep-deprived night. Who could say? He remembered asking Brickhouse a personal question when they had worked together for the second time. Brickhouse had been married back then. Eddie had just met Irene, his future wife, and things were already starting to get serious. He had asked Brickhouse how he made his marriage work with the demands of the job. Brickhouse hadn't even hesitated in his response. "It's simple," he had said, "I'm just not that into her. It's comfortable for both of us, and I don't think she really minds me being away. We have a great house in Hollywood. I get laid when I'm home and she's a beautiful girl, but if I was way into her, I don't think it would work. I'd miss her."

Looking down at the bloody mess at his feet, Eddie reflected that Brickhouse had been a good guy and a great engineer, but after a funeral that could be mistaken for an awards show, with all of the moguls and rock stars in attendance, who would really miss him?

Eddie turned back to Gribbens. Now he could hear the faint wail of sirens through the woods. "I don't get it. Did you kill the deer or was it already dead in the road? It looks like the birds have been at it for a while."

"It was already dead. There was a crow eating it when we hit it. Kevin swerved to miss it and we wiped out."

"Alright. That sounds more like an accident. I'm sorry I yelled at you."

The ambulance came over the hill, flashing and wailing, and nearly slammed into Eddie's Jeep, but at the last second, they cut around it, somehow missed the trees as well, and came to an abrupt stop beside the tangled corpses of deer and man. Paramedics jumped out. One opened the back doors and pulled out a stretcher, the other knelt beside Gribbens and started asking him questions about his vision and where he felt pain. More sirens sang on the morning air, police cars on the way.

As he was lifted into the ambulance on the stretcher, Gribbens called out to Eddie, snapping him out of a daze.

"Yeah, Ron?"

"Would you call my mom?"

"Sure."

* * *

Trevor Rail called a three-day break in the sessions so he could fly to L.A. for the funeral. Jake, in a state of shock, had used the first of the three days to catch up on sleep. On the second day, he tried to hang around the apartment with Ally to catch up with her. They ended up hauling their laundry to the local Laundromat together and watching the spinning clothes in silence.

Later, Jake told her he was going to the studio for an hour or so, just to check in and see what Eddie was doing about the outboard gear that had belonged to Brickhouse. If it was being removed from the signal chain and shipped back to L.A., Jake wanted to make sure the project could still run without it. After all, Rail had only called for a three-day break.

Ally sighed and said, "Does it really matter? I mean, hasn't the engineer himself been *removed from the chain?* Jesus, Jake, these people act like it's the arms race or something. Rail should cancel the project after this. But oh, what will the world do without a new Billy Moon CD?"

"Honey, it's my job until someone tells me it isn't."

When he returned to the apartment, she had dinner cooking on low heat, trying not to burn anything. At the sound of his key in the door, Marla the cat jumped off the banister and hopped down the first three stairs to greet him. Ally scooped the rice and stir-fry vegetables onto plates and lit a candle on a bookshelf in the living room. They didn't have room for a kitchen table, so they usually ate sitting on the couch if Jake was home for a meal.

Tonight she'd borrowed a folding card table from their landlord, Sam, who lived on the first floor. It wobbled, but she'd wedged a cardboard shim under one leg and tossed a small tapestry over the tacky surface to serve as a tablecloth. She was setting the plates down on it when Jake topped the stairs and gave Marla a quick scratch behind the ears. The cat arched her back, and her tail floated up like a charmed snake.

Jake looked up and smiled, made a soft little sigh through his nose. "This is nice," he said. He kissed Ally on the head and took a seat. She opened a beer and put it down beside his plate.

Before he could lift the bottle to his lips, the phone rang.

"Let the machine get it," Ally said. But Jake was already reaching for the receiver.

The caller introduced herself as Danielle, Billy's manager. After politely thanking Jake for all of his help so far, she asked, "So how are you handling Kevin's death, Jake? It must be difficult for you, having worked so closely with him."

"I only knew him for a few weeks, but yeah, it's pretty heavy trying to process it. He was a good guy. Treated everyone with respect."

"From what I gather, you earned his respect."

Jake didn't know what to say to that, so he asked, "Have you all decided who will be coming on for the rest of the project?"

"That's what I wanted to talk with you about."

"I don't know if I could recommend anyone," Jake said, "I haven't worked with many engineers yet."

"The thing is, Jake, Billy takes some time getting comfortable with new bodies in the room when he's writing. Kevin worked on the previous two albums, so it felt natural working with him again. But now, starting over with someone new when the material is in a vulnerable early stage, well… we're afraid it could hurt the record."

"Does Rail have someone in mind?" Jake asked.

"I don't know, but *we* were thinking of asking you."

"Like I said, I don't think I could recommen—"

"Don't be so dense, Jake. We want you to engineer."

He felt as if someone had told him he had just won the lottery and all he had to do to claim the prize was swim across that little pool, with the sharks. He said, "But it's Rail's decision, isn't it?"

"Ultimately, yes. But if Billy doesn't feel comfortable with Trevor's choice, he'd rather postpone the sessions. And if that happens, I think even the brass at Gravitas would let Billy have his way, considering what's happened. You seem unsure. Are you not getting along with Trevor?"

"No, I think we're okay. I just don't want to overstep my bounds. I wouldn't want to engineer a record if the producer didn't think I should be doing it."

"Of course not," Danielle said. "Let me talk to Trevor on Billy's behalf. I'll let him know that we're very comfortable with you and that Billy doesn't want to change the vibe. He doesn't have to know that we discussed it with you. Billy says you've taken the wheel a few times already when Kevin needed a break. Are you up to it?"

"Yes. I could do it. I mean, we already have most of the sounds set up. If Billy likes what he's hearing so far, I could keep running it."

That seemed to be all Danielle needed to hear. "Okay," she said. "Then between us it's settled. I'll speak with Trevor and Eddie."

Jake hung up the phone and turned to Ally. "They want me to take Kevin's place."

She threw her arms around his neck and planted a kiss on his cheek with an audible smack. "Congratulations," she said. "That was fast."

"It's not for certain."

"They want you."

He laughed. "Yeah. Weird, but kinda cool, huh?"

"It is. You should let yourself feel good about it."

"It's just a strange way to get your first gig."

"That's not your fault."

"I know."

"I knew you'd go places sooner than you expected."

He kissed her, this time on the mouth. She studied his eyes and asked, "Are you excited?"

"Terrified."

TEN

Rachel Shadbourne's black nail-polished fingers fluttered over the dirty keypad of her cash register, ending with a swipe of her thumb across the ENTER key in the corner. The drawer ejected, she counted out change, slid the three discs of shit you couldn't pay her enough to listen to into an orange Velocity Records bag, swung the bag over the counter—hooked on her finger as if it were indeed a doggie pickup baggie—and deposited it into the hands of the sorority girl customer with a big fake smile. She looked up at the line, sighed, and slapped the little silver bell on the counter as the next patron stepped up with a basket full of Country and Classic Rock. The bell was a joke anyway with Tupac pounding out of the house system at bowel-churning volume. Where the hell was Paul now?

She walked away from her register without so much as a word to the miffed-looking Baby Boomer holding out his plastic and stepped into the DJ booth where she cranked the volume dial down. She returned to the register and slapped the bell three more times, making it jump across the counter, then picked up her scanner gun, and fired the little red laser at each disc as if she meant to kill Garth Brooks, George Strait and Peter Frampton.

No one appeared in response to the bell. Of course not. Paul was probably downstairs in the basement where the Art Department kept shop, chatting with his guitarist, Andy, who spent his days applying his Bachelor of Fine Arts degree to the creation of the three dimensional Styrofoam signs that hung from fishing line throughout the store. For a moment, Rachel almost regretted ever having sex with Paul Yurgovich, or Paul *LeStadt*, or whatever he was calling himself this week in the Hemoglobin flyers he and his imps stapled to every telephone pole in Minneapolis.

Sure, he had stage presence, but after you got over how he looked under the red lights without a shirt, you couldn't help eventually noticing that the music kind of sucked. And yet he didn't seem to be reaching that conclusion himself in spite of the fact that even with his indie CD loaded in the first listening station you came to at the top of the escalator in the biggest record store in the only city where his band played regularly, it wasn't selling at more than a trickle. He still strutted around the floor like a visiting celebrity, conferring with his band mates and avoiding the register at all costs, except to look up his own disc three times a day and see if it had sold another copy.

Rachel was a supervisor. She shouldn't have to ring down a line like this by herself. Did he think their tryst had made him exempt from doing his job? Well she might have to let him know it wasn't Hemoglobin she'd been listening to in her headphones when she hitched up her skirt for him in the break room that night. It was Billy Moon. And despite Paul's well-toned body, it was also Billy Moon whom she had imagined sliding her thong down between her knees as she pressed the palms of her hands against the Employee Rights poster and closed her eyes, using her hips to teach him the tempo of the music in her private halo.

She guessed a better singer would have known the groove wasn't one of his own. So he was in a band, so what? So was every other wage slave in the building from the grunts in Shipping and Receiving to Steve Singledon himself, their black-clad, more-salt-than-pepper boss who spent his weekends working on his drum chops and his beer pouch. Passion, she had learned after a short time on the retail front lines of the music business, was the most exploitable commodity on earth.

She hit the bell again, this time hard enough to send it bouncing off the counter and over the velvet rope that kept the cattle in a neat line. But she couldn't prevent her train of thought from reaching the conclusion that Paul had exploited *her* passion for Moon by presenting himself as an adequate substitute.

She looked at the line again. It had grown. At this rate she was never going to get a spare minute to run downstairs to the magazine section and snag a copy of *Billboard*. Why couldn't she have found out about the article before she'd taken lunch? Then she could have read it by now.

Ah, here was the poseur now, striding up to the checkout with that ever so serious look on his face, all purple hair and leather—the plastic name tag swinging from a black lanyard around his neck like a backstage pass the only indication that he worked here. He actually stooped to pick the little chrome dome from the carpet and set it next to his register before typing in his password and uttering a barely audible, "Help someone down here."

When the line had disappeared, she noticed Paul starting to type his log out and stopped him in his tracks. "*Wait,*" she said in a tone she usually reserved for her roommate's corgi. "You're first ringer until somebody gets back from lunch." And before he could begin arguing, she slipped into the stockroom to close the web browser she'd left open on the computer they were only supposed to use to check the CD database. Of course every employee in the place also used it to check their hotmail, and to surf porn and the assorted musical fetishes that had led them to the job in the first place.

This morning, like clockwork, she had pulled up the Lunar Sightings message board and tucked it behind the Velocity home page where she could refresh it obsessively every half hour or so when she ducked back here on the excuse of topping off her coffee. She was looking to see if any of her anonymous friends had any tidbits about the new album, already rumored to be in production. But there was nothing new on the board. Just the same old stale posts that had devolved into flame wars and lame attempts at wit by the end of last week, when there were three days of wild speculation touched off by a rumor that Billy Moon had been attacked by a pit-bull in Japan and that he had subsequently been seen wearing a scarf over his now mutilated face at his father's graveside.

Rachel knew at least some of that was false—she had found his father's obituary by a search of Long Island newspapers using Billy's birth name (after striking out at asking the webmaster of billymoon.com for the name of a funeral home so she could send flowers) and the obit had mentioned cremation. So there was no graveside for him to be seen at. As for the dog story, she couldn't know either way but she doubted it. Billy had been the subject of dark and violent rumors before.

And yet today's rumor, the violent death of an engineer during the recording of the new album, would have fit the profile that Billy's publicist seemed to thrive on. Wouldn't that be big news for a spooky gothic rocker, an opportunity for some pre-release headlines? But no one on Lunar Sightings had made mention of it, and she wasn't going to be the one to put it up there. If it were true, and there was no press release about it from Billy's people, it could only mean that they were trying to keep the media away from him while he worked. Maybe only she and Karen had made the connection.

Rachel read the email again before closing it.

Sender: nikonsniper@ibishead.net
Recipient: shadowgirl76@wickedmail.com
Subject: Stalking on the Moon

Hey Rachel,

i'm gonna give you a tip today that i won't post, because i think you might be crazy enough to actually use it. my way of saying thanx for the live mp3s. check out the new issue of Billboard, pg. 33. there's an obituary for Kevin Brickhouse, who i'm sure you know engineered the first two discs, if you go through booklet notes with a magnifying glass like yrs trly. Says he died in a motorcycle accident while working at a studio in upstate New York near Woodstock. They don't name the artist he was working with, but i'll bet you your used BM water bottle it's him. remember that MTV music news blip in sept. that said he was going to be recording on the east coast after the tour? anyway, i just know it's him. i can feel it. of course, with a member of their crew dead, they might have canceled the sessions, but you should check it out. i'd pack my camera and go with you if you really mean what you said about tracking him down, but i wouldn't have an apartment or a job to come back to if i did. you MUST keep me

posted if you do it. and get him to sign
something for me!
xoxo

Karen

Rachel closed the browser and walked out onto the floor, past Paul who was ringing down a small line and straight to the escalator, down to Magazines where the oversized cover of *Billboard* beckoned to her in its colorful header. She plucked it from the rack and waved at Matt, the brawny deadhead who worked this section, then retreated to the stockroom where she sat on a box and flipped to page 33. The article said everything Karen had paraphrased and nothing else useful, except maybe the names of the other artists Brickhouse had recorded.

She knew that *Eclipse* was recorded at Electric Ladyland in New York and *Lunatic* was done at A&M in L.A. Billy had never worked at a studio in upstate New York before, but obviously someone had recommended it. That could have been anyone. It could have been Trevor Rail. It could have been Brickhouse himself. These were the names she had to work with. Maybe she would get lucky.

She did a quick walkthrough of the rock department and found Steve Singleton having a hushed talk with Bobby, a clerk in his thirties, who did a good enough job when his medication was working. She paused to straighten some disheveled discs nearby and tuned into their conversation long enough to hear suave Steve telling flannel-clad Bobby that, no, he wasn't fucking Bobby's wife. Bobby was just being paranoid, and he regretted ever fucking her in the first place because it almost broke up his own marriage— it was months ago and Bobby was going to have to get over it.

Rachel moved on, cruised over to the end of the alphabet and picked up a copy of the only disc Upchuck had put out. She took the long way back to the registers, avoiding the quiet Jerry Springer moment her boss was having over there among Pearl Jam, Pink Floyd and Prince. She also pulled copies of Guttermonkey and the Drowning Lisas before returning to the stockroom where she immediately sliced the three discs open with the little razor knife that hung from a nylon cord around her neck beside her nametag. It wasn't stealing if the merchandise didn't leave the store.

Brickhouse had recorded Gutter Monkey in Jersey City, the Drowning Lisas in New Orleans and Upchuck (bingo!) at Echo Lake Studios, New York. That sure didn't sound like the name of a studio on Fifth Avenue. Back to the web. Google: Echo Lake Studios. The studio home-page roster of previous clients included producers and engineers and showed not only Kevin Brickhouse for Upchuck, but also Trevor Rail for Cradle of Fire. She felt a tingle in her belly. *He* was there. Right now.

The pictures looked nice. It was like a summer camp in the woods, only with more buttons, dials and lights than a 747. There was even a studio in an old church. Of course. That's the one he would be in. She jotted the mailing address on a piece of register tape. Two more stops on the web and the printer was spitting out schedules and fares for Amtrak and Trailways. Rachel folded the pages and put them in her purse, tossed the opened CDs in the defective bin and returned to her post at the register.

Before her break, she had been tired. Now she worked through the rest of the day in a flurry of busy energy as if she'd taken a double espresso instead of a research binge.

Shortly before her shift ended, Steve Singleton plodded past her register on the way to his office.

"Steve," she called over her shoulder and received the best *What now?* look he could muster.

"I need to talk to you about my vacation time."

ELEVEN

Jake was in the driver's seat now and Ron Gribbens had been assigned to assist. Jake had asked Eddie if he thought that was a good idea considering Ron might still be shaken by the accident. Should he be working on the last project Kevin Brickhouse had set in motion when he felt responsible for the man's death? They had been friends, after all. Jake had said all of this in a single breath before pausing to think about what he was doing: questioning Eddie's judgment to his face.

Eddie replied that Gribbens wanted to work, and he was the only body available. "If they want you behind the desk, he's all I can spare right now. All three rooms are working. Is it a bad idea? The whole fucking project's probably a bad idea at this point. What do you want me to do, tell Gravitas I don't want their money? Moon will probably have a breakdown before Ron can do any real harm. Just keep an eye on the kid, would you? Try not to let him do anything stupid." Eddie looked down at the paper on his desk and the pen in his hand, indicating that the matter was settled.

Jake knew better than to push it.

Eddie sighed. "I wish I could give you a better assistant. But he's been here a long time. It's his turn. And he may know more than you think."

In fact, the first few days back at work had introduced Jake to a new Ron Gribbens, much more sober-minded and focused on what he was doing. Jake was relieved that he didn't need to have the talk with Ron he had imagined might be necessary, about keeping a low profile. He'd wondered, before they resumed the sessions, if Ron's nervousness might manifest as an overdriven sense of humor.

Fortunately, all of the comedic flair seemed to have been drained right out of the younger man, who now walked with a slight limp and wore a temporary knee brace. Jake figured that the new demeanor could mostly be attributed to his brush with death, but he wondered if some of it wasn't also the result of Gribbens possessing some ability to read the tension in a room after all, and attenuate his personality accordingly.

Because there was no denying the vibe in the room. In the days after work resumed, the tension between Rail and Moon droned underneath everything like a sixty-cycle hum.

The subject was a ballad called "After the Storm." Billy had spent the morning laying down the acoustic guitar and vocal live to a click track, and Jake was pretty happy with the sounds he was getting. Rail had maintained silence. He was either satisfied enough with the sound not to comment, or he didn't care how it sounded because he intended to shit-can the song after indulging Billy for a little while.

A couple of takes in, Rail finally spoke up and asked Billy for the lyric sheet. His pen hovered over the page, tracing empty lines in the air. Then he dropped the paper onto the field of knobs and leaned back in his chair, looking at a fixed point on the ceiling as if something intensely interesting was occurring up there on one of the acoustic tiles.

After an adequately suspenseful silence, he said, "It's too optimistic for you. And too literal. Your audience expects darker, angrier material." He looked at Billy. "You could have your publisher shop it around and find an artist who could make a killing on it for you in the triple A format, but if *you* put this song out, I promise you the critics will crucify you. So will your fans. They'll say you're selling out, that you've lost your edge, gone soft."

"I guess I have more faith in my audience than you do."

"And that, mate, is why I'm here. Take a cue from Nine Inch Nails, Billy. If you're going to write a ballad, at least have it be about self-mutilation, not getting *better*. You don't even know your own demographic," said Rail, and before Billy could argue, he turned to Jake. "Put 'Black Curtain' on the machine. We're going to focus on something that's working, because this isn't."

Gribbens had the "Black Curtain" master off the shelf before

Jake could get out of his chair.

"Fuck this," Billy said. He snatched his pack of cigarettes from where they lay atop the left monitor speaker and stormed out of the control room through the side exit, climbed the stone path beside the building, and disappeared in the direction of the creek and the woods beyond as the glass door hissed shut behind him.

Rail turned to Gribbens and said, "What are you waiting for? Cue the bloody song up. He'll be back."

The studio clock ticked out most of an hour. Rail listened to "Black Curtain" over and over again, making notes on the lyric sheet. He went out to the big room and picked up Billy's red Les Paul.

For some reason he couldn't quite put his finger on, Jake felt unsettled watching Rail tune Billy's guitar. Then it came to him: it reminded him of a story he'd read about how Robert Johnson had handed his guitar over to the Devil at a crossroads, to have it tuned by the arch fiend, in effect, selling his soul.

Rail put on the headphones and told Jake to keep rolling the song and give him some guitar in the cans without recording it. Then he played a tight mechanical riff that locked in perfectly with the hi-hat, giving the song a chugging, metallic pulse. Jake and Ron exchanged an astonished look, but didn't say a word.

Rail had just finished tracking his first pass at the song when Billy reappeared at the side door, walked straight through to the big room, and yanked the cable out of the amp, eliciting a loud crackle of static followed by a brief hum, then near silence, except for the tinny chatter of the backing track in the headphones when Rail took them off and handed them to Billy, who was now holding out his other hand for the guitar neck.

"Give me my guitar, you fucking hack."

Rail slipped out of the strap and handed the guitar over. Billy slung it on and pulled the headphones over his neck. The two men stared at each other. Rail said, "Can you play that part or shall I teach it to you?"

"I can play it better than that. Go back to your side of the glass."

They recorded guitar overdubs for the next three hours with scarcely any talk. Billy's playing became more ambitious with each new take. Some of it was brilliant—a dissonant little melodic hook he played on a Stratocaster—and some of it was mere noise. Jake estimated maybe half of what they got would make the final mix and half of that would be buried in the background.

While they worked, Rail kept turning up the master volume of the monitors. Then he switched from the little near-field speakers to the big ones the size of refrigerators suspended on chains from the ceiling on either side of the glass doors. He turned it up some more, eyes closed, snakeskin boot tapping on the scuffed floor. Jake pulled a tissue from the box on the side of the console, ripped a couple of pieces off, rolled them into balls between his fingers and stuffed them in his ears. Just then, the left speaker went dead. Rail switched back to the small monitors, their white cardboard cones visibly jumping to life. He shot a look at Gribbens and shouted, "Fix it!"

Gribbens looked at Jake, who was keeping an eye on the pumping needles in the meter windows. Jake waved him to lean in and shouted directly into his ear. "The fuse is in the back of the speaker cabinet."

Gribbens sprinted to the amplifier closet and rummaged through some plastic drawers looking for a replacement fuse. The control room was dimly lit, making the closet even darker. Gribbens pulled the chain to switch on the light.

Jake saw something fly past his face across the front of the console and only realized it was a beer bottle when it smashed against the metal chassis of a power amp inside the closet, right above Gribbens's head. Gribbens flinched and looked up, foam splashing over his arm. Rail yelled, "You're killing the vibe!"

For two seconds Jake feared Gribbens was going to yell back, but the guy's face just twisted into a look of horrified indignation. Then he stood and pulled the chain again, vanishing into darkness.

Jake realized he'd been holding his breath when he exhaled at the sight of Gribbens disappearing back into the shadows. He took a small red Maglite from his pocket (he was never without it) and rolled it across the floor toward the closet. There was a brief moment of dim, dancing light from the darkness, during which Jake watched Rail out of his peripheral vision, but the producer was swaying his head to the deafening music, eyes half closed.

Gribbens, fuse in hand, emerged from the closet and pushed an extra chair over to the dead speaker. Jake saw he intended to stand on the wheeled chair to reach the speaker, and ticking his head firmly from side to side, pointed at the stool Billy had sat on while playing the acoustic guitar that morning. Gribbens moved the stool to where the chair had been, and stepped up onto it with fuse and flashlight in hand. When he stepped down, he gave Jake a thumbs-up and Jake tapped the button to switch the big speakers back on. The bass vibrations shook the glasses on his face. The left side was working again. Rail opened his eyes and gave Jake a tight smile.

Sometime later Billy spun the volume knob on his guitar down, took it off and laid it on the couch. He said to his microphone, "I'm done. Go home." And without looking up for a reaction, he climbed the spiral stairs to the loft.

* * *

21 November
11:23pm
Hey Jake — I finally decided to stop procrastinating about this communicating by way of journal thing and just get started. I find that I think more clearly in writing anyhow, so maybe this will help us figure some things out. It sounds like you have some questions to answer for yourself lately about what you really want from this career you've chosen, and while you may need to find the answers on your own, I know that I've been carrying around a lot of questions in my head too. Maybe we can clarify just what we're doing here, living together but never seeing each other.

I just read that last sentence over and thought about erasing it because I don't want you to worry when you read my first entry at four in the morning, or during a break in the studio tomorrow. Don't think that I'm questioning my decision to move here or to be with you. I just want to be with you. I'm proud of you. You're in the right place at the right time and you're ready for it. If this is your big break, I wouldn't want to hold you back. I knew what I was getting into when I met you and you were talking about your hopes for a placement at a big studio. I just wonder if your hopes and dreams are still the same now that you're here and it's really happening. We haven't had time to talk about it and you probably haven't had time to even think about it. But I see the pressure you're under and I'd just feel a lot better about what you're going through if I knew you were happy.

I've seen how happy you get, like a little kid, when you're recording a band you like, and I know you're trying to do something that few people succeed at. But when there's no room for anything else in your life and I catch these glimpses of you between crashing at dawn and running out the door a few hours later to do it again and you look like the walking dead (I'm sorry but you do, lately), I have to wonder if this is what you really want.

So tell me what you think about this whirlwind you're living in. Or just tell me something that happened to you during the thirteen hours I didn't see you. I feel better already having started writing in this thing. Let's see where it takes us. I love you.

Goodnight,
Ally

23 November
12:08am

Jake - There is an enormous bug on my desk. Seriously, it is huge. I wish you were here to get rid of it. I don't think I can smash it with my shoe. Not only would that make an absolutely nasty mess, but I'd feel bad. I mean it's not his fault that he's gross or that so many houses got built in the woods where his little bug family has probably been living since forever. But I *don't think I can pick him up either. Yuck. Maybe if I give him a name I won't mind picking him up. He looks like some kind of beetle. Is there a nuclear power plant around here? I shall name him Herman. YIKES! It moved. Here, I'm going to draw you a little picture of Herman the beetle. This is going to be ACTUAL SIZE. Really. Wait — I hear a key in the door. You're home! I'll show you the critter himself.*

xox,
Ally

Nov. 24 3:20 AM
Ally,
You're sleeping right now and you look beautiful. I like looking at your face when it's totally relaxed and there are no signs of worry on it.

I'm glad you started this journal. I'll take it with me when I can, and write to you on dinner breaks. Speaking of dinner, don't hate me, but we have to work on Thanksgiving. The album is getting more ambitious all the time, and the deadline is coming at us like a train.

One more thing—please switch from pencil to pen. I'm glad you didn't erase that bit you were worried about, but you could have. I don't want you censoring your feelings if we're going to communicate this way. And I don't want my half of the journal to be all that's left when we're 80.

Goodnight.
Love, Jake

* * *

Billy's lead guitarist, Flint, apparently didn't have any family obligations for Thanksgiving. He arrived around noon on Thursday in a chauffeur-driven Lincoln Town Car with three guitars in the trunk. His amps were already on site, and he seemed pleased to find that while Jake had put the Marshall stack in the big room, he had chosen a tight little closet space for the vintage Fender tweed: the confessional. Flint laughed out loud when Gribbens opened the door on the priest's side of the box to reveal a binaural head—a Styrofoam mannequin head on a stand, with microphones in the ears. It would pick up a stereo image of the little guitar amp through the metal grate, reflected off the claustrophobic mahogany walls.

"It's just an idea," Jake said. "Probably looks cooler than it sounds, but we'll find out."

"Cool. I can play out my sins."

Flint wasted no time. He plugged in and got right to work. The verdict was instant and unanimous—he was brilliant.

They spent the afternoon watching him writhe around with his cowboy boots firmly planted on the red Persian carpet, a sinewy spectacle of tattoos and silver jewelry bathed in the soft purple glow of the stained-glass windows, a joint smoldering from the headstock of his guitar like a stick of incense. He threw his body into every note he played, as if this wasn't a studio, as if to play at all was to perform one hundred percent. And yet, for all the rock-star swagger, there was no pretension in him.

He knew if what he had just played wasn't his best, and he didn't need someone else to tell him. He would immediately ask them to wind it back a few bars and record over a particular passage. This kept Jake on his toes, punching in at exactly the right spot to seamlessly merge the old track with the new one until they had a guitar part that invariably opened up new dimensions of a song without overshadowing anything essential. Moon and Rail were both delighted with the results, and Jake noticed that the shift in focus away from Billy for a day had the effect of lifting a dark cloud from the church.

Flint played until the sun had set and the studio had darkened before announcing, "Man, I could eat a pig."

Billy called his friend into the control room and announced, "I hired a caterer in honor of Flint's bottomless stomach. He set up shop right across the road at the farmhouse. Says it's almost ready. We'll all eat together tonight, like the Waltons."

The food was topnotch country cooking: shepherd's pie and a

big colorful salad with warm bread. The chef was a tall fat man who went by J.T. He scooped heaping piles of steaming food out of casserole dishes onto the farmhouse's blue-and-white china, all the while talking around the cigarette that dangled from his lower lip. He had a British accent of a different region than Trevor Rail's—to Jake's unfamiliar ear, it sounded more working class. When they all complimented the food, J.T. said, "Payple seem to loyk my meals." Jake had to guess again; maybe the guy was Aussie.

Back at the church after dinner, they tried out the confessional guitar amp. It was a pretty thin sound and not very usable except for a strange little intro riff that Flint came up with for one song. Jake switched him back to the big amp, and they worked until one in the morning with diminishing returns. Finally, the session devolved into a listening party with Flint and Rail playing CDs for each other and telling war stories about people they had both worked with, over a bottle of Chivas Regal scotch. Gribbens listened eagerly from his perch on the couch at the back of the room, while Jake wondered if they would ever get tired and call it a night. Billy was already passed out on a couch in the big room.

"You know, I think we might have almost worked together once before," Flint said. "When I was in Kama Sutra, our A&R guy told us you were going to produce our second record but then it fell through. We ended up working with Andy Wilson instead."

Rail nodded and said, "You ever hear about how Andy got that gig?"

"No, how?"

"Wilson, what a character," Rail said, swirling the scotch in his glass. "I *was* supposed to do your second record, but it was a very competitive gig after your indie disc hit big. Columbia called me up as soon as they signed you, and I said, of course, I'd love to do it. We even booked the time. It was my idea to record at The Black Lab."

"Great room," Flint said and sipped.

"It is. Anyway, as it happens, one day about a week before the first session, Kit Holzinecht opens the door of his office and sees Andy Wilson's asshole staring at him from across the room with that million-dollar view of the New York City skyline in the background. Wilson, fat bastard that he is, is standing on Kit's desk, bent over with his pants around his ankles yelling, 'Come on, you wanna fuck me? Go ahead and fuck me then, huh? You gave the Kama Sutra record to Trevor Rail? Come on, then, fuck me again, if you like it so much.'"

"It's a shame Kit had to see that, but needless to say, he let Wilson have the record."

"Oh my God," Flint said, "How did I never hear about that before?"

"I'm sure Andy didn't exactly want to brag about it."

Jake and Gribbens locked eyes and burst out laughing. They couldn't help it.

Flint rubbed his temples and said, "Unbelievable. And I knew Andy was the wrong producer for that band. The record sucked. It's probably why we broke up."

Gribbens was laughing harder now, apparently tickled even further by the idea that a great band could blame their breakup on a producer's plea for sodomy in a corporate office. When he caught his breath, he said, "That record *did* blow," a tear streaming down his cheek as he held his hand to his belly and tried to get it under control.

Jake saw the gun sliding out of Rail's pocket and froze. The draw had a leisurely quality to it. He thought of yelling, but he didn't know what to yell. He thought of kicking off from the floor to roll his chair away from Trevor Rail, but there was no time.

Rail fired. It was incredibly loud, even in the little room designed to absorb sound. Flint jumped to his feet, spilling scotch and ash on the floor. Gribbens' laughter was clipped off as if someone had pressed a mute button. White dust rained down from the ceiling onto the assistant's head. He looked up at the bullet hole in the acoustic tile above him, swallowed, then met Rail's unblinking gaze.

Rail said, ever so gently, "Our guest may piss on his own record, but you may not."

The control room doors swung open. Billy stood there taking in the scene from over the front of the mixing console, red-eyed, hair tousled. To Jake, he said, "What the hell was that?"

Jake didn't answer. The gun was back in Rail's coat pocket.

Rail rotated his chair to face Billy. "Go on up to bed, Billy. We're done for the night."

TWELVE

Jake didn't tell Allison about the gunshot incident. He almost wrote about it in the journal that night while she slept, but he could hear her telling him to quit the job, that this was no way to live, that the long hours were bad enough, but at least she hadn't thought she was living with someone who was likely to get killed when he went to work, like an inner city cop. Not until now, anyway. He closed the book without writing anything and went to bed beside her, feeling that to write anything about the night and omit the gunshot would be an outright lie.

He woke up early and went straight to Eddie's office. Gribbens wasn't there. Eddie was on the phone. Jake hung back by the door and listened. Eddie was saying, "I don't know what to tell you, Bob, there's no standard anymore. I should replace at least one of the old analog Studers with a new one, but I don't even know if they'll still be making them in a couple of years. Analog is on the way out.

"The pity of it is that the musicians who are coming up now don't even know that it really does sound better…. I know. You know what I tell them? I say it has an *infinite sampling rate*. Yeah, I do. Digital can suck my dick; analog tape is the only format with infinite resolution. But who cares, right? At the end of the day, it's coming out of some guy's car speakers over the engine noise with the radio station compressing the shit out of it…. Uh-huh. I don't know what to tell you. None of it's a good investment. Here today, gone tomorrow. Yup. Alright. Best to Laura. What's up, Jake?"

"Hey, Eddie." Jake walked in but didn't sit down. He said, "Have you seen Gribbens today?"

"No. Why, is he late for the session? If he's sleeping through, I will wring his neck," he said, picking up the phone again.

Jake raised his hand and said, "No, he's not late. We don't even start until eleven."

Eddie put the phone back in the cradle. He sat back, studying Jake. "How's the project going? Are you getting anything you can use?"

"Yeah, we have basics for about nine songs done. Some are really good. Yesterday we started lead guitar overdubs. Everybody seems happy with the sounds."

"Good. So you're confident about driving the desk? I mean, I haven't heard any complaints."

"Yeah, I think I'm doing alright."

"Well, I'm waiting to hear back from Danielle Del Vecchio. I told her the studio only includes an assistant with the day rate. Told her they need to find some real money for you, now that you're engineering."

"Thanks."

"You have to make sure Rail gives you the proper credit, too. An engineer credit on a Billy Moon CD could kick-start your career. Of course, then I'd be stuck having to replace you already, so don't let it go to your head before you have good reason to make the leap. Maybe your phone will start ringing in five months. You never know."

"Yeah. Uh, listen, Eddie, last night Trevor Rail fired a gun in the studio."

"In the studio."

"Yeah, the control room."

"No shit. He didn't hit anybody, right? If he did, I would have been woken up, *right, Jake?*"

"No, no, he didn't hit anybody. I think he was aiming for the ceiling."

"Why?"

"You mean there could be a rational reason? I don't know why. To make a point, I guess. He's pretty dramatic to say the least."

"So I'm told."

"Well, what do we do about it?"

"What do you mean?"

"I don't know, are people allowed to fire guns in the studio? I didn't see anything about firearms in the facilities handbook. Are you going to call the police or talk to him about it?"

Eddie sighed through puffed cheeks and fat lips. He looked at the paper-strewn blotter on his desk and said, "Jake, I know you're new at this, but don't talk about calling the cops again or I'm going to start worrying about you. If I called the cops every time I heard about one of our clients using illicit drugs, or having an orgy with a bunch of prostitutes, or, hell I don't know, practicing animal sacrifice to invoke their muse for a vocal track, I would have put us out of business in the seventies.

"The biz is full of people who are highly unstable, theatrical, and emotional. Our job is to stay sober, levelheaded, and non-judgmental about their lifestyle choices. It's really none of our business, if no one gets hurt."

"Somebody *could* get hurt. Eddie, I don't know about this guy. He's kind of a loose cannon. Definitely, somebody could get hurt."

"Rail is an intense character, but he's not going to *kill* anybody. It's like how some film directors establish a tense atmosphere on the set to motivate the crew or to provoke inspired performances. People hate those guys, but they make some of the best movies. Are you sure he wasn't firing blanks?"

"There's a hole in the ceiling."

"Hmm. I'll have Buff spackle it when the project's over."

"I'm not getting paid enough to take a bullet."

"Are you saying you want off the project? Do you want me to tell Danielle they need to find another engineer?"

Jake considered. Then he said, "No. I just thought you should know what's going on down there. We've already had one fatality."

"Come on, that was an accident. Look, Jake, it's not the first time a producer or artist ever put his gun fetish on parade. Phil Specter was legendary for waving a gun around on those Wall of Sound sessions. Fuckin' David Crosby, the gentle hippie? He's a gun nut. Just chill. If you let this kind of thing get to you, you won't last long."

"Forget I said anything, then."

"Good. I'm glad to hear you're getting decent tracks. Let me know if you need anything."

Jake turned to leave. Eddie called after him, "Hey, Jake! You let me know if he puts a slug in any of our equipment. The ceiling's one thing, but if he shoots up any vintage gear, Gravitas is gonna have to pay for it."

* * *

Billy woke to the sound of a fist banging on the front door downstairs. He crawled out of bed and pulled his black kimono over his pale, naked body on his way across the catwalk. When he opened the heavy double doors, he found Flint, fist cocked for the next round of pounding. Billy said, "You should be careful with that hand. We still have to get another day or two of tracks out of it."

Flint looked like he had forgotten to take his sense of humor with him when he left the rectory across the road. He appraised his red knuckles and said, "Motherfucker must be solid oak. I thought you'd never hear me."

Billy looked beyond him at the fog-bound woods, pulling the thin silk kimono close around his chest. "What time is it?" he asked.

"I dunno," Flint answered. "Early. Get dressed. Let's go into town and get some breakfast."

"You crazy? It isn't even light out. I'm not hungry. Just come in before I freeze."

Flint stepped into the church and Billy closed the doors, pressing his weight against them to make sure they sealed. He scratched his head and said, "You want some coffee? I'll make some."

"Yeah, good."

Billy pointed at an antique couch where his acoustic guitar lay, the neck jutting over one arm. "Have a seat," he said and set about opening and closing cabinets. Usually when he woke, the housekeeping staff had already been in and brewed the first pot of the day, so it took him a while to find the filters and get it started. His first domestic chore in recent memory accomplished, he returned to the couch where Flint was finger-picking a variation on McCartney's "Blackbird" riff over the gurgling sounds of the coffee maker.

Billy sat down beside him and said, "Be ready in a minute. So… what's up?"

"I wanted to talk to you before everyone else shows up. I couldn't last night with Rail kicking us out all of a sudden."

Billy said, "That *was* a gunshot, wasn't it?"

"Yeah, man. Dude's a first-class nut job."

"What happened?"

"That kid Gribbens said something that pissed him off, so he fired a… a warning shot. Fucking gun came out of nowhere. Kid must have pissed his pants."

Billy set his elbows on his knees, his temples in his hands, and stared at the floor.

"I didn't like it one bit," Flint said. "It's not that he carries a gun that gets me. If he liked to shoot it off in the woods, whatever. But not in the studio. Nuh-uh. Not at some guy who's running his ass off for crumbs. I don't trust him with it. If I were you, I'd fire him."

Billy nodded. "It's not that simple," he said. "Lemme get that coffee."

He returned with two mugs and handed one to Flint. He put his own down on top of an amp, lit a cigarette, and began pacing the rug, talking between drags. "I have a three-record deal with Gravitas, but it doesn't allow for much creative control at this point. The last record, well, they let me do it my way because *Eclipse* was a hit. This one, I have to do what they say. If this one bombs, I'll get dropped from the label."

"Billy, I've heard stories about ol' Third Rail. Stop thinking about your contract for a minute. What's your *feeling?* Is he dangerous?"

"He's probably more dangerous than you'd think in your wildest dreams, but I don't really see a way out for me. He's the captain of this ship, and I've been press-ganged."

"Well, I'm sorry, Billy. I guess you have an obligation, but I'll work today and then I'm out of here. I'm not gonna end my career in a backwoods ditch because some psycho producer had a breakdown, you know? Use me the best you can today, okay?"

"Yeah. Alright, man. Can't say I blame you."

"You shouldn't have to deal with this shit while you're trying to write. Talk to Danielle. She's a ballsy lady. If you're unhappy, she should be talking to the label."

Billy took a long drag.

"Dude, are you alright? Hey, man, look at me. Am I way off base here? The fucking guy fired a shot at an assistant. Why do I get the feeling you don't want to tattle on him?"

Billy stamped the butt out in the crowded ashtray. He said, "I hear your concerns, I do. But I have a strange relationship with him."

Flint set the guitar down, turned his palms up in a prompting gesture.

"He showed up in my life at a time when I really needed help. He... intervened when I was at rock bottom. I was gonna kill myself. "

"Wow. So you feel like you owe him your life?"

"I don't know. In a way, maybe."

"That's bullsh—"

"No. Let me finish. In a way, I owe him the life I've been living. *The* life. Being a rock star, what I dreamed of as a kid. It's the only thing I know how to do, the only thing I'm qualified for. Nobody wanted to give me a chance until he showed up. And then doors opened where I didn't know there *were* doors."

"But you don't owe him anything. Do you know how much money he's made off you? You're the one who wrote the songs. You're the one who sang 'em. Hell, it's you living on the road, working your ass off. The only reason he's an in-demand producer is because you were a success. You're the goose that laid the golden egg. But your self-worth is all fucked up because he's messing with your head."

"I don't know."

"It's subtle. He's got you here in the middle of the woods, isolated. He's the one with the power, and he's intimidating the engineers, playing with your ego. There's no one else around to give you any perspective. If you ask me, you should be in the city with a band."

"It means a lot to me that you're worried. Seriously, I don't think I have too many real friends these days who would talk to me like this. Truth is—yes, he scares me, but I believe in what he can do for me. He's done it before."

"That's the label talking. *You* did it before."

Billy looked at the floor and said, "People are starting to forget about me. What am I gonna do, go back to working in retail? You'll think I'm crazy, but I think he can make me a legend. He's done it before. For other people."

"What the hell are you talking about? You're his only platinum record."

Billy shook his head, "I'm pretty sure he's been involved with other records behind the scenes, or under pseudonyms. Really big records. He's a lot older than he looks."

"Dude, you *do* sound crazy. That makes no sense. You think he wouldn't want credit? You really believe that?"

"I do. And it doesn't matter anyway because my contract pretty much says I have to stay on this train until the end. They won't let me off."

Flint stood up and nodded at Billy, "Alright, man. I tried. I'm gonna go have some breakfast."

"Hey, Flint," Billy said when the guitarist had his hand on the iron door handle. "Do they have a piano over there in the old rectory?"

Flint's face turned a whiter shade of pale. He stared at Billy, opened his mouth, and closed it.

"I just wondered what could have woken you up at six."

"It's a piano, Billy, not an alarm clock."

"You sure the gun's the only thing you're afraid of?"

"Sorry I woke you," Flint said, and closed the doors behind him.

Billy showered, dressed, and started work on a new beat in the computer. With the headphones on, he immersed himself in the project for a few hours, only looking up each time a wedge of subdued sunlight fanned across the floor to herald the morning arrivals—first Jake, then Flint again, then Gribbens.

Billy took off the headphones and nodded at the assistant. "Hey, Ron."

Gribbens flashed Billy his usual enthusiastic smile and said, "Billy, my man. Wassup? Flint, baby. Hey, is that 'Blackbird' I hear you pickin'?"

"Indeed," Flint replied. "Well, my variation on it, anyway."

"*Nice.* I fucking love the Beatles. Wanna hear *my* variation on a timeless classic?"

Flint looked at Billy and said, "Sure."

Gribbens slid the piano bench out with a grinding of wood on wood and straddled it. He stepped on the sustain pedal, flipped up the lid, and with a dramatic tilt of the head, struck a chord, singing:

There's nothing you can shoot that can't be shot...
He hit another chord and let it ring out.
There's nothing you can snort that can't be snot.

Billy and Flint started laughing. Jake looked up from his notes in the control room. Gribbens picked up a bouncy, slightly stilted descending bass line with his barely adept left hand, which he more than made up for with his voice as he sang out full and loud:

There's nothing you can't smoke, but you can learn how to take a joke
It's easy...
All you need is drugs!
All you need is drugs! Dot dah diddle dah,
All you need is drugs, drugs
Drugs are all you need

Flint clapped and whistled as the door swung open and Trevor Rail strode in, black overcoat whirling around him. Gribbens cut it short and scurried away like a field mouse in the shadow of a hawk. He was in the control room gathering papers before the sound of the piano lid slamming down finished reverberating in the rafters. Flint slid off the couch and intercepted Rail with a lazy, tilting gait that seemed slower than it was. He said, "Hey, Trevor, I've been thinking about that bit I did in 'Language of Love.' I might have an idea for how to make it support the vocal more."

Rail said, "Okay, we'll try it. But the vocal itself isn't etched in stone. I may have Billy try something different as well."

Billy followed Rail into the control room and heard him telling Jake and Gribbens to build a makeshift vocal booth out of gobos and packing blankets in the big room.

"I thought it was a guitar day," Billy said.

Rail turned to him. "There's little point in having Flint play around your vocal if I'm not sold on *your* performance. I'm hearing 'Language' as the single at this point, and I'm not going to waste time having him poke around in the dark until I know we have a vocal that's a keeper."

Billy blinked. "I wasn't expecting to start the day with lead vocals, Trevor. I didn't get much sleep and my voice is shit this early in the morning."

"Don't fret. It'll warm up."

"But Flint is only sticking around for today. We should use him while we can."

"I was told we had him for three days."

"He changed his mind."

"Changed his *mind*?"

"Talk to *him*."

Rail turned to Gribbens who was hovering nearby, listening to the exchange. "What are you waiting for? Didn't I just tell you to build a booth?"

"Right. I'm on it," he said and wobbled around, trying to choose which side to pass Rail on.

Rail leafed through the lyric sheets.

Through the glass Billy could see Jake and Ron rolling sections of modular padded walls with plexi-glass windows into position in a corner of the kitchenette. Flint was sitting on a stool near a stained-glass window that depicted one of the Stations of the Cross, tuning his guitar. Billy said, "Well, are you going to talk to Flint about how long he's staying? 'Cause if he's leaving today, we should focus on him."

"I don't have a single yet," Rail said, "and this studio is booked to someone else in just a few weeks. If Gravitas is going to pay for additional sessions at another studio, I need to have a single in my hands when we leave here. 'Language of Love' could be it, but I won't know that until I hear you sing it like you mean it. I'm not going to piss away the day dressing up a song with guitar parts if the song might not even make the cut. Do you think I'm making a guitar record? I'm making a Billy Moon record. So get out there and sell me the song."

Billy went to the kitchenette, lit a cigarette, and made himself a cup of Throat Coat tea. Jake was telling Ron which vocal mics to set up in the booth for Billy to try out.

"Billy, is there a favorite mic you've used in the past?" Jake asked.

"Not really. It always sounds like me no matter which mic. What's the big black one that's shaped like a gun?"

"An SM-7?"

"Yeah, I like that one."

Jake called into the booth, "Put up an SM-7 too."

A little while later Gribbens poked his head out of the control room and told Billy, "Ready when you are."

Billy pulled a blue horse-blanket aside and stepped into the dead air of the booth, where he found his worn headphones hanging from a hook beside an assortment of expensive mics on stands. He put the cans on and looked through the window to the control room. Jake's voice in his ears told him to sing through the song once, starting with the mic on the left and moving over to the next one for each new verse or chorus until he had tried them all.

Even in the headphones he could hear a sweet spot in the spectrum of his voice when he tried the third mic, singing:

> *Do you write a check?*
> *Do you write a song?*
> *Do you risk your neck?*
> *To right a wrong?*
> *Do you toss your change in a beggar's cup?*
> *Run into the flames, does it raise you up?*
> *When you're tied to the chair,*
> *Will you lie, do you swear?*
> *How do you speak the language of love?*

They settled on the third mic. Gribbens took the others away and placed a windscreen in front of the keeper. Billy asked for a touch of reverb in the cans and Jake dialed it in. Time to sing it for real.

Billy closed his eyes and went inward, letting the dark details of the music carry him to that place where the studio disappeared and the part of him that was half poet, half character actor stepped up and laid it down. But in the middle of the take, he was jolted out of the flow when the backing track abruptly fell out from under him. Rail's voice clicked into his ears, thin and distant, but as saturated with willful command as ever. "Pick a fucking beat to end each note on, Billy. They shouldn't be that long. You're running out of air and getting pitchy at the end of every line. Try ending it on three."

And so it went for the next few hours. Billy sang until his voice was warmed up, rich and fluid. Then Rail had him sing the same chorus over and over in falsetto, full voice, and a raspy scream until his tone passed into a zone that was ragged and weak. The shadows of mic stands on the wood floor shortened as the sun climbed to its zenith. Purple and gold puddles moved across the room from the stained-glass panes. Rail's criticism chattered, metallic and tireless in the headphones.

In the afternoon, the room darkened with storm clouds and snow flurries dusted the ground around the little church. The song played on and Billy sang:

> *Do you raise your voice?*
> *Drop your pants?*
> *Do you even have a choice?*
> *Did you ever have a chance?*
> *In a dirty phone booth,*
> *Do you swear to tell the truth?*
> *How do you speak the language of love?*

Dark gray shapes trotted out of the woods in the falling snow. Dogs? Surely not a whole pack. Billy glimpsed motion much closer through the vocal booth's distorted Plexiglas window and the kitchen window beyond. Something lunging past, too quick to focus on.

Wolves. He stopped singing and took the headphones off. The music marched on without him, now reduced to a trebly clattering from the headphones hanging in his hand. They were wolves—bony, motley gray wolves running in the field around the church. The playback in his headphones stopped. He dropped them absentmindedly and stepped out of the booth. Slowly, like a man in a trance, he walked across the room to where Flint was standing on a stool, peering out through a clear segment in one of the Stations of the Cross. Flint looked down at Billy, his face blanched, and said simply, "Wolves."

"Over there too," Billy said, nodding in the direction of the kitchenette. "They're circling the church."

Flint laughed. A dry, humorless chuckle that reminded Billy of the sound of a motorcycle engine sputtering out on an empty tank.

"Told you, you should have booked a room in the city."

The control room doors swung open. Rail leaned out between them and snapped his fingers like a hypnotist. The sound echoed in the space above them.

"I brought you here so you could work without distraction," Rail said. "Back in the booth." He pulled the doors shut without waiting for a response and took his seat beside Jake with an imperious stare that never left Billy. Behind him, the reels of the tape machine whirred, rolling back to the top of the song.

Flint said, "Do you think they're hunting deer?"

"Deer would be in the forest where they came from," Billy said, walking back to the booth. He slipped the headphones on, pulling his long black hair out of his eyes with them.

He tried to focus on the song, but then, halfway through the next take, he heard something in the mix that hadn't been there before: a voice whispering in some strange clipped dialect. Billy stopped singing. The song cut off, followed by a short reverb trail.

The air inside the booth suddenly felt at least five degrees colder.

"What now?" Rail said.

"Did you just say something to me, while I was singing?"

"No."

"I thought I heard you saying something. But it sounded like it was in Russian. Never mind, just roll it back to the top of the chorus and punch me in."

This time he sang all the way through, but there it was again—a whispering voice at the fifth bar of the second chorus. It had to be on the recording, but he had heard this mix at least twenty times today. If the voice was on the tape, he should have noticed it before now. When he finished the take, he asked to hear it back. As the song played, he dialed down the knob labeled VOX in red sharpie on his personal headphone mixer so that his own voice vanished from the mix. No one in the control room would know he wasn't listening to his own last performance for flaws. He turned the master volume up, holding his breath as the second chorus came around. *There.* It sounded like a woman's voice saying, *scar hath woluf.*

What the hell did that mean and who said it? He was certain

the whispered fragment hadn't been there until two takes ago. Billy's mouth went dry, as if all of the moisture in it had drained down to his palms, which were now slick with sweat. He wanted very badly to get out of the booth, to get out of town.

Rail's voice blasted in his ears, loud and metallic. He jumped and swatted at the little mixer, cranking the volume down again as Rail said, "I want you to put the emphasis on the second syllable. *On the beat.* Got it?"

"Yeah, okay." Billy wiped his hands on his jeans, sipped his tea, and set the mug down with a tremor in his hand.

Two takes later, Rail was satisfied, and he called for Flint's overdubs. Billy stepped outside for a moment to take in the air while the engineers were setting up for guitar. The snow flurry had ceased and the wolves were gone. Scanning the gray sky and the silent tree line, the only sound Billy heard was in his memory where an old song, a song that never really stopped playing, marched on—the dull jangle, twang and thump of Robert Johnson's battered steel string guitar, and that reedy African voice that sounded so old Billy could imagine it issuing from the dusty throat of a Canopic jar: *Got to keep on movin', blues fallin' down like hail. Got to keeeep on movin', hellhounds on my trail.*

Rail declared the session over just after midnight. The producer offered his hand to Flint as they walked down the church steps together. Flint switched the handle of his guitar case over to his left hand to receive the gesture. Billy thought his friend looked a little weaker after that handshake.

Rail continued on alone across the gravel lot, lighting up the BMW with the key fob. When the taillights disappeared, vanishing over the crest of the hill beyond a mist of glowing red exhaust, Flint looked up at Billy standing in the open door.

"I'm glad he didn't press me to stay on another day," Flint said.

"I think he knows you won't take any shit from him."

Flint smiled thinly at the overestimation. "You could give him the same idea, Billy."

"Easy for you to say. You're not under contract."

Flint wanted to say more and they both knew it, but all he said was, "I'll be taking a car back to the city in the morning, probably before you get up. Take care of yourself, eh?"

"Thanks, man. You were brilliant."

"Any time."

Billy watched Flint walk across the field to the rectory. Gribbens jogged down the steps, slapped Billy on the shoulder as he passed and said, "Later, Billy."

Billy started back up the steps, the sound of Gribbens handling his mother's car like a stunt driver receding into the night behind him. Jake appeared in the doorway, shaking his head, and said, "You'd think the accident would have made him just a little more careful."

Billy shrugged, then jutted his chin out and said, "Hey, Jake, can you hang just a little bit longer and play something back for me?"

Was that a sigh Billy heard? He couldn't read Jake's face, backlit in the doorway, but if the young engineer begrudged him for extending the day's work, his voice kept the sentiment in check when he said, "Sure thing."

Jake flicked on the lights in the control room and asked, "What song?"

"'Language of Love'."

"Of course. The song of many vocals," Jake said, pulling the box from among its fellows, all lined up on the windowsill next to the multi-track, their spines labeled in Gribbens's neat hand. He threaded the tape onto the machine, typed a number into the transport, and set the reels spinning, the pitch of the motor rising as it picked up speed and lost the resistance of a full spool, then falling again as it slowed to a stop at the head of the song.

Billy said, "Take me to the top of the second chorus."

Jake checked Ron's notes and shuttled to the proper cue. The room was filled with the thick rhythms of bass, drums and keyboards, as well as the newly minted cacophony of layered guitars and a choir of Billy's vocals. They listened to the chorus until about the halfway point, when Billy reached past Jake and hit the STOP key, rewound a few beats and hit PLAY.

"What are we listening for?" Jake asked.

Billy shushed him and leaned into the speakers. "There, you hear that?"

"Sounds like talking in the background," Jake said, sitting up.

"Doesn't it? You didn't hear that when I asked Rail if he was talking to me during a take?"

Jake looked embarrassed. "If we didn't have some of the tracks muted right now, I think it would be harder to pick that out. You probably only noticed it because you had headphones on."

"Yeah, but what is it?"

"Dunno. I mean it's obviously someone talking. Could be on one of the drum tracks. Steve might have said something while he was playing. Or even Jeff. One of them cued the other and it got picked up by a drum mic. Don't worry about it. I'll sift through the tracks and find out where it is when we have some down time. If I can't spot erase it, I'm sure whoever mixes the song can hide it. It's only there for a second or two."

Billy furrowed his brow, then said, "Find it now."

"That could take a while. Why's it so urgent?"

"I want to know what it's saying. And it sounds like a woman's voice. I don't think it's Jeff or Steve."

Jake ran his hand through his hair and sighed. "Alright." He hit the rewind key and said, "If you want to watch TV upstairs or something, I'll give a shout when I have it isolated."

"Nah, I'm good," Billy said, planting himself on the couch and flipping open a copy of *Rolling Stone*.

Jake started muting entire groups of tracks, running his finger across a row of buttons, leaving a trail of red lights and snuffing out entire swathes of the mix. First all the drums. The voice was still there, clearer now with less to obscure it. And it *was* a woman. He wondered if a radio station had been briefly picked up by a poorly shielded cable. Next, all the guitars. Still there.

Billy listened as Jake carried out the tedious process of looping the three bars in question to repeat over and over again, isolating the vocal tracks in solo mode and marking the strip of masking tape that identified each track with a penciled X to rule out one after another. Billy had never liked hearing his own voice naked, without musical accompaniment or reverb—especially early takes of a new song with all the rough edges still showing, but he endured it, forcing himself to listen carefully. Jake had been right about how time-consuming it was. He almost drifted off but startled back to a state of alertness when his chin touched his chest. He tuned in again. The rollers engaged. The spools revolved.

Scar hath woluf

"Got it," Jake said.

Billy leaned over the console. Now he was fully awake, adrenaline saturating his sinews.

Jake pushed a fader up and played it again. The whispered phrase sounded distant compared to Billy's sung lines before and after it.

"So it's on one of my vocal tracks."

Jake nodded and made a note on the track sheet. "Track seventeen. A harmony part. And it doesn't overlap with your singing, so I can erase it no problem."

"Don't erase it!" Billy yelled, his hand out, fingers splayed. He rubbed his eyes and pondered. "I think that might be the take I was doing when I first heard it. If it's on my track, that means *my* mic picked it up while I was singing."

Jake bit the inside of his cheek, eying Billy sidelong.

"It's like someone was in the booth with me, whispering over my shoulder. Whispering into my ear."

Jake raised an eyebrow and opened his mouth but nothing came out.

"What?" Billy asked.

"Nothing, I just... I just think it's late and you're tired and maybe more than a little stressed out."

"You hear it too, Jake. It's on the fucking tape. The needle moves when it goes by. Shit, you found it yourself. Don't tell me I'm hearing things."

"I didn't say that."

They stared at each other until Jake looked away.

"You think it's me," Billy said at last.

Jake looked down at the field of knobs before him.

"That's not my voice."

For a moment neither of them said anything. Then Billy asked Jake to play it again.

Scar hath woluf.

"It sounds like the last word might be 'wolf,'" Billy said, "and those wolves were outside when I heard it."

"Billy... have you ever heard of an artist going into a kind of... creative trance?"

"It's not my voice."

Jake pulled his chair closer to the console, rested his elbows on the leather pad, and rubbed his eyes with his fingertips.

Billy said, "I'm sorry, but if I said it, why don't I know what it means?"

"My girlfriend majored in psychology. She talks about this kind of thing all the time, and according to her, trance states work like that. Maybe it means something to you subconsciously. It slipped out while you were getting into the song."

"I don't buy it."

"What *do* you think it is?"

"A ghost. There, I said it."

"If you don't mind my saying so, the possibility that you went into a trance for a few seconds and whispered some gibberish you don't remember saying requires a much smaller leap than the idea that a ghost was in the booth with you and we caught it on tape."

Billy made a sour face and said, "Play it backwards."

"Huh?"

"Can you play it backwards?"

Jake glanced at his watch, but nodded. "I can do it, yeah. Let's see... uh, flipping the tape over and finding it again could take some time. I'll boot up the computer and fly it into Pro Tools. Take a couple of minutes."

Billy paced the big room, smoking a cigarette, and eyeing the vocal booth with suspicion while Jake worked. When Jake waved him back in, there was a small blue waveform on the screen.

Jake tapped the spacebar. The sample played in reverse.

Billy clutched Jake's shoulder. "Did you hear that? It says, *follow the tracks.*" He looked excitedly at Jake for confirmation, but Jake kept his eyes on the screen and clicked the mouse to cue it up again.

Jake played it again.

Billy said, "Well? Right?"

"It could sound like 'follow the tracks.' Especially now that I'm listening to it with that in mind."

"What the fuck, Agent Scully? It's as clear as day."

"It's clear to you. But we're both really tired."

Billy sat down hard and sunk into the couch. Jake was right, he *was* tired, but why couldn't the kid admit that he heard the message? What was he so afraid of? He said, "You know, if you want to talk psychobabble about subconscious states and such, I could point out that the reason you're in denial about what you heard is because it scares you."

"I'm not scared."

"Listen, Jake, this is not the first strange thing I've experienced in this church. You know what I'm talking about, don't you?"

Jake's gaze drifted through the glass doors toward the loft where the grand piano slept under its black canvas cover.

Billy leaned forward, hands clasped, stubbled chin perched atop steepled fingers. He said, "You told me to transpose that melody to D. It spells 'dead.' Why did you tell me to do that?"

Jake kept looking through the glass, but he said, "I've heard it too. When I was alone in here."

"The piano playing itself?"

"Yeah."

"So then why are you busting my balls about this voice? It's another manifestation of the same thing."

"It could be. I'll admit that, because I don't even have a *theory* about what that piano did. But there could be other ways to explain the voice. It doesn't have to be connected."

Billy sighed. "Give me a theory that doesn't involve me speaking in tongues."

"A burst of radio interference."

Billy folded his arms and gave Jake a stare that said, *That all you got?*

Jake turned his chair to face Billy. "Have you ever seen a UFO?"

"No." Billy could feel anger welling up now. "I'm not some fucking psychedelic casualty who believes every weird story he's ever heard like it's his civic duty as an artist. Believe me, I know guys like that, who won't even do a guitar track until someone balances their chakras with crystals and does a banishing ritual."

Jake held his palm up to ward off the tirade. "I'm not suggesting you're like that. Just hear me out. I *have* seen a UFO, technically. Many times. I've seen something fly by that I couldn't identify for certain. Could be a plane, could be a helicopter. Maybe a satellite at night. *Maybe* even a bona-fide alien spacecraft. The point is, sometimes you have to file things under 'unknown.'"

"Yeah, but there isn't any normal explanation for a piano playing itself. Or a voice besides mine getting into that mic. It doesn't sound like radio. I've used cheap pedals and cables that pick up all kinds of crap. I know what that sounds like."

"And I know that damned piano makes no sense. I admit it— it's fucking scary. Maybe that is a real poltergeist. But if we have to get on the crazy train about one thing, that doesn't mean every other weird thing has to be connected to it, or we're just running full tilt off the tracks. There may be different explanations for these two things. That's all I'm saying."

"Let me get this straight, because now you sound crazy to me. You think it could be a ghost playing the piano, but it could still be me leaving myself backward messages in a hypnotic trance in the vocal booth."

"Maybe."

"You'd rather believe in *two* weird things happening instead of just one cause for both effects."

"Billy, I'm trying to help you keep one foot on the ground. I just think you should keep your options open for as long as possible when you're tempted to start believing some really weird shit."

"Okay, I get it. But I'm still more concerned with what it means. It says, *follow the tracks.* How can you not hear that? Do you think it means the railroad tracks?"

"What railroad tracks?"

"When I was walking in the woods the other day, after he pissed me off, I saw an old railroad track. Maybe I'm supposed to follow it."

"I guess a walk in the woods just to see where it goes for a mile or so wouldn't hurt. It's not like the voice is telling you to jump off a cliff. Or kill someone. At least not yet," Jake said with a strained grin.

"I'm serious."

"So am I. Sorry. If it means something to you, you should follow your instincts and try to figure it out." A few beats of silence passed. Jake said, "Do you think it might be a reference to Rail's name?"

"Could be. But that still wouldn't necessarily mean it's my subconscious playing tricks on me. Not where he's concerned. If it refers to him, it's even more likely to have an otherworldly origin." Billy looked out through the side door at the stepping-stones that led to the creek. The wood beyond was a tangle of black shadows, the sky above only a shade or two lighter than the tree shapes. When Jake spoke again, it snapped him out of a reverie in which his mind tumbled down a railroad track through the cold night. "Why would a message about Rail be more likely to come from the other side?"

Billy got to his feet slowly, arched his back and said, "You should go home, Jake. It's late."

"All of a sudden you've given up trying to convince me?"

"I appreciate you staying late to let me hear it, but I just don't think you'd understand what I'm going through."

"Did I say something?"

"No. Just, you're skeptical about a spirit playing the piano and you've even heard that for yourself. You're not ready to go where this conversation leads next."

"Try me."

"You'll think I'm completely burnt out. And maybe I am."

"Well now I'm awake and totally curious. Tell you what: if you tell me what you mean about Rail, I'll tell you what I heard about the ghost and the piano."

"I could probably get that story from Gribbens for a beer."

"I won't judge you."

"People always say that. It's impossible not to judge, even if you keep it to yourself."

Jake waited.

Billy sighed and said, "I think he's the Devil incarnate. Okay?"

Jake smiled and said, "I won't argue with *that* wild theory."

"I'm serious."

"Okay... So you sold your soul?"

"I believe I did. It's an idea that has kind of gathered around me lately when I look back at my experiences with him. I know it's crazy, but once I thought of it, a lot of things just seemed to fit. For a while I couldn't put my finger on how it happened exactly, but now I think I know." Billy gave a rueful little laugh and tapped his right hand nervously on the corner of the console, the platinum ring on his finger rapping out a nervous rhythm. "There you have it. Devil. Now what about this ghost?"

"A deal's a deal, but I'm afraid this is going to feed your fire. Her name is Olivia. What I heard is she was a witch back before the Civil War. They hanged her for consorting with you-know-who."

"Go on," Billy said, feeling his gooseflesh rising, having that sensation of wanting to look at what might be over his shoulder, and *not* wanting to.

"She played the organ back when this was a real church."

"Before they hanged her as a witch, she was the church organist?"

"According to the legend. Everybody around here has a different version of the story. The studio grounds keeper told me they got the idea she was a witch because she played so well. Apparently, her interpretations of certain hymns were a little too hot to handle. They say she played them with rhythm and odd chord voicings, like in a black gospel service, sweating and writhing on the bench."

"Really."

"Yeah, but who would really know, after all this time, about the details. There's probably a sparse record of what happened at the Town Library. Far less titillating, I would bet."

"That might be worth looking into. Records of the trial."

"I'm not so sure it would have been a real trial. Hanging witches went out of vogue after Salem in the late 1600's. If there's a grain of truth behind the story, it would've been the act of a small-town vigilante mob. But there might be a Historical Society of Echo Lake you could check with. I never leave the studio, so I couldn't tell you what we have in this town."

"Okay, go home already. Get out of here. Thanks again for the help."

Jake stepped around the console and was almost through the glass doors to the big room when Billy said, "Hey, Jake?"

"Yeah?"

"Can I borrow your flashlight tonight? I'll buy you new batteries."

"Sure. Just don't lose it. My mom gave it to me."

Jake took the little red anodized Maglite from the nylon holster that hung from his belt beside a folding knife for stripping cables. He handed it to Billy. The barrel was etched with his initials, JC.

THIRTEEN

Billy stepped outside and looked around. There was a half-moon beginning its descent toward the southwestern horizon and enough clouds around it to confirm that he would need the Maglite. He twisted it on to check the batteries, and a puddle of milky white light splashed out between his fingers onto the snow-frosted grass at his feet.

It was just about three hours before dawn, and the night was cold. He pulled his leather jacket close around his chest and walked into the field toward the road. Looking back at the church from this vantage point in the middle of the field, the little white building was backlit by the half-moon, the stained-glass windows dark. The place looked peaceful standing alone in the virgin snow against the black spires of the forest. The wind picked up, raising the pine boughs with a gentle murmur. He thought of going back inside and burying himself in thick fleece blankets. From here, the church looked like a safe place in contrast to the dark forest. He felt a coldness that seemed to emanate from *underneath* his coat, from under his skin; he knew that tonight, whatever spirit haunted this place, it awaited him not in the church but in the woods.

He squeezed the flashlight, rubbing the texture of the scored grid that served as a grip into his palm, finding in its tactile reality the resolve to go there. Maybe it *was* all in his mind. Maybe his poet's imagination was extracting too much meaning from the random chaos of his life. There was a way to put that theory to the test now. *Follow the tracks.* Follow the thread of meaning to its end and see what he found: an overstressed mind thrashing and drowning in its own secretions or the tangible teeth of a soul eater.

Billy forced his feet forward, toward the tree line, where he could hear the icy brook gurgling. As he pulled his combat boot from the suction of the muddy ground and took the first step, the moon seemed to sink like a stone dropped in water through the underside of the cloud cover, suddenly illuminating the thin crust of snowfall covering the field in patches.

There was an unbroken skirt of snow around the church where the shadows of the pines had sheltered it from the slanting rays of the afternoon sun. Now, as the cold moon reflected that same light down from high above, it revealed a pattern of small shadows, little craters running in a circle around the building. Backtracking, Billy saw what they were—wolf tracks, preserved like fossils by the night freeze. They encircled the church and then ran beside the creek before vanishing into it at a shallow place, then continued on the other bank, climbing up the snowy slope between mossy stones.

He walked across the running water, splashing his black jeans. The combat boots were waterproof, but they were old and worn and some icy water sluiced through around the tongues under the laces, making him catch his breath. He shone the flashlight on the ground ahead. The tracks vanished for a couple of yards where the overhanging boughs had caught the snow. As he stepped over the stones and under the conifer canopy, his beam fell onto a sparkling crust of snow up ahead, and the paw prints resumed—the trail of the pack of gray wolves that had paid him a visit while the ghost of a witch whispered over his shoulder into his microphone.

So it wasn't railroad tracks he was supposed to follow. He thought of how that Robert Johnson song had been inverted in a way. *Now it's me on the trail of the hellhounds.*

He focused on the beam of light shuddering ahead of him. What if he found their den and they attacked him? The thought made him stop to consider just what he was doing. There would be daylight in a few hours. He could borrow a shotgun, just to be safe, come back, and see where this led without the prospect of a pack of hungry wolves lunging out of the dark at him. But he didn't know how long the trail was, and daylight might melt it before he reached the end. If he waited, the opportunity to find out what it meant could literally evaporate. With that possibility in mind, as urgent as it seemed to make haste, his growing fear that the flashlight beam would catch the golden fire of lupine eyes at any moment almost corroded his will.

His intuition told him to trust whatever had summoned the wolves, summoned the snow to take the impression of their tracks. Whatever purpose he was serving, it had to be greater than feeding the pack this night. And he needed to know. If a dead witch was leading him on, he needed to confront her and get some answers about the nature of his situation. If she had once walked the same path, made the same deal, she could tell him what lay ahead.

Follow the tracks.

He pressed on.

The soft laughter of the creek faded in the trees behind him. An owl hooted somewhere off to his left. Pinecones hit the ground at odd intervals, triggering his taut nerves. Every animal sound sparked his synapses and spiced the air around him with fear pheromones like tendrils of blood in shark-infested waters.

At one point, he heard what sounded like footsteps behind him—twigs crackling and leaves crunching with the slow impact of stealth. He spun around and swept the beam of light across the woods in an arc.

"Who's there?" he called and held his breath.

Silence.

He could have called again, could have demanded that his pursuer step out, but talking to the shadows would only grant uncomfortable credence to the notion that he was not alone, so he moved on, straining to listen through the sounds of his own stride for evidence of another.

Dense pine and oak branches now blocked what little remaining light was cast by the setting moon. The trail faltered in places. Twice he had to stop and scan the ground with the flashlight to find the next spot where the gaps between the trees widened enough to allow the snow crust he depended on for continuity. Each time when he found the tracks again, he felt a strange sweet-and-sour reaction in his stomach.

At length he came to a moonlit glade in the heart of the forest. Here the pristine snow formed an unbroken disc of crystal cover around a large pool of still, black water in the center. Over the past hour, he had often seen the tracks of other animals bisecting the wolf trail. There had been deer tracks and those of some small animals. But he had scarcely noticed these while he was focused on the distinctive shape and direction of the wolf prints.

He realized now how ubiquitous those other tracks had been when he registered their total absence here. In this clearing, only the wolf tracks cut the snow. They spiraled inward, the overlapping pattern of the pack thinning out as the spiral closed until only the sparse tracks of a solitary wolf completed the final circumambulation around the brackish pool, then vanished at its edge.

There was only one way to read it. The tale these tracks told, even to an urban eye, was singular and impossible: a pack of wolves trotted into this glade, encircled the pool and vanished one by one into thin air, or condensed their numbers one into another until a lone wolf remained—the pack leader—and this wolf then dove into the pool and was gone. Gone as if the pool were a window to another world.

Billy no longer wanted to know what was going on here. He had found the end of the trail. Now all he wanted was to turn tail and run through the woods as fast as he could with no concern for the branches that would cut and bruise him along the way. This had been a bad idea. It would be an even worse idea to stay. Time to haul ass. Time to find out if his pack-and-a-half-a-day lungs could pump his boots back to yonder haunted church before the Devil could catch him.

But then what? Didn't he have a session scheduled with the Devil at noon this very day? Wouldn't he also be running *to* the monster, if he ran? At least if he confronted the undisguised threat here in this primeval place, he might see things as they really were, without the pretense that the relationship had anything to do with the everyday concerns of people like Jake and Danielle, profit and loss. Here the game would be stripped of the civilized trappings that kept him wondering if he was going insane. Burning out. Wouldn't it be better to stare it in the face?

Maybe not.

Something stirred the air around him. He picked up a fluttering of blue-violet light in his peripheral vision, like a wavering propane flame or the afterimage of a camera flash on closed eyelids.

Only, when he turned toward it, the image didn't flee in the direction of his gaze as if riding his vision – it clarified itself: an ephemeral body standing beside him, a naked woman drawn in migraine-hued light.

Her figure was voluptuous, her face darkly beautiful, with strong, northern-European features. Her long hair was braided and wrapped around the crown of her head, exposing sensuous shoulders and the milky hollows of her collarbone. He could see the trees through her skin. It was like looking through wet rice paper he had seen in Japan. She turned toward him and he saw that her nipples were hard, as if she could feel the winter chill in the nocturnal air.

Maybe she's always cold now, since she's been dead.

The ghost raised her hand toward him and he recoiled. But she didn't reach to touch him, she merely cupped her hand over the lens of the flashlight. It went out like a snuffed candle.

Now he could see her more clearly, her own light seeming to glow more brightly in the absence of the profane electric stuff. She almost looked solid as she walked into the center of the clearing and touched the surface of the water with her toe, like a timid little girl deciding whether it was warm enough for a swim. The water didn't exactly ripple from the specific point she had touched, but rather quivered as if a gentle breeze or an electrical current was stirring every atom. Then she raised her hand again and gestured toward a solitary tree at the water's edge.

The moon dropped through the clouds again, and she was gone.

Billy swallowed. His mouth tasted like he had been sucking on an old penny. He approached the pool in the pale light, noticing as he did that a tangle of thick roots were woven into the earth around the hole, reaching down into the dark water. He saw some silver thing flash and dart away in the depths. A fish? Was the water clearer than he had at first judged by its blackness? Any mud would have settled to the bottom in its utter calm. The smell of it was not as swampy and stagnant as he expected it to be. He detected a note of rot, but there were also overtones of rosewater and cut grass. These seemed impossible in late November with snow on the ground.

He knelt at the edge and sniffed the air above the water. There was something relaxing about it. He couldn't see the bottom. The basket weave of thick, rough roots appeared to continue below the surface, but that was only a reflection of their upper segments. His breath formed wispy ribbons of mist that clung to the water. The odors, both foul and sweet, were stronger down here, so close.

Billy banged the Maglite against his thigh a couple of times for good measure, then twisted the emitter back and forth. Nothing. Maybe that placed a merciful limit on his curiosity. Maybe it was better not to see too deep into the pool.

But then he did see, all at once in a flash, as if lightning had formed in the heart of a mud cloud deep in the water, hovering over the bottom of the pool. In that flash, he saw the white corpse of the witch, laced with a blue web work of gossamer thin veins through her throat and breasts, staring up at him from the twin tunnels of empty eye sockets picked clean by fish. He imagined how their thorny teeth would have peeled those eyes like boiled onions. Her lips were also gone—her mouth an abomination of shredded tissue dancing in tendrils around her bloated, black tongue.

His breath caught in his throat, but as he saw the harrowing image of the corpse, he also continued to see the flat impenetrable surface of the pool reflecting the tree roots and the setting moon and his own silhouette. That deeper vision had to be in his mind's eye. It was scary how vivid his inner vision was getting—maybe he *was* going insane—but it was only that, a vision of what he expected to see. Not what was actually there in the water now, but perhaps what had been there once, long ago.

What does she want me to see?

Could she help him somehow? Was that why she wanted his attention? Was it possible that she was not the Devil's servant, but one who had found a way to escape his grip? He felt a rush of hope as physical as a surge of blood. *She must have!* How else could she persist at all as a spirit on earth unless she had evaded the snare of Hell? But then his heart contracted as quickly as it had opened.

Maybe that was the definition of Hell—wandering these woods forever, freezing and starving and haunting the place where she had been executed. Or maybe this ghostly guide was just an echo. He had to admit that for all his inarticulate fear of the arch villain of his childhood religion, he lacked a coherent notion of the soul and its anatomy. Perhaps what the witch had left behind was merely the residue of who she had been and what she had done in life. The real substance of her consciousness could have been devoured lifetimes ago, or it could be elsewhere right now, like an animal in a trap, suffering all this time. Or maybe Rail had plucked her from the underworld and given her a job on the ground for a little while—play with Billy Moon. Toy with what little sanity he has left.

What if she never knew Rail? This thought surfaced in a voice that wasn't his own, but Jake's. *Maybe she was falsely accused. It could have been hysteria, like in Salem. It could have been a rumor started by a woman in the congregation who noticed her husband's musical appreciation was on the rise.*

Whatever she was, maybe she did mean to help him. The moon was low enough now to illuminate Billy's face and cast his reflection onto the surface of the water. The shadows under his eyes were long.

"I look like shit," he said aloud, and lunar light or not, he knew that he did. He suddenly felt bone tired. The weeks, no, the years, were catching up with him.

"Look at you, losing your fuckin' marbles. Ghosts and devils and wolves, oh my."

His jeans were soaked through the knees and his calves were cramping, but he felt like he could fall asleep kneeling there. He leaned forward to take the weight off his calves and let out a long exhalation. When he breathed in, he tasted ozone on the air. He looked at his haggard face, framed by his long black hair and saw that he was going gray. How had he missed that in the mirror in the mornings? Then he realized that the gray hair wasn't the only thing different. He stared, transfixed, at his own face, and watched it transform.

His nose elongated into a snout. His eyebrows turned snowy white, curling upward at their ends. His eyes remained green, but the pupils expanded. The transformation of his face into a goat's was completed by a final dramatic cadence in which his ears grew outward, parallel to the ground, while heavy gray horns spiraled out from his temples. And yet he felt none of this in muscle or bone as he watched it happen.

He raised his right hand to his face and saw it in the mirror pool, just as it appeared before his eyes—a human hand. Touching his face he felt only flesh—not fur—and the same features he had known his whole life. Turning his head from side to side while keeping his eyes fixed on the face in the water, he saw that it did not pivot with him. The face looking back may have used his reflection as a basis to take form, but it wasn't him.

If seeing his face become that of a beast had failed to terrify him (his slow-dawning reaction had been more akin to fascination), this knowledge, that the goat face was independent of him, plunged him to the very bottom of the deep well of fear he had been drinking from of late. He dropped like a bucket breaking free of its frayed rope, filled with the knowledge that what he was seeing was *not* in his mind's eye in the same way the vivid image of the witch's corpse had been. This wasn't a flash of what he feared to see. He was seeing it.

"What are you?" Billy asked.

A third eye opened in the creature's forehead as the other two closed. Billy felt the hair on the nape of his neck rise, but he could not look away. Vines appeared and formed a crown around the goat's head, leaves writhing and crawling, red-globe grapes blooming into existence. Then a horrible thought occurred to him, and he forced himself to turn his head, sure that he would see the creature standing over his shoulder. He saw only a hanging grape vine drooping down from the branches of the rowan tree beside the pool, the tree the ghost had pointed at. When he looked at them, the grapes popped like boils, spraying his face and neck with dark juice and pulp, making him jump.

Slowly, he turned his head and looked into the pool again. The face was still there. In a resonant baritone, it said, "I am the blood."

"Are you the Devil?"

"So say some. I am the blood. I am come."

Billy didn't know how to continue. For a time, the only sounds were his own pulse in his ears and the rustle of the wind in the boughs.

"What do you want from me?" he asked.

"I want not. I am the blood. I hiss and foam in your very veins. Close your eyes and I am there, open your flesh and I am there, spit your seed and by the feast of be-with-us, I am there. I want naught but unremitting surrender to me in thee."

"I don't understand," Billy whispered.

"You lie. I am the truth. I am the blood. I would taste your inmost fruit, unsullied by the machinations of your mind. I am the spark in every fish, the flame in every egg, the apocalypse in every star. When you coughed out the fluid of your mother's womb and drew breath, you sucked me in. When you screamed your first wail, sang your first song, I was there. When you first ate of the fungus of madness and felt the girders of your soul tremble, you knew me. Behold."

The face was obscured by a rippling of the water. A pallid sheen spread across the surface, flickering like a film screen. Billy watched a silver and black image take form. In a barren field, the dome of a mushroom broke the dirt and sprouted, leaning to one side under the weight of its cap, transforming as it grew, morphing into a penis. It glowed as if an incandescent filament had been ignited at its core.

The light spread outward until it blasted stark shadows across the ground, emanating from the little clumps of soil that had fallen around the stem. A flash, and the earth and sky were erased in the fury of that light. When detail returned to the image, it had become a towering pillar of dirt and smoke vomited against the stratosphere, mushrooming against heaven's floor.

Billy's field of vision swarmed with purple phosphenes, but he managed to maintain consciousness while the water dimmed again and all he saw was the horned head staring at him, wavering in the black mirror. The creature's heavy eyebrows arched sternly below the expressionless third eye, and its snout drew back, revealing teeth. It bellowed, "You have betrayed me. You will suffer." The water vibrated with the words.

"I haven't betrayed you! I did what you wanted. I'm *still* doing it."

"You haven't *begun* to honor me. Defy me again and you will know me next when the hemp rope snaps your neck and the nectar of your last spasm lands upon my tongue."

As if to illustrate the threat, a serpentine tongue dropped from the creature's open jaws and traced a slow orbit in the atmosphere of the black water.

Just when Billy thought he couldn't take any more, the face softened and withdrew into his own reflection once more, his own head, but now with a thick, rough rope around his neck. Physically, he felt no such thing, but the sight of it made him retch. Then the mirror picture shifted slightly, gaining depth of perspective, and he saw the rope extending upward behind him into the tangle of grape vines in the tree branches.

He tried to turn his head away, but the pull of the pool was too strong. He was transfixed. But he had to look, had to see if the rope was somehow really there. He was about to force his head to turn, half expecting to feel the coarse rope burning his neck despite the absence of its weight on his shoulders, when his reflection transformed back into that of the goat creature. The noose was gone.

Billy said, "Are you the true face of Trevor Rail?"

A clawed hand appeared below the face. It reached toward Billy. He recoiled from it, but when it reached the place where it should have penetrated the surface of the water, he heard a sharp tap. The water had become a solid sheet of black ice. The claw scratched thin white lines across the surface, forming crooked letters, with a screeching sound. Billy watched the letters form, four of them, appearing from right to left on his side of the black mirror.

LIAR

Billy's vision swarmed again. He fell forward into darkness.

PART III
AND THE FOREST WILL ECHO WITH LAUGHTER

"Don't you know there ain't no devil?
There's just God when he's drunk."
-Tom Waits

FOURTEEN

Rachel Shadbourne stepped out of hiding when she saw Billy fall face-first into the puddle he had been talking to. Tossing her caution like clutter from the top layer of her purse, she ran to him, grabbed a fistful of his hair, and pulled his head out of the water.

He didn't cough.

That wasn't good.

Her leather pumps sank into the mud under his weight—bad footwear for this midnight Girl Scout expedition, but she didn't own anything more appropriate. She had never been a Girl Scout, never owned a pair of hiking shoes, never learned CPR.

"Fuck, oh fuck, oh fuck," she whispered, dropping him to the ground. She realized she was afraid to touch him and almost laughed out loud. Here was her idol, alone with her in the dark woods, perfectly vulnerable, and after dragging him out of the water, she was afraid to touch him? But she was aware of her limits: all she knew of resuscitation was what she'd seen on TV and in movies. And how did that apply to someone who had inhaled water?

Did you need to do something different, or just start pumping their chest like usual? She had seen countless actors over the years, rolling victims onto their backs and lifting under the neck to clear the airway. But what if rolling him onto his back made him drown? Was she supposed to do the opposite and try to drain the water out of him? Force him to expel it with that Heimlich thing? Oh fuck, indeed.

She knew that if she did nothing, he would probably die. But the caution and self-protection she had tossed when she'd left her voyeur's post behind the tree were crowding in around her. *You're a crazy fan who's been stalking him. If you touch him and he dies, people will accuse you of killing him.*

Superimposed on the face she knew and loved so well, now glazed with a thin coat of muck, she could see the front page of a newspaper.

Below

KENNETH STARR TO ADDRESS HOUSE JUDICIARY COMMITTEE,

a smaller headline,

ROCK SINGER BILLY MOON DEAD AT 27, FEMALE FAN SUSPECTED OF FOUL PLAY.

Rachel rolled Billy over and tilted his head back. He wasn't breathing and he *might* have water in his lungs, but she didn't know what had caused him to pass out in the first place. Heart attack? Was he on drugs? Which ones? This was a subject she knew a little more about. Coke could give you a heart attack but it wouldn't make you hallucinate a conversation with someone who wasn't there. Acid might get him talking to his reflection, sure, but it wouldn't give him a heart attack. Heroin? She didn't know. It didn't matter. Could be a combination. Nothing she could do about it.

She placed her hands on his stomach, one atop the other and pumped three times. She knew it wasn't CPR but hoped it would make him throw up the water and maybe even some pills or something with it.

No reaction.

She squeezed his jaw, and his mouth opened. She could smell garlic on his breath. Was that Chinese food? Gross. Not quite how she would have imagined getting this intimate with him. She put her finger down his throat, careful not to scratch him with her long black nail.

Nothing. His gag reflex was disconnected.

Now she tried her best imitation of CPR, pumping on his sternum and puffing hard into his mouth. The fear of cracking his ribs made it a half-hearted effort, but that other fear—that he was slipping away to a place where even paramedics wouldn't be able to reach him—was fast eclipsing the first. She pumped harder.

The thought of paramedics brought her cell phone to mind but even if she could get a signal, it would mean abandoning the resuscitation attempt at the crucial moment. There was no time.

But I don't know what I'm doing. I could be killing him. Her own heart was pumping enough beats per minute for the both of them. It occurred to her that she hadn't even checked him for a pulse. Now she tried, feeling his wrist, then his throat, but all she could feel in her fingertips was her own.

She didn't know if you could get 911 on a cell phone, and even if it worked, where would she tell the dispatcher to send the ambulance – the woods near Echo Lake Studios, by the tree and the puddle? Yeah, right.

What the hell was he doing out here in the middle of the night, anyway, talking to a puddle? Just what in the hell was he doing, flirting with death when he was supposed to be finishing his new album? Without thinking, she slapped him across the face, hard.

You like his Gothic death trip just fine in the lyrics and photos. What's the matter, girl? The real thing a little too real for you?

She wound up and slapped him again. Harder. Three things happened. He sprayed blood from his nose, spewed swamp water from his mouth, and drew a loud, ragged breath. Her eyes widened. She used all of her strength to roll him onto his side and beat the heel of her hand between his shoulder blades.

He squinted through a coughing fit, then rolled onto his back of his own volition, his head settling in her lap. He blinked, confused, at the dark shape of her against the indigo sky now infused with the first dirty light of November dawn. His brow furrowed. He said, "You're real."

"Shh. Don't try to talk yet. Take it easy."

"Why did you lead me to him? What do you want from me?"

She didn't know what he was talking about, and for a moment, she no longer knew what she wanted from him. She brushed wet hair from his forehead. Billy swatted her hand away, wiped his mouth with the back of his hand, and looked at the blood on his fingers. Then he was reeling like a cornered animal, scrambling in the dirt, trying to get his cramped legs under him, muttering, "Get away from me. Stay 'way from me."

Rachel held her hands up, not moving but ready to catch him, watching him try to stand. Billy stumbled, but when she reached for him, he pointed a finger at her, staggering and groping for the nearest tree with his other hand. Now that he was conscious, he looked dangerously deranged: eyes blazing from his dirty face through a mask of blood and drool. Then he said something she'd never imagined hearing from him, "Get back, witch!"

She laughed. She knew it probably didn't help to laugh when you were being called a witch, but she couldn't help it. It was just such a relief that he was alive, even if he was out of his mind on some crazy trip. But the laughter seemed to make him worse, so she shut up. Then, gathering her composure, she said, "Billy, you almost died. Calling me a witch is a funny way of thanking me for pulling you out of the water. You hafta calm down. And I always kinda thought you were *into* witches."

For a little while he said nothing, just stood there swaying from a branch, examining her in the fast-growing light. She rummaged in her purse.

At last, he said, "You're not Olivia."

"Rachel," she said, holding out her hand to him, a small cellophane-wrapped peace offering glinting on her palm in the first real rays of sun through the misty air. "Mint? Might do you some good. I'm giving you the benefit of the doubt and chalking all of this up to low blood sugar."

Billy took the candy and looked at it like it was a fuel cell for a jet pack from the third star in Orion's belt. Clearly, he was reassessing the situation. When he unwrapped it like an idiot child and popped it in his mouth, she took a wad of tissues from her bag and dampened them in some crushed snow. "I'm going to clean that blood off your face, okay?"

"Uh-huh." He nodded.

Wiping his face clean, she got a pretty good look at his eyes. The pupils weren't overly dilated for someone in low light. It struck her as strange that she knew those eyes so well and yet this was the first time she'd seen them in person.

"Are you on anything, Billy? If you don't mind my asking."

"No."

"No, you don't mind the question, or no, you're not on anything?"

"I'm not on drugs. Who are you?"

"I'm Rachel." She said with a crooked smile.

"Yeah, you told me that, but who are you? What are you doing here?"

She really didn't have a good, plausible excuse for being here, of course. She hadn't expected to need one tonight because she'd only intended to watch from a safe distance when she saw him leave the studio with the flashlight. A lot had happened since her decision to leave her lookout post beside the farmhouse and follow him into the woods. She couldn't predict how this would play out, but she felt sure there was nothing to gain by lying about what she was doing here. There were no excuses he wouldn't see right through. Then again, he *would* be dead right now, if she hadn't been following him. And that couldn't just be a coincidence. A man of his sensibilities would see that.

"Actually, I'm a fan. I wanted to meet you." She bit her lip.

His eyes shot to her purse and back. His face formed an expression that, as best she could read it, was made of equal parts disbelief and horror. He said, "At four in the morning, when I'm taking a piss in the woods, you wanted to meet me?"

"It's not exactly like that. And you know, I doubt you crossed a creek and walked a quarter of a mile to relieve yourself, okay? At least *I'm* being honest with *you*. I was hoping to meet you at a better time, but I followed you out of concern."

"Concern?"

"And curiosity."

Staring at the ground, he said, "When exactly did curiosity become concern? When you found me face down in the water?"

"Actually, I was full-blown terrified by then."

He took a step toward her now. She stepped back.

"So you were watching me the whole time," he said with an edge. "What else did you see?"

"I don't know."

This was so weird. She already knew what his angry voice sounded like. Knew it like the feel of her favorite fingerless gloves. And now it was directed at her, not at some mythical ex-lover or authority. She felt a warm awakening between her legs and was surprised by it. Still, she gathered her wits, tucked a lock of hair behind her ear, and touched the almost heart-shaped glass pendant that hung from a black choker at her collarbone. Finding courage, she said, "*I saved you.*" Nothing more in her defense, just the plain fact.

It had the desired effect, for a few seconds his face mixed a dash of guilt into the simmering anger. He softened his tone and asked again, "What did you see, Rachel?"

She hesitated, couldn't think of a polite way to put it, so said it in a quieter voice, as if a lower volume would cost him less, "You were talking to yourself. Talking to your reflection, I think."

"Did I answer myself?"

"Maybe, I don't know. I don't know what you mean. And I didn't hear everything you said, I swear. Look, could we go somewhere indoors to talk? It's freezing out here."

"Go somewhere? You mean like the police station, so you can explain about how you were stalking me?"

"You'd be dead now if I wasn't."

Billy took a pack of cigarettes from the inner breast pocket of his jacket, examined the limp cardboard, and gingerly withdrew one far enough to see how wet it was. Too wet. He pushed it back down. "Where do you live?"

"Minneapolis."

"You came cross-country to stalk me? Are you staying with someone?"

"I'm renting a cabin."

"Do you have a car?"

She shook her head.

"How long's the walk to your cabin?"

"Fifteen minutes."

"Okay, let's go there."

Her heart jumped into her throat. She said, "You don't want to go back to the church and get cleaned up?"

"No. I can't go back there."

"Why not?"

Billy only shook his head and said, "I just can't go back there. I need to think first. I need to sleep and think before I go back there. Can I do that at your cabin?"

"Of course. You can take a shower too."

Billy looked intently at the black pool. When he pulled his eyes away to look at her again, she thought he looked like the shocked survivor of a car accident. He shivered and ran his hand through his hair. "Come on," he said. "Let's get out of here."

FIFTEEN

While Billy Moon was following wolf tracks into the woods, Jake was at home standing under the twenty-watt bulb that illuminated the stovetop in the kitchen of the apartment he shared with Allison, reading her last journal entry while she slept. He read the words a second time, a soft dread compressing the air in his lungs.

Jake,

It's almost 1:30 and you're still not home. I really miss you lately. I tried to stay up to talk to you. It makes me sad that even though we 'live together,' I'm stuck with writing to you if I want to tell you how I feel, or even if I want to bounce something off of you like how tonight I was thinking it might do me some good to go visit my parents for a while. I haven't called them yet, so I don't know if I'll go, but I was thinking of maybe leaving next week.

Seeing as I haven't found a job yet, there's no reason not to and with you gone all the time, there isn't much reason for me to hang around here. Would you care if I go? I'm lonely. Maybe going home would cheer me up. Talk to you soon, I hope.

Goodnight,
Ally

His eye kept retracing that one line, *Would you care if I go?* It revolved in his head like a skipping record. Then a charge of anger illuminated the oppressive atmosphere within him.

I'm working for us, *and all she can think about is how bored she is.*

Jake read the entry again, this time reminding himself that, if he didn't read between the lines, it only said what it said. Nothing more. There was no reason to jump to the conclusion she was leaving him. Of course she was lonely. Would he prefer it if she *didn't* miss him? Or missed him but didn't tell him? He had to admit that he had been too busy and under too much pressure to dwell much on missing her.

But when the smoke cleared at the end of each session, and he longed to tell someone just how crazy these fuckers he was locked in a soundproofed box with really were, and how scared and thrilled he was to be pulling it off, it was Ally he wanted to talk to. Always. He took it for granted that living the dream he had worked for was ultimately pretty meaningless if he couldn't share it with the one who had stood by him and watched as he reached for it, the one who had come this far with him and would love him whether the record went platinum or collapsed under the weight of the egomaniacs making it.

The one who will love you if you're there for her, *as more than a pen pal.*

He took a pen from the drawer where they kept the books of matches and batteries and wrote a short entry.

> *Ally,*
> *I'm sorry you're sad. Just remember, please—this is a phase, and it will pass. You should go home if you want to. I would say I'll miss you, but I guess I already do. Just be back by Christmas, okay? The project will be over soon and if you're back, maybe I'll even give you your Christmas gift early.*
> *Love,*
> *Jake*

He staggered to the bedroom like a drunk and crawled under the blankets beside her. She stirred a little, but settled without waking.

Despite his fatigue, sleep eluded him until right up to the threshold of dawn. He slept through the alarm and woke up to Ally shaking his shoulder.

No time for a shower. Only a few hours had passed since he went to bed, but the light in the room looked like about nine o'clock. He tried to force his fatigued body into motion. It was stubborn and heavy. He stood up, wobbled, and pulled on some clean clothes, almost falling over in the act, leaving a pile of laundry on the floor and hanging out of the dresser.

In the bathroom, he splashed cold water on his face, glanced at his wild hair, and made a mental note that if he shaved his head, he could save time in the morning and get by with fewer showers. He ran deodorant across his pits, squeezed toothpaste onto his finger and rubbed it around in his mouth as he jogged down the stairs. He could rinse when he got to the studio.

Allison yelled his name as he yanked the front door open. He looked up just in time to see his car keys flying in an arc over the stairs and caught them, noting that they sounded like a hi-hat when they smacked into his palm. He blew her a kiss, trotted out to his Pontiac Shitbox and still managed to arrive at the studio twenty minutes before the session start time.

Half an hour later, Rail walked in, looking rested and rejuvenated. Billy had still not descended from the loft. Rail approached Jake and, in his most polite British tone, asked, "Jake, where the fuck is Billy Moon?"

"Still upstairs sleeping, I guess. I haven't seen him yet."

"I see." He took the revolver from his jacket and fired it into the rafters. The gun barked fire and sounded a deafening blast. Jake and Ron cowered with their hands to their heads. "Billy!" Rail shouted over the fading sound of the gunshot. There was no reply, no sound at all from above.

Rail ascended the spiral stairs. Jake and Ron exchanged a wary glance but neither ventured a word. When Rail returned a moment later, his gait was lazy and resigned. He simply said, "Not here."

Jake asked, "What do we do?"

"Wait. We wait for the artist."

It was a long, tense wait.

Billy came in at one thirty in the afternoon with a scarlet-haired goth groupie clinging to his jacket.

Rail didn't shift from his reclining position in the control room with his feet atop a road case when Billy arrived. "Decided to take the morning off, did we?" he called out.

Billy picked up his acoustic guitar and started tuning it. The goth girl cracked her gum and gazed wide-eyed at the guitars and microphones scattered everywhere. Rail swept his eyes over her like a scanning laser, reading her price and moving on. Then without warning, he stood up, shot through the double doors with feline grace and, within a second, was towering over Billy.

Rail said, "Gravitas is shelling out two grand a day for this room and you decide to spend half of that having your knob polished?"

Billy strummed a chord and adjusted the tuning.

"I'm talking to you."

"You're fired," Billy said softly.

Rail laughed, turned toward the control room glass and called for Gribbens to put up the current reel.

Billy finally made eye contact. He said, "Didn't you hear me? You're fired."

Rail sighed as if losing his patience with an insolent child. He said, "You can't fire me, and you know it. You are centimeters away from landing in the bargain bin. Gravitas will drop you like a burning coal if you tell them you're firing me, *and* you will be contractually prohibited from releasing new material on any other label for *years*. Put the guitar down. We're doing vocals today. And get your pussy out of here. It's time to work."

The goth girl said, "Hey, who do you think you are? That's Billy Moon you're talking to, and I'm the one who talked him into showing up here at all today."

"Really. So what are you, his number one fan?"

"My name is Rachel."

"Rachel, then, let me ask you: which record did you like better, *Eclipse* or *Lunatic*?"

She shot a look at Billy. His eyes were riveted to a spot on the floor. She said, "*Eclipse*."

"Then you have me to thank. I produced it. And if I can do my job today, you will have another brilliant Billy Moon album to cherish. So please sit down and shut your gob."

Rachel cleared some clutter from the couch at the back of the control room and laid down on it. Gribbens took a not-so-inconspicuous mental snapshot of the shadow in her plaid miniskirt before she adjusted it. Reclining there, she looked like a piece of art the studio had selected to add ambiance to the room: stainless steel studs gleaming under the track lights, vampire chic makeup faded in perfect gradations of violet around her black eyeliner, a tattoo of the letters and numbers from a Ouija board exposed on her stomach when her short black shirt rode up.

Billy went into the makeshift vocal booth looking like he wished it had a proper door he could slam.

"From the top," Rail ordered as he sat down beside Jake at the console. Jake rolled the tape. Everyone leaned forward into the sound field when Billy's raspy whisper entered after the chugging guitar intro.

You wear those boring clothes and think that nobody knows
You try to conceal it, but girl I can feel it
I can't see it, but I know it's there
I can't see it, but I know it's there

"Stop tape," Rail said. Toggling the talkback button on a wand in his hand, he told Billy, "Your rhythm is off again. Listen to the snare drum. It's supposed to be pushing forward, not hanging back. It sounds uninspired."

Releasing the switch, he told Jake to run it back to the top of the song, and to turn up the snare in Billy's headphones.

Jake knew this take was worse before Rail even called, "Cut." When Rail did stop it, he swiveled his chair to face Rachel on the couch. She raised her eyebrows theatrically. He said, "You fuck his brains out all morning? He's clearly spent."

"None of your business," she replied, holding his stare until he swiveled back around. Then he laughed.

She couldn't help herself, she said, "*What?* What's so funny?"

"I guess you didn't or you would have said so. Your kind usually wants everybody to know. Especially when you're getting credit for wearing him out."

"Fuck off."

"Careful, now. Remember, I can show you the door."

Rail clicked the button and asked, "What is it, Billy? You're killing me here. Can you sing this like you mean it or not?"

"Trevor, I don't want to do this song."

"This is the song I need, Billy."

"Well, I'm not into it. I don't even think this one is right for the album. It's an old song. It didn't make the cut on the first record, so why are we reworking it now when I have new material?"

"Because, Billy, I'll decide what belongs on the record, and frankly, I don't think a lot of the new material is up to snuff. This one has radio written all over it now that we've added Flint's guitars. Come, now. Do it again."

Jake rolled the tape, but this time Billy skipped his cue entirely. He just stood out there and lit a cigarette as the music passed by. Rail's hand swept past Jake and swatted the STOP button like he was killing a fly.

"Am I wasting my time here?" he said with a note of remorse to the little mic on the desk. "Are you throwing it all away, Billy? The houses, the cars, the freedom to make a living doing what you love?"

"I don't love this."

"What's not to love? Do you know how many younger men would kill to be in this room with me?"

"It's got nothing to do with love, what you're making me do."

"What am I making you do?"

"Singing this fucking song when I'm not feeling it. I thought we were done with this song. You know I wrote it with Jim."

"So? You don't have to pay a dead man royalties."

"You're a sick son-of-a-bitch."

Rail laughed. "You take yourself too seriously. This is the same old game of egos and echoes it's always been. You made the choice to play a long time ago. So sing, lad."

Billy threw the headphones on the floor and stormed out of the booth, then out of the church. Rail reclined in his chair, put his feet up on the road case, took a penknife from his pocket, and set to work cleaning his fingernails. Rachel got up and went after Billy.

Jake waited long enough to determine that no orders were forthcoming, then slipped out of the control room and up the stairs to the bathroom in the loft.

Ally had pointed out on a couple of occasions that social tension seemed to give him an over-active bladder. She said it was a physical response to confrontation that gave him an excuse to get out of the room. He had argued that it wasn't psychological; when he had to go, he really had to go. She had countered that it was still a nervous reaction. He didn't know if he believed her theory that this was the flight half of a fight-or-flight equation, but he definitely had to go pretty urgently right now. As he stood there pissing and pondering how much it had to do with his expectation that Rail would shortly be applying the little knife to more than his manicure, he was reminded of how much he missed talking to the woman who knew what made him tick.

The sound of the flushing toilet trailed away, and Jake heard voices floating up through the screened window. Peering out, he could make out the little shapes of Billy and Rachel below, standing under a pine tree, passing what was probably a flask between them.

"I think it's a great song," Rachel said.

"Really?"

"Yeah. You should at least record it, even if you don't put it on the album."

"I dunno. Things went bad between me and the guy I wrote it with. I don't think he'd want me to make a dime off of it."

"But it's your song, too, isn't it? I mean, don't you have the right to record a song you co-wrote?"

"Well, sure I have the *right*. But that's not really the point."

"You're upset because your friend died."

Jake couldn't hear what, if anything, Billy said next. The wind picked up and a tree branch scraped against the building. Rachel said, "I've lost friends, too. It sucks. But you can't always fix things."

They both let the statement hang there in the space between them. Maybe she was touching his hand. Jake started to feel creepy about eavesdropping but he wasn't quite ready to go back down while Billy was still outside.

"Here," she said, "finish it."

Jake heard the metallic clink of the cap being screwed back onto the flask.

"Whatever else you and your friend had between you, there was chemistry. You should honor that."

"We were just stupid, horny kids when we wrote it. Now it just reminds me that I miss him."

"How did he die?"

"The house I used to live in with him and the rest of my old friends burned down. Three people died, and he was one of them."

"Oh my God."

"It was right after my first record came out, not long after the band broke up. We were on bad terms. Never had a chance to reconcile. How am I supposed to sing a sex lyric when it just makes me feel guilty?"

"Sex and death go together like peanut butter and chocolate, Billy. Guilt, too."

At that, he uttered a dark laugh.

"Seriously," she said, "the song would suck without that kind of tension. You must know that. The lyrics might make it a sex song, but the music is darker."

"I guess."

"Trust me. I can help you find your way on this one."

Billy made no reply to that.

Jake rinsed his hands and went back downstairs. Rail was clapping his hands slowly. He said, "The lovely Rachel talks our star back into the studio for the second time today. Bravo."

"I can do more than that," she said, in a low voice, sidling up to the producer.

"What might that be?" Rail asked.

"I think I can provide some much needed inspiration."

"I wouldn't get carried away, love. Why don't you have a seat?"

"Why don't you blindfold him?" she said.

Rail seemed to reappraise the girl. A dimple appeared at the corner of his mouth. He said, "Why should I?"

"The lyric is, *I can't see it*, right? So why don't you have him sing it with a blindfold on?"

"Because despite what you may fancy you know about producing music, it's not about role playing. I have a deadline, and I just need him to sing the damn song and move on. I don't have time to indulge your bondage fantasies."

"Oh, okay. I guess I thought the problem was that he sounds uninspired."

Rail snapped his knife shut.

Rachel said, "Let me inspire him."

"You know what? Fine. I'll sit this one out. But if we don't have a track in half an hour, Ron is going to drive you to the bus station.

"Jake, record this amazing bit of inspired singing, would you? It'll be a novel experience for you to take direction from a groupie."

Jake rested his chin on his folded hands, his elbows planted on the console. He fixed his eyes on Rachel. Beyond her he could see Billy fidgeting in the vocal booth, swaying a little on his feet.

She said, "Hey, Jake, nice to meet you. Can you lower that mic stand so he can sing sitting on the floor?"

"Yeah, I can do that."

Ten minutes later Jake swiped the PLAY and RECORD keys with two fingers. Red lights came on, the tape machine engaged, needles jumping across the softly backlit VU meters. An explosive drum fill cracked the air followed by the psychedelic crescendo of a backward piano chord before the pumping pelvic rhythm of distorted minor key guitars launched into full swing.

Beyond the glass doors and through the dusty window of the vocal booth, Jake could see Rachel gyrating by the light of a candle, eyes closed, one hand pressing the headphone into her ear, the other hidden from view below the window's edge, below the hem of her skirt judging by the way her shoulder was moving.

The boom stand was angled downward, the pole passing between her legs. Her black thong dangled from the weighted end of the stand that pointed toward the ceiling. Jake couldn't see Billy, but he knew he was sitting on the floor behind her, blindfolded with a purple silk scarf, unable to see the microphone or the flesh that framed it when she bent forward, keeping her balance by pressing one hand against the glass, fingers splayed.

Gribbens floated away from his post at the patch bay, drawn to the glass doors like a bee to an orchid. Rail lay on the leather couch, eyes closed, hands locked behind his head, listening to the take. Jake tried to focus on the meter for the vocal channel, but couldn't keep himself from getting hard imagining what was going on out there below the window. The fact that he couldn't see it made it excruciatingly hot.

Billy couldn't see it either, but that was the whole point, right? And if the microphone was level with Billy's mouth, then Jake knew what had to be inches from Billy's nose. His eyes kept drifting away from the controls and up to the black thong draped over the boom arm. He imagined Rachel's glistening fingers just inches from Billy's nose, just inches from the mic. He was afraid she would inadvertently tap the microphone grille with a fingernail while gyrating and mar the track with the noise. Just as easily, she could bump the stand with her inner thigh if she wasn't careful. The tension raised the hairs on his arm.

It only got more intense when Billy started singing. Immediately, the quality of the performance surpassed anything he had heard from Billy in weeks. He nudged the fader up to hear more of the detail in the vocal. Was there another texture blending into the track? It occurred to him that Billy's lips and Rachel's were equidistant from the microphone in a salacious duet.

> *You try to conceal it, but girl I can feel it*
> *I can't see it but I know it's there*
> *I can't see it but I know it's there*
> *I can't see it but I know it's there*
> *The rosebud in your jet black hair*

It was perfection in one take. When Jake hit the STOP key at the end and the drum reverb trailed away, Rail opened his eyes and proclaimed, "That's a keeper. Put a star on the track sheet."

They tracked vocals for three more songs before midnight, with the mic back in its normal position and Rachel sitting like an attentive schoolgirl at the back of the control room, listening to every syllable. For tonight, at least, Billy Moon was back in the groove.

When Rail called the end of the session at twelve thirty, Rachel followed Billy upstairs without a word.

SIXTEEN

Jake bought his first pack of cigarettes while Ally was away. He chose American Spirits, probably because they were what Billy smoked — they were heaped in every ashtray in the studio, like the collapsed remains of little log cabins burned to ash. Everywhere he went he saw them atop guitar amps, pianos, and road cases. It was a tobacco tycoon's dream: ubiquitous advertising in a closed environment.

The first time he drew the pack from the pocket of his denim shirt and lit one up with the awkwardness of a neophyte trying not to look self-conscious, Rachel wrinkled her forehead.

"Jake, honey?" she said.

"Hmm?"

"The fuck're you doing?"

"Smokin' a butt, what's it look like?"

"Uh, it looks totally asinine."

Now everyone was looking at him. Heat rose in his face, and not from the cigarette. He said, "Look, just sitting in this room, I'm doing what, about a half a pack a day? If I'm going to be taking up smoking anyway, I'd at least like to be an active participant."

The answer satisfied everyone because it was so obviously true. Confined to the smoky control room a minimum of twelve hours a day, seven days a week, Jake had probably been hooked long before he put the first one to his lips. Gribbens set an ashtray down on Jake's side of the console and the session resumed.

It was the second week of December, and Trevor Rail was in the throes of a creative frenzy. Time was running out, and he was piling on overdubs, the album sounding more menacing and seductive, more eerie and epic with each new layer. Only one primary element was still needed to bring the tragic drama to a climax: orchestra.

Rail arranged for a string section to come up from the city on Monday morning to track backgrounds in Studio A, the big room up the hill. On Sunday night, he called an early end to Billy's vocal session and sent Jake and Ron up to the main building to get a head start on preparing the room. "These are real musicians," he warned them, "not rock sidemen. That means they make union wages. I get them for cheap in the morning but when overtime kicks in for a room full of the bastards, it's insufferable. There will be no time to spare for things like dead headphones and faulty cables. Gather everything you need tonight and *test it*."

The pair nodded solemnly.

"If I have to stop for technical wanking, heads will roll," Rail said. Then turning to Rachel, "You need to sit this one out tomorrow. Billy won't be singing anyway. Stay at your hotel or go sightseeing."

"You think I'm still paying for a room I'm not even staying in? I've been living upstairs with Billy. If you're recording your orchestra up the road, I'll just stay here in the church."

"No offense, love, but I don't think the studio manager would care for a groupie hanging around unsupervised."

"Don't call me that. And what do you think, I'm gonna steal some mics and pawn them? I would never do that to Billy."

"Your words, not mine. And I'll call you whatever I like while you're shacking up here on my tab. Just make yourself scarce for a day."

"Whatever."

Rail looked her over more seriously, as if he knew very well that from this type of creature "whatever" most certainly meant more mischief than a flat refusal. He reached into his blazer. Jake held his breath and waited for the gun to come out, not at all sure what he would do if he saw Rail pull it on her. But Rail drew his wallet instead and held out a crisp bill folded between two fingers.

"What's this for?" she asked.

"Go and have your hair done tomorrow. Tell them to dye it black, like Billy's."

"Why would I do that?"

"Because bright scarlet is distracting. And Billy likes girls with dark hair. Have them cut it to the same length as his, and he may even find you attractive without a blindfold."

"Fuck you," she said with true contempt, but she took the money.

"Do what you like," Rail said, "but I've seen Billy go through a lot of girls. *He* may not be aware of it, but the ones who resemble him tend to last a bit longer."

"And you want to keep me around?"

"Who knows? You may yet have a part to play."

"You're a strange bird, Rail."

* * *

In the morning, the thirty-piece string section arrived at Studio A. They poured out of a small fleet of white Econoline vans and milled around the big room, drinking bitter coffee in paper cups with powdered creamer and generally getting in the way while Jake and Ron hastily arranged the placement of microphone stands and headphone mixers among the folding chairs. Jake had even ordered Ron to spray the chairs' joints with WD-40 the previous night to prevent creaking from getting into a mic when a cellist leaned forward.

By ten o'clock, when Michael Lambert—the arranger and conductor for the session—walked in with his portfolio under his arm, the musicians were settled in and tuning up. Lambert requested a less wobbly music stand , and Jake sent Gribbens hunting for one in another studio, which left him short-handed and personally catering to thirty musicians, each of them with a different opinion about how comfortable the headphones, chairs, and room temperature were.

Jake didn't realize how tense he was until Gribbens returned with the music stand, entering the room with Trevor Rail on his heels. Jake found himself breathing a little deeper when Lambert approved of the stand. He took his place behind the big, less-familiar console, and triple checked his setup, while Rail briefed the conductor on which songs were the highest priority.

Billy dropped in to listen from the back of the room, smoking in silence. But he only got to hear one take before a headphone amplifier blew out, leaving the players to taper off into chaos with no reference to the song they were accompanying. At first, Jake didn't know it was the amp that had failed. This was a problem he hadn't encountered before, so it took him a few minutes to test other areas of the signal chain and narrow it down. Time spent with Rail literally breathing down his neck while he tapped buttons, asked Gribbens questions, and broke a sweat.

Jake was stretched over the console, reaching for a button in the routing matrix when Rail seized his left wrist and twisted it. He pinched the winding knob on Jake's watch between the long, tapered nails of his thumb and forefinger. The watch, a stainless steel Timex with a second hand, stopped ticking. Overcome with revulsion at the man's touch, Jake pulled his arm back and felt a flare of bright pain, like a bee sting. A bead of blood welled up in the scratch left by Rail's fingernail. Rail made a *tsk* sound and pointed that same fingernail at the clock on the wall. The message was clear: *keep checking that one, and your watch will show you what you've cost me.*

Out in the big room, the musicians were laying violins in cases and stretching their legs when Jake burst out of the control room with a screwdriver and a flashlight. He slid to his knees like a baseball player coming home, frantically unscrewed the faceplate of the power amp and slid it from its housing in the wall. Realizing that he was moving too fast without thinking, he paused to unplug the amp from the wall outlet, uttering a nervous laugh at how close he'd just come to poking a screwdriver into live circuitry. Truth was, he had never seen the inside of one of these babies before, and his abilities as a maintenance tech were slim to none. Either there would be a fuse in there with a broken filament, or not.

When he pulled the chassis open, his heart dropped. You didn't need to be a tech to see that the power transformer was melted. The acrid odor of burning plastic wafted up at him. Not a quick problem to rectify. Out of habit, he glanced at his dead watch.

He hustled back into the control room, and without looking at Rail or Moon, went straight to the phone and dialed the shop extension. No one picked up—probably at lunch—but as he listened to it ringing, he saw a red light pulsing on the base station of the phone. Was the shop calling him on the other line? Before he could switch over, Gribbens picked up the call with the other phone in the room, a cordless. "Yeah, he's right here," Gribbens said, and held the second phone out to Jake. "It's Allison."

Jake turned his back on Rail, holding one phone to each ear. "Hello."

Ally's voice sounded choked and strangely unlike her. It was unsettling, and for a second, he wondered if it was really her. "Hey, Jake," she said, "I'm sorry to bother you at work. Is it a bad time?"

He risked a quick glance at Rail, who was swirling the ice in a glass of Scotch while whispering in Billy's ear. Rail's eyes were fixed on Jake.

"A bad time?" Jake said. "Yes, it is. Can I call you later?"

"I'm home," she said. "At the apartment, I mean."

"Okay, I'll call you there."

"Jake?" Was her voice breaking with emotion?

"Yeah?" His mind was cloven in two by the sound of her strained voice. Half of it detached from the escalating tension in the studio. He could feel this part of himself breaking away as a wave of concern and compassion, moving toward the despondent voice of the one person in the state of New York he loved, drawn into her world, her worries, wanting to know what these were. But the other half retreated into the other phone, listening to the desolate unanswered ringing, counting the rings, icing over with anger at the shop crew for not being there, anger at Ally for choosing this moment to need him.

"I need to see you. I know you're busy, but you will be no matter when I call, and I don't know when I'm going to see you. If they take a lunch break, could you come home for just a half hour? I really need to see you."

"I don't know. Things are a little out of control right now." Jake noticed a bead of blood running down his arm toward his elbow from the scratch on his wrist. He wondered if Gribbens could find him a Band-Aid.

"I did a lot of thinking this past week. Jake, I don't want to do this on the phone. I just... don't want to try to write it to you in the damned book. I need to see you. I just really need to see you today."

Jake hung up the unanswered shop phone and whispered, "Are you leaving me?"

"I don't know." She sobbed. "I don't know if I can keep living here. I'm sorry. I know you're busy. Please try to come home later?"

"I'll see what I can do."

Jake hung up the phone, looked Rail in the eye and said, "It's the headphone amp. It's toast. I have to go see about swapping a replacement in from one of the other studios."

"Make it happen," Rail said. He tossed back his scotch and crushed the ice with his molars.

Jake found the shop crew in the kitchen amid the remains of Chinese takeout. They pulled an amp from Studio B, and tape was rolling again by one o'clock. The session wrapped by five, narrowly avoiding overtime.

Jake felt jittery from too much caffeine and no lunch. He also found himself in the unusual position of having a night off. Strings had been the only item on the agenda for the day.

He stood in the parking lot watching the vans roll down the dirt road that would soon join the pavement and carry the little orchestra back to the city, crushed his cigarette in the icy gravel underfoot, and fished his car keys out of his pocket. "Okay," he said aloud to the first cold stars, "I'll fix this. I just haven't been able to talk to her lately, but maybe this happened for a reason. A night off. A minor miracle."

* * *

Ally was standing at the top of the stairs when Jake pulled his key from the door and closed it behind him. He couldn't read her face in the gloom. Night had fully settled, but she hadn't turned on any lights yet. Even in the dark, something about the set of her shoulders told him she was depressed. He thought of asking her why she was standing in the dark, but when he opened his mouth, he only sighed gently and said, "My girl."

"Hey, Jake. Did I get you in trouble?"

"No. Are you dressed? I want to show you something."

"Show me what? I thought we could talk before you go back to work."

"We can. I don't have to go back."

"You have the night off?"

"Yeah, crazy, huh?"

"Because of me?"

"No. Come on, put your coat on."

"Where are we going?"

"It's a surprise. Your Christmas present. We can talk at dinner. We'll have dinner in Kingston, okay?"

"I don't know."

"Please, Ally. Just come with me. You'll feel better. We have all night to talk."

She nodded and said, "Let me get my shoes."

They drove in silence. Jake unfolded a crumpled piece of notepaper to consult his own scribbled directions. He soon made a series of turns down empty side streets. There were no shops in this part of town. Even the houses soon petered out.

"Are we lost?" she asked.

"No. We're almost there."

"Almost where?"

"The Christmas Surprise Place, silly."

She looked out the window as the car rolled down a dark, tree-lined lane, ending in a parking lot with a long, low cinderblock building flanked by chain link fences. As soon as the car cleared the trees, they could hear it—even with the windows rolled up—a cacophony of barking dogs echoing inside the building, spilling out into the quiet night.

Jake parked the car and cracked his door open to see her face by the dome light. She looked surprised, but more scared than happy.

"It's an animal shelter?" she asked.

He nodded. "We're going to rescue a puppy. I would have just brought one home to you, but I wanted you to be able to pick it yourself." He waited for her reaction.

"You're giving me a dog for Christmas?"

"I know how much you've wanted one. Ever since we met."

"You always said the apartment was too small."

"Well, puppies start out small, too. And things are going well for me. Maybe we'll have a bigger place before long. I know it's hard for you, being alone. You should have a companion."

She started to cry and turned her head away from him to look at the kennel building. He touched her hand where it lay in her lap.

She squeezed his fingers tight and a deep sob wracked her body.

"Ally? Honey, I thought you wanted a dog. What's wrong?"

The silence spun out between them, punctuated only by the sound of desperate, lonely animals, crying out from their cages. When she looked at him and tucked her hair behind her ear, he realized it was the first time in weeks he had really seen her face close enough and long enough to read it. It required no interpretation. She wore a sadness so complete it seemed to fit her like a pair of jeans she had already broken in.

She reached out and brushed his sandy hair away from his glasses with a slight wrinkle of her forehead as if she was only now noticing that it was getting shaggy.

"You smell like cigarettes," she said.

He didn't say anything, just looked into her eyes.

She said it softly, but it hit him hard, "A dog isn't going to fix this, Jake."

He started the car and shut his door. The darkness enveloped them again.

SEVENTEEN

Jake felt something pushing his shoulder. He hoped it would stop. It came again, hard enough to wake him. Ally was shoving him. "Summuns at the door," she said through the pillow. He blinked the sleep out of his eyes and interpreted the thin promise of light on the ceiling. It could hardly be dawn. His second coherent thought of the day startled him into action: if that banging woke the landlord... He got on his feet and looked at the alarm clock. 4:48. Wearing only boxers, he plodded down the balding carpeted stairs to the foyer door. Before he reached the bottom, he recognized Billy's haunted face, framed by cupped hands, peering through the dingy, bubbled glass.

Jake unbolted the door, swung it open to the tune of a loud creak, opened his mouth to ask Billy if he knew what time it was, and instead found himself saying, "What happened?" Billy looked more intense than Jake had ever seen him. Was the church burning?

Billy looked at him wild-eyed and asked, "Do you have a portable recorder?"

Jake chuckled humorlessly. It became a cough in his dry throat. He said, "Are you fucking kidding me?"

Billy shook his head.

Jake turned and climbed the stairs, scratching the back of his head. Billy closed the door and followed without invitation. Jake looked back at the sound of Billy's boots on the stairs and pushed his palm down beside his knee, *keep it down*. Billy gingerly crept up the rest of the steep stairs with a gait like Elmer Fudd's in the old Bugs Bunny cartoons.

In the kitchen, Jake turned on the coffee machine, which wouldn't have automatically started to gurgle and hiss for another three hours. As he took the half-and-half from the fridge, he tried to ignore Billy, who was shifting his weight anxiously from one foot to the other as if he had to pee. At last, Billy said, "Listen, Jake, I'm sorry about the hour, but this really can't wait. Can you please just get dressed and come with me?"

Jake said, "With a recorder."

"Yeah, do you have one? I left my mini-disc recorder back home in San Fran."

"Billy, you sleep in a studio in case inspiration strikes. You know how to plug a mic into your computer. You don't need me to make a demo at five in the morning."

"It's not in the studio, it's in the woods."

"What is?"

"What I need you to record. It's in the woods. Do you have a handheld DAT or something?"

"Yes, but what are you trying to get, bird calls at dawn? We could set that kind of thing up in advance with a little notice. Hell, we have an FX library full of stuff like that."

"It's not birds, it's... You'll see. You have to see for yourself. I can't tell you. Just get dressed. I'll show you," Billy said, fumbling in his pocket for a cigarette. His hand was trembling.

"Don't smoke in here," said Jake. "Wait for me outside."

"Okay. Cool. You're coming, right?"

"Sure. You're killing me with curiosity," Jake said.

"I'll be out front."

"Hey, how did you find my apartment?"

"Just looked for the shitbox car on the main drag." The little grin that curled one side of Billy's mouth at the end of the remark won Jake over, and he almost forgot how aggrieved he was. The guy had charisma, you had to give him that.

"I'll be right out," Jake said.

He hastily poured the coffee into his travel mug and spilled some when he heard Allison's voice behind him say, "Oh. My. God." She was standing in the hall, pulling her bathrobe tight around her chest. "Billy Moon."

"Yeah," Billy said, lowering his head boyishly, clearly expecting to be scolded for waking her.

She looked past him at Jake. "Jake, darling?" she said, "Why is there a rock star in our kitchen at five AM?"

"He needed to borrow a cup of sugar. Why don't you go on back to sleep?"

She started laughing nervously and Billy joined in. It became a warm, genuine sound before it trickled away.

"I'm sorry," Billy said. "I'm very sorry to have woken you."

"S'okay," she whispered.

Still looking like she'd seen a ghost, Ally pivoted on her heels. As she shuffled back to the bedroom, Jake called after her, "Uh, I'm going to work early."

"Whatever."

* * *

The story came out as they drove in the gathering dawn up the winding dirt road to the church.

Billy had dreamed that night of taking his acoustic guitar to a little pool he had found in the woods. Once there, he sat on a tree stump and sang a new song—one he had not yet written. It was a beautiful haunting melody. When he awoke from the dream, his head was clear for the first time in weeks, but he couldn't remember how the song went.

He felt sure that if he took his guitar to that glade in the heart of the forest, like in the dream, the song would come to him. So he slipped out of bed without waking Rachel. Deep in the woods, he came to the place he had been visiting on his walks, and with fingers numbed by the cold, he was able to hear the song in his head and find it on the fret board.

And here was the part he didn't think Jake would believe, the reason he had gone into town to wake him. While he was working out the chords, and scribbling little notes on a legal pad, he heard fragments of flute on the air playing a counterpoint melody against his guitar. At first, he wondered if it was just the wind sounding in the hollows of dead trees. But the more he played, the more convinced he became that it was there, a clear melody.

"Your musical imagination is just really vivid," Jake interjected.

"Like the piano in the church? C'mon, Jake. I can tell the difference between what's in my head and what's in my ears."

"But you were half asleep."

"Look, that's why you're here—to record it and *prove* it's not in my head, okay? I know what I heard. Maybe I'm crazy. You're gonna let me know."

Jake waited outside the church while Billy ran in to get his guitar. When he reemerged, they crossed the creek using the stepping-stones and started up the trail into the woods. A thin cover of snow reflected and amplified the scarce light. Jake checked the recorder slung over his shoulder on its strap. The batteries had enough juice in them for a good hour.

The not-yet frozen ground made for a mucky surface to walk on, and Jake had to stop twice to pull his foot free, one time losing his work boot when his foot slipped out of it, leaving him to balance on the other foot while pulling the boot from the mud with the sound of greedy suction. Billy watched with an impatient glare until Jake was moving again. After that, Jake tried to follow Billy's course more carefully, placing his boots on the same thick tree roots and grasping the same overhanging branches for balance. Billy seemed to know the path well.

Jake wondered what Eddie would say if he knew a client had dragged him out of bed at dawn to do a little field recording in the middle of the woods. Probably something like, "Better not end up on your time sheet, you make enough OT as it is. And if you drop one of our mics in the creek, I'll have your head." Eddie might also wonder what Moon was on at the time. Probably mushrooms purchased on the village green.

Jake's problem, however, was that he didn't think Billy *was* high. His pupils were a little big out here in the semi-dark, but they had looked normal in the kitchen. Besides, Billy just seemed like himself. Excited, yes, very excited, but not zoned out. No, he was pretty sure Billy wasn't on drugs, just batshit crazy.

Jake was so accustomed to the stress he imbibed daily now—like a low dose of a poison he was developing an immunity to—he wasn't especially miffed about this latest violation of his personal life. Even the notion of a personal life seemed like a joke. He knew he could have refused Billy's request, so why exactly was he cooperating with this madness? Was it because he saw more of Billy than Ally these days and had come to regard him as a friend? Would proof of delusion in the form of a recording with no flute break Billy's psychosis?

Jake was also aware of a less virtuous motive underlying his cooperation. He felt a boon from the simple fact that Billy was trusting him and confiding in him. It placed the two of them on a different side of the fence from Trevor Rail, and that seemed important. That they were about to record something, however bizarre, without Rail's knowledge gave Jake a thrill. This was, after all, a new Billy Moon song, written with just a guitar in the woods, and he was going to be the first person to hear it and record it on the spot. Just the two of them.

What if he captured something special? Something even usable. Maybe a demo version that had some magic that just couldn't be recaptured or surpassed in the studio. It was unlikely, but such things had been known to happen. Sure, Billy's voice and hands were probably too cold to deliver a clean performance of something so new and fragile, but it was possible. Magic was always possible, every time you pressed the record button. That was why he had taken the job in the first place, and that was why he was tromping through the mud at dawn.

Lost in his own thoughts, Jake bumped into Billy's guitar case before noticing the singer had stopped. They were in a little clearing with a black pool in the center ringed with mossy stones under a lonely, gnarled rowan tree. The sight of that tree gave Jake a chill, though he could not say why.

Billy laid the case down on a relatively dry patch and popped the latches. Taking the acoustic from its plush shell, he sat down on a fungus-riddled tree stump and did a cursory tune up.

Jake said, "Strum a few chords while I get a level."

While Billy strummed idly, Jake walked around him in a semi-circle, microphone in hand, listening through headphones. Jake stopped when he found the sweet spot and said, "Okay, I think I'm all set. Thought I'd be picking up wind and bird sounds, but it's dead quiet here. Birds should be going nuts at this hour."

Billy nodded gravely.

Jake pressed the record button and a tiny red LED came on. The slightest breeze stirred the trees like a curtain parting on a stage. Tiny ripples moved across the pool. Jake felt a tingle of fear, like a splinter edging under his skin, as Billy started to strum a syncopated minor key progression. *He's going to turn on me in five minutes. He won't forgive me for not hearing it too.*

But then he did hear it, and that little shard of social fear seemed to grow and radiate throughout his body, mutating into a different thing entirely, a multifaceted blazing star of spiritual dread.

They were not alone in the woods. The flute wove in and out of the chord changes. Billy sang a wordless melody in his husky tenor, the notes spinning and dancing with the lilting flute line.

Jake focused on keeping the mic from shaking too badly.

Toward the end of the song, Billy's voice shifted direction slightly, and Jake glanced up to see him looking at a little stand of birch trees in the bracken while he sang. Following the direction of Billy's gaze, Jake saw a flash of ridged animal horn that reminded him of the color and texture of a conch shell. Then a glimpse of brown fur and ruddy flesh—*human flesh*—in another narrow gap between two papery white birch trunks.

But before he could focus on it, it was gone with the flute melody, punctuated by the percussion of hooves on stone. Jake knew in that moment that if he had caught those hoof beats on tape, it would freak him out even more than the flute because he wouldn't be able to convince himself they belonged to a deer.

Billy let the final chord ring out and then stowed the guitar back in its case. He didn't comment, just stared into Jake's eyes, daring him to contradict what they had just witnessed. Jake, who still trusted machines more than his senses, looked down at the digital Walkman in his hand. It was trembling. He pressed rewind, listened to the whir and click, then pressed play, holding his breath, feeling his heart in his throat.

In the headphones he heard the guitar intro, followed by Billy's voice, but no flute. "It's not there," he said. He took the phones off and held them out to Billy, who didn't accept them.

"But you heard it, right?" Billy said, "You heard it."

Jake nodded.

* * *

Ally was throwing clothes into a duffel bag, missing the mark half the time, the volume of her voice rising as she ranted at Jake, who stood dumbstruck behind her in their bedroom. "It's wrecking you, Jake. This job is wrecking you. You're going *gray*." She punctuated the word with a thrown garment. "You don't get any *sleep*, or *sunlight*. You live on takeout. That producer is going to give you PTSD, or at the very least a good case of tinnitus. And now you think you're seeing *devils* or something."

"It was more like a satyr," he muttered.

"What you saw was probably a deer," she said, turning to face him with something new on her face—pity. "You know that, don't you, Jake? It was a deer. You can hardly drive down Main Street without hitting one."

"But what about the flute?"

"There's nothing on the tape but Billy, right?"

"Billy and the hooves at the end. I'm telling you, I saw human skin, human muscles, not just animal fur."

She held up her hand for him to stop.

He had come home to shower before the day's session and found Ally waiting for him at the kitchen table. Over eggs and toast, he told her about the encounter in the forest and what Billy thought it was, and now she was leaving him.

She gently placed the hand she was holding up in a stop-don't-say-any-more gesture on his cheek. "Jake, this isn't like you," she said, "You're sleep deprived, and you're spending a lot of time with a charming but delusional man. It's affecting your judgment, and you're scaring me. Tell Eddie you can't do it anymore."

Jake took her hand from his face and dropped it. He felt his cheeks flush with heat. "I can't just quit my job in the middle of a project. That'd be the end of me. The deadline is just two weeks away now. There are a lot of guys who would give anything to be in my position."

"Give anything? Give what? A life? A wife? You're giving everything, and it wouldn't amount to peanuts if it wasn't for the overtime."

"Yeah, well, it's been enough to support you."

She cast her eyes down. "I guess you won't have that expense anymore."

"You're breaking up with me for Christmas?"

She laughed. "You won't even know it's Christmas. It'll be just another day in the studio."

She was right, of course. Rail and Moon probably would work on Christmas to make the deadline. Maybe Rachel would make hot chocolate and string the control room with popcorn.

"There's nothing here for me, Jake. We're in the middle of the woods. I came here for you and you're not even here. You won't even know I'm gone."

He could think of nothing more to say. He plucked his keys off the hook at the top of the banister and lumbered down the stairs. Time to go to work.

His wrist itched where Rail had scratched it.

EIGHTEEN

There was no aspect of the album that Trevor Rail lacked a vision for, including the cover art. In his wildest fantasies, the cover would feature Billy's autopsy photos—just imagine how that would sell—but Rail knew how to attenuate his vision for what the market would allow, and he would settle for pictures of Billy posing, in the church and winter woods, with the suicide knife.

"The setting has been a big part of Billy's creative process," Rail told Don Lamar on the phone. "We should carry that influence over into the artwork. Give the fans a sense of place."

Eddie had put Rail in touch with a local photographer, Joel Eastman of nearby Woodstock, who had begun his career photographing Bob Dylan back when the bard had walked these same woods. After leafing through a coffee-table book that Eastman had donated to the studio lounge, Rail decided that the old-fashioned documentary quality of the work had just the right gothic undertones. There was something about the shadows under Robbie Robertson's sunken eyes and the tragic aspect of how Jimi Hendrix's psychedelic clothes rendered in black and white. It was perfect. Eastman would capture Billy Moon with a realism that would make his spooky persona even more disturbing than if it were played up in a conventional way.

Lamar agreed to the shoot, but it took a little extra finesse to talk him out of sending an A&R guy to oversee the thing. Rail argued that he wanted to get pictures of Billy at work, in addition to the posed shots. Didn't Lamar understand the concept of candid photos? An unfamiliar body in the studio would only distract Billy, make him self-conscious. It would kill the vibe.

As it happened, Joel Eastman was skilled in the art of invisibility. After warm introductions in the morning, the tall, skinny photographer in a fleece pullover and jeans (sporting an afro that made him look even taller) somehow managed to draw almost no attention to himself during several hours of overdubs, which he spent roaming the church with his Nikon, capturing Billy from odd angles: through windows and doorways and from the loft overhead with a zoom lens. After a break for lunch, which ended the recording session for the day, the focus shifted, and Billy had his hair and face done by a pair of makeup artists up from the city who worked quickly to beat the early setting December sun.

Then it was show time, with Billy posing in a long black overcoat. Eastman was up close now, the new music playing loud as they moved from one stained-glass window to another, capturing Billy in front of the purple-robed Virgin, the Stations of the Cross, standing in the arched Palladian doorway as a silhouette, or striding up the spiral staircase in an out-of-focus blur of moving hand and swirling coat.

Rail kept his distance at first, letting Eastman coax Billy out of his shell into performance mode. Once the ice was broken, he inserted himself between them with small comments and suggestions until he was directing the shoot, selecting the next background, the next pose, moving Billy outside among the trees, placing the *tanto* in his hand and encouraging Eastman to romance the blade with his camera.

A change of lenses brought out the details of the silver cherry blossoms on the handle and the watery grain of the folded steel blade. Billy, ever the showman, did not disappoint. Even without his heart in it—this music, this image all seemed to have lost its luster for him—he could still slip into character. Rail supposed it was a mark of pride that even when Billy was being typecast against his more authentic inclinations, as a person he no longer was, he refused to give his fans a half-hearted version.

He may only be playing a role at this point in his career—the role of his younger incarnation still beloved by legions of Rachels—but he still played it to the hilt, slipping into that dark mystique with ease and authority. Billy might secretly wish some other, older and wiser version of himself could land on the record store shelves, but if that was not to be, if it had to be the Dark Moon yet again, then at least he was committed to making sure that fellow didn't come off as some clumsy poseur or mere caricature.

Billy Moon had arrived. There he was in the intense green eyes. There, wrapped around a wet tree branch with the blade in his teeth, exuding sex and violence. And there, pulling the waistband of Rachel's skirt down with one hand while holding her shirt up with the knife blade in the other, exposing her Ouija board tattoo, and licking the crescent moon that was a part of it, on the underside of her left breast.

They finished the session back inside the church with a series featuring Billy naked, a dim silhouette, his own tattoos a muted blue in the fading light from the colored windows. He stood behind a mic stand in the center of the empty floor. Inserted in the clip where a mic should have been was the red silk-wrapped handle of the *tanto*, blade arched toward his rouged lips.

Then the light was gone, and they wrapped for the day, Jake and Ron leaving first for once while Eastman packed up his own minimal equipment. "That's a beautiful knife," Eastman said to Billy, his eyes on the LCD window of his camera where some detail of the hilt was magnified.

"It was a gift from Trevor," Billy said. "He has impeccable taste in wine and weapons."

"Ha. What's that texture under the fabric?" Eastman asked.

"Stingray skin," Rail answered. "The Japanese use it in much the same way Europeans use leather."

"Fascinating," Eastman said, slinging his camera bag over his shoulder.

Rail continued the lesson for both Eastman and Billy, who was still within earshot, buttoning his black cotton shirt with Rachel's assistance. "A samurai would have used this knife for close combat, and it would have been presented to him on his empty dinner plate when he finished his last meal and composed his death poem, if he was called upon to commit *seppuku*."

"What's that, like *hari kiri*?" Eastman asked.

"Yes. Ritualized suicide to avoid shame. Leaving a legacy of honor was supremely important to the Samurai. More important than life itself. If that honor was jeopardized in any way, suicide would redeem it."

"Huh." Eastman looked like he found the alien practice distasteful, his enthusiasm for the artistic merits of the knife waning. He glanced at his watch.

"This blade," Rail continued, "is an antique, refurnished with new fittings. It may once have served the very purpose we speak of."

"Interesting. Alright. Well, pleasure working with you all. I should have a contact sheet for you tomorrow, Trevor. Then you can select some proofs."

The four of them strolled out of the church together, Eastman in the lead cutting a brisk path to his own car, Billy and Rachel lingering on the stone steps, sharing a cigarette. Rail could hear the girl asking Billy if she was really going to be in the CD booklet. He gave a non-committal answer about how her ink very well could be. It had been a good bit of improv on Billy's part to include her tattoo.

Maybe he did understand his audience after all. Rail wondered if the girl would want financial compensation for modeling. He doubted it. For now she seemed intoxicated with the mere possibility of her skin being immortalized in print. Billy offered to take her to the Mountain Lion for dinner to celebrate. She accepted, of course, with a joyful pirouette, and then in a small, reluctant voice, asked, "Should we ask Trevor to come along?"

Before Billy could answer, Rail spared him the anguish, saying, "No, no. You two lovebirds go and have a proper date. I have some phone calls to catch up on. But here, why don't you take my car so you don't have to ride with dirty laundry in some runner's rust bucket? The walk up the hill will do me good."

Now she was glowing. Billy caught the keys Rail tossed at him and opened the car door for her. He was almost in the driver's seat before he remembered to dash back up the steps and lock the studio doors.

Rail felt one of his own psychological levers sliding into place as he watched Billy do this—the satisfaction of knowing that Billy would remember locking the church when he discovered what would be waiting for him inside upon his return. Billy was the only person outside of studio staff who had a key, because the building was also his lodging.

Rail ambled toward the road, but when the taillights vanished below the hill, he turned back and climbed the steps.

The art of lock picking came back to him easily—one of those skills rooted in muscle memory and intuition—even though he had long since moved onward and upward from the simple crimes and cons of earlier years when such tricks were practiced daily. Looking around the empty church, he was reminded of just how far he had come.

It had been a career forged from nothing but gut instinct and the sheer force of charisma. Now that he was a legitimate professional, he saw that many of his peers, producers and entertainment moguls alike, could claim to have invented themselves in similar fashion, but none with the degree of existential heft and artistic flair he had employed in using Billy Moon as a foothold. Perhaps it was akin to the intuition a brilliant stockbroker employed to make a fortune out of a volatile investment.

When Rail had discovered Billy playing scummy dives in Boston, the kid had been a fractured rung at the very bottom of the ladder he intended to climb. And that very fragility (in combination, yes, with the talent of a diamond in the rough, but those were scattered everywhere) had made him perfect—malleable. The kind of diamond that could be cracked from a shell of blackest coal, set ablaze in the heavens as a beacon to a generation of lost souls who felt the same, and then hurled to the earth in a tragic flash to live on forever as legend.

But it had been work. An honest trade would have been easier by far, but what honest venture could contend with the exhilaration he felt in this game that was more than work, this art that was more than game? His great opus: The Rise and Fall of Billy Moon.

Other men could claim to be self-made, but only one in a generation could claim to be the Prince of Lies.

He had created the persona of Trevor Rail for himself and had inhabited that form to guide Billy in the creation of another persona: a dark rock god. He had known from the start that his ultimate aim was not merely to make Billy famous but to make him immortal, like Cobain, who had reminded the world so recently that it could still happen.

Immortality could still happen, even in this transient culture, even among the legion of jaded cynics who hungered for something, anything, authentic, be it even authentic nihilism in a wasteland of calculated marketeering. Billy could be both. The suffering was real in him, the voice true, but the Life and Times, the Rise and Fall, the Final Act could be larger than life in the hands of an artist. Why leave anything to chance, when you could manufacture fate?

Looking around this beautiful room, the state of the art crucible in which he was forging that final act, Trevor Rail brimmed with pride and delight. The end was near indeed, and events were falling into place with a curious grace and symmetry. Some of these auspicious circumstances were part of his plan, but even the random elements could be tethered to his will. The unexpected arrival of the girl, solitary representative of the masses Billy spoke to, showing up at just the right time to put him back on track—that was serendipity.

Rail laughed aloud as he rounded the top of the stairs and strolled down the catwalk toward Billy's sleeping quarters. He idly dropped his left hand into the pocket of his overcoat and felt the small device he kept there at the ready. His ring finger slipped it on with fluid, practiced ease, and for his own amusement he swept his hand from the pocket, licking up a thin sheet of nitrocellulose flash paper with his thumb as he did so. He waved his apparently empty hand through the air, admiring it, then flicked the ignition wheel of the finger-flasher and watched as a ball of fire drifted from his splayed fingers, incinerating into thin air in the gulf between the catwalk and the polished floor below.

Ah, the tools of the trade. The right clothes, the right car, a ten-dollar trick from a magic shop in Brooklyn. Satan at your service.

The primary tool in this game, though, was more difficult to manipulate. If Trevor Rail was an artist, for he felt certain that the creative fire informing his game was the self-same impulse that drove any artist, then Billy Moon was his instrument. Experience had taught him how to put that instrument through its paces: when to push it to a triumphant crescendo, when to detune it with despair and self-loathing, when to tighten the strings to near breaking with anxiety and fear, and when to play the minor key motifs of remorse and regret. Now was one of those times.

In the curtained-off bedroom, Rail found the sort of disheveled mess he had been expecting—clothes, papers and gadgets cast about at random, most of Billy's personal effects spilling out of a suitcase beside the bed. It took some discrete digging to find the prescription bottle of Zoloft. He dropped it into his pocket, patted the black wool and said, "It's no wonder you misplaced your medicine, Billy, living like this."

Billy had once confided in him that he occasionally experimented with going off the antidepressants in order to feel his emotions more acutely, and as a consequence, write more songs. But these trials invariably resulted in unproductive meltdowns. The pills were a necessary evil, Billy had decided long ago.

Now that the album was ninety-percent recorded, a little meltdown would be just what the doctor ordered.

From another pocket, where he also kept the Ruger SP101 Snubnose, Rail took a pair of 3x5 photos and two votive candles. There were two small nightstands in the room, one on each side of the queen bed, each topped with a small lamp. Rail placed one photo on each table, leaning them against the lamps to stand them upright, handling them with the handkerchief they had been wrapped in. Then he took the votive candles by the wicks and set them down in front of the photos, lit them and stood back to admire his work: two faces glowed in the dark room, seeming to sway in the dancing light.

He had acquired these photos in a basement in Boston years ago, had discovered them in a cardboard box that had been packed up by Billy's old friends and roommates after he abandoned them. Maybe Billy's friends had imagined he'd return someday. Rail had known better and saved these two photographs from the fire that would consume the house. The fire that would take three lives, including the two whose faces were preserved here: Jim Cassman and Kate Wilson.

Rail had approached Billy on a bridge. And on the night he found these photos, he had burned Billy's bridges.

He turned to go. The pills rattled in his pocket as he walked. It was unlikely he would cross paths with anyone who would notice the sound, and almost certainly no one who would connect the small tell to Billy, but he couldn't be sure of that. Billy might enlist a runner to try to have the prescription refilled. Small chance of that working out so far from home and without the bottle label, but if said runner remembered the rattle of pills… It was the kind of loose end he found unnerving. He had not come this far by being cavalier about such things.

He went to the little bathroom adjacent to the sleeping area. It smelled of cedar planks and Pine Sol. He took the prescription bottle out, unscrewed the cap, and dumped the little pink pills into the toilet. The empty bottle could be discretely disposed of back at the Mountain House, tucked deep in a trash bag. He flushed the toilet and stood meditating for a moment on the downward spiral. Billy's downward spirals had always ended with him finding his level again. Slowly but surely, equilibrium had returned. Not this time.

He turned to go and heard the voice of Ron Gribbens, the idiot assistant. "Yo, Billy, came back to fetch my bag. You wanna smoke up?"

The curtain parted and the young man's clueless grinning face emerged, framed by those ridiculous sideburns and Buddy Holly glasses. The grin flatlined instantly as their eyes met.

"Trevor," was all the kid could think to say.

Now it was Rail's turn to grin. "Hello, Ron. I would suggest that you learn to knock before barging in, but I suppose one can't knock on a curtain."

"S-sorry. I heard the can flush. I thought it was Billy."

"Billy is not at home."

Gribbens's eyes ticked to the candle-lit photos and back to Rail, then straight down to a spot on the floor. "Sorry," he said again, "I'll go. I just... forgot something and came back for it, that's all."

"Of course, your bag of marijuana. Because we all know how vital it is to the success of a million-dollar project that the technician and record keeper be adequately stoned," Rail said. He stepped forward, his grin widening to the point where he just might burst into giddy laughter, sharing a joke with the class clown.

Gribbens stepped backward, away from the slit in the curtain as Rail glided through it. He waved his hand in the gesture of warding off, of signaling innocence. "No, no, no," he said, "Not on the job. Only after hours."

Rail drove him out onto the catwalk, one slow step after another. Gribbens walked backward, his eyes fixed on Rail, his hand running over the waist-high wooden railing.

"Do you like getting high, Ron?" Rail asked, breaking his predatory stare and casting a theatrical glance over the expanse of space between the catwalk and the floor below. "Because we're pretty high right now, wouldn't you say?"

Gribbens's panicked eyes darted downward and Rail used the diversion to sweep his thumb through his jacket pocket before the frightened little creature could refocus on him.

"I don't smoke on the clock," Ron said. "Please don't tell Eddie I do, because I don't."

"It's alright, Ron. I would be the last one to judge a man's vices," Rail said, dropping his voice to a low drone, barely more than a whisper, as he leaned in closer. "It's not about that."

Gribbens swallowed. "Is it about those pictures in Billy's room? 'Cause I didn't even see them. I didn't see *you* here. How about that?"

"It is about the photographs, Ron. About what I'm doing here. It is very much about that. You see—catching a little runt like you sniffing around my territory is something I do have a problem with." Rail's voice twisted with an anger that hardened the seductive tone like cold water quenching molten steel.

"I swear I didn't see you here. I didn't see *anything.* Just let me go home."

"Maybe you forgot you were here at all. Is that it?"

"Yeah."

"They do say the Devil's weed impairs the memory."

Gribbens giggled, nodding his head, but still walking cautiously backward, matching Rail step for step.

"Perhaps I should encourage your habit then, help you forget."

Gribbens's face darkened with confusion at this new tack.

"Need a light?" Rail asked, waving his hand at Gribbens's chest, a flower of fire unfolding from his fingertips, flaring up in the tight space between them, and rising toward the interloper's astonished eyes with a gentle roar.

Gribbens arched backward away from the fire, threw his arms up to shield his eyes and lost his balance. He tumbled over the railing with a wild cry and fell toward the floor, toward the mic stand that held the upward pointing *tanto.*

Rail watched the body twisting in the air, listened as the cry became a shriek cut short when Ron Gribbens had the wind driven out of him. The blade impaled him through the gut so cleanly that the boom stand followed, running right through the gash.

Rail watched as thick, round globules of blood leapt up toward him from the tip of the knife and then rained back down like hail on the varnished wood floor, pattering and exploding in exquisite starbursts. The spatter was a gorgeous thing to behold from above. The beauty of that knife just continued to unfold. If only Eastman were here to capture it. *Ah, well,* he thought, looking at his wristwatch,

Time to find that Pine Sol.

NINETEEN

Billy fumbled with the key for a moment, finally got it in the slot, and tumbled through the church doors with Rachel draped around him. She was singing his own lyrics in his ear—not a real turn on—and attempting to undress him with less than nimble fingers. For his part, he didn't feel particularly horny tonight, at least not on a conscious level, but his body was showing signs of voting yea anyway as her hands roamed and plucked, chipped black nail polished digits flitting in and out of his shirt and jeans. Then she stopped.

"What's that smell?" she said, suddenly distracted from the task at hand. They were staggering across the floor, which was cleared of the couches and guitar stands that usually covered it, all moved aside for the photo shoot. Billy had noticed the chemical bite in his sinuses immediately upon entering the room. "Some kind of cleaner," he said. They usually come in the mornings before I get up. Looks like they took advantage of the empty floor and gave it a polish while we were out."

"Stinks like a darkroom," she said, wrinkling her nose. "Lez go upstairs. You can carry me, like Dracula."

"I don't think so, baby. It's a pretty tight spiral. How about the control room couch?"

"Fine, be a wimp. I'll climb it myself. Couch sex is pretty lo-fi after a nice dinner," she said, sauntering away from him with a weave. It had been good wine, no doubt, but he was a little surprised to find she had such a low tolerance. Well, she was petite.

He noticed that her trajectory had put her on course for the sole object on the empty floor: the mic stand that still held his Japanese dagger. "Ho! *Rachel*, watch the knife, girl. *Jeez.*" He stepped forward to remove it from the clip and tuck it away somewhere, but now that she was focused on it, she beat him to it and had it in her hand before he could get there.

Holding the knife seemed to sober her. She turned it this way and that, watching the light play over the blade, transfixed. When she met Billy's eyes again, it was with a whole new intensity. "You ever play with this in bed, Billy?"

His heart beat a little faster. "Not really my cup of tea," he said.

She held the tip of the blade to her lips as if to shush him, then gently pulled her lower lip down with it. "I used to cut sometimes," she said. "Acshully, all the time. Not so much anymore. Used to *need* it. Now it's more of a treat."

"That thing's super sharp, Rach. Lemme put it away."

She ran her tongue along the unsharpened spine of it in reply.

"Come on," he urged, "Lemme have it. You're kinda drunk. You shouldn't be playing with knives."

"*I can teach you things,*" she almost sang. Then the knife was behind her back, held tightly in her right hand, the wrist of which she gripped with her left. She solemnly marched up the stairs, grasping the knife that way, where he could see it.

Billy followed.

Watching her pace across the catwalk intoxicated and holding the knife made him deeply uneasy, but as they approached the bedroom, he felt the disquieting sensation increasing at just the moment when seeing her on safer footing should have eased it. Something wasn't right. It was the light. A dim illumination flickered through the white curtain, shifting the tone of the canvas through a range of muted hues. Candle light. He had left no candles burning here, in his private space. What new game was this?

He almost told her to stop, to wait, as if some physical danger must lie on the other side of the curtain, something that even the razor-sharp knife in her hand could not defend against. But he said nothing. He watched as she parted the veil, needing to know.

She hesitated, taking in the room he could not yet see beyond her. Turning to face him, she asked, "Who are these people?"

Billy stepped through beside her, and saw Jim and Kate

looking back at him across the gulf of years. Twin shrines flanking his unkempt bed. Kate was looking over her shoulder, caught in the candid instant before noticing the camera pointed at her. She had always been camera shy, so he'd had just a few photos of her, each acquired on the sly, and all lost in the house fire, along with the woman herself.

He remembered taking this one. The humidity of the summer day on the porch, the yellow jackets hovering in the rose bush by the mailbox. Her placid inscrutable eyes, so soft on that day, somehow managed to pierce him right through here and now. This picture could not be here. He looked again at Jim's photo, this one not candid at all—tie-dyed t-shirt obscured by a big, red disposable cup of keg beer in one hand, face so overly stern and serious as to be comical, chest puffed out, stomach held in for the shot, a prince in the castle they had once shared.

Heat overwhelmed him, flushing into his ears and cheeks from some eternal source, ever at the ready, flooding his eyes with tears in an instant, shattering the unframed photos into splinters of refracted candle light. Suddenly it was all here with him in this unexpected defenseless moment: the profound emptiness at the core of his body, the sorry burden of abandonment and betrayal. Unfinished business.

Worst of all, the firm knowledge that he had gotten what he wanted all those years ago by casting these friends from his heart like worthless cargo from a ship caught in a gale. The treasures he had found on the other shore had been worthless in his isolation. And he had raised anchor again, kept on moving. From the day Trevor Rail had set his course, he had kept on moving. But it was all catching up with him now.

Who had put these pictures here? Was it the ghost who haunted this place? He didn't think so. This smelled like Rail.

Without thinking about what he was doing, he plucked up the photos, walked over to his acoustic guitar perched on the chair in the corner and slipped them between the strings into the sound hole where he wouldn't have to look at them. Where they would be safe.

"Who are they?" Rachel asked again.

"Friends I lost. I told you about Jim."

"And her? Was she your girlfriend?"

He nodded. "Her name was Kate."

"They're both dead?"

"Yes."

"Who put them here?"

"I think maybe Rail. He's been fucking with my head for a long time."

"That's pretty sick. You two have some old feud?"

Billy laughed. "I guess you could say that."

"He said he produced *Eclipse*, right?"

"Yeah. A lot of those songs were about her. Even if I didn't know it at the time."

"That CD saved my life."

He looked at her, really looked at her for the first time since they had entered the room, maybe for the first time since she had entered his life. He said, "Then maybe we're even."

"My step-father used to rape me. By the time I was sixteen I couldn't feel anything."

"That's horrible."

"Then I heard your song 'Empty Vessel' on the radio, in a parking lot, and for four minutes and twenty-eight seconds I could feel *everything*. I can't tell you how many times I played that CD."

He reached out to touch her wrist. She let him. Scar tissue under his fingers.

She said, "I found out everything I could about you. It opened a lot of doors I didn't know were there. Other bands, books, people like me."

"It's good to hear it helped somebody."

"It did. And not just the music, but the artwork, the images. It taught me to look under the surface of things. Everything my mother ever wanted is worthless in the end. No meaning at all in it, all that materialistic crap. But you taught me to celebrate death, because it's the ultimate truth for everyone. And everyone denies it."

"I don't know if I ever meant to teach anyone that."

"Well, you did. And I'm better off for it, because knowing it and facing it, I can finally *live*."

"Is that why you got the tattoo? To celebrate death?"

"Yeah. You like it?"

He touched the Ouija board on her belly. "It's pretty intense.

You ever use it?"

"Sometimes. That's what this is for," she said, touching the teardrop shaped silver and glass pendant that dangled from her black silk choker.

"Does it work?"

"The first time we ever tried it, me and my friend Christine, we called up my Aunt Judy. She's the only one who ever gave a shit about me. It works. Better than a regular Ouija board because, when you think about it, it's written in blood and pain, not just ink." She bit her lip.

"I want to try it."

He wasn't sure what response he expected from her, but when she didn't answer, just clawed at her shirt and crossed her ankles, he realized he had asked for something more personal than sex.

"Who do you want to talk to?" she asked, "Kate?"

Billy hadn't even considered the possibility and the idea chilled him. "No. Someone I've never really met. Her name is Olivia. She haunts this place."

"Really? There's a ghost here?"

"They say she was a witch. Or people thought so, anyway. They say she walked with the Devil in the woods out there."

"You're not lying to me, are you, Billy? Making shit up?"

"Just telling you what I heard. I know it sounds like a campfire story, but I've heard her play the piano, believe it or not."

"I believe you."

"And I caught a glimpse of her on the night you followed me, the night we met in the forest. She wanted me to see something, but I don't know why. And I need to know. I need to ask her, and I can't just wait around for her to come calling. Not anymore."

"Why's it so urgent?"

"Because I've been talking to devils." He breathed a short laugh. "Crazy, right? Even you must know that's crazy. A dead Aunt is one thing, but..."

"Yeah, you might want to keep that one in Siouxsie's cupboard at your next interview."

Billy smiled. "Well, between you and me, I think it's time I talked to someone else who might know the Devil. Someone who can tell me what the hell's going on here. Because I'm just lost."

"And you think Olivia can help you."

"Maybe. Are you game?"

She set the *tanto* down on the bed and touched the pendant in the hollow of her throat again. She lifted it, kissed it lightly, and asked, "Where do you want to do it?"

He led her to the grand piano and put the hood down. He laid a horse blanket over the black lacquered surface and asked her how it worked. She told him she would need candles and some massage oil or other lubricant for the pendant to move freely.

Billy went downstairs to rummage through the drawers and cabinets. When he returned carrying three candles in glass jars (he didn't want to touch the votives that had appeared with the photos) and a bottle of olive oil, she was stark naked except for her rings, studs, and choker pendant. He studied the tattoo: an arch of black letters above her navel, a line of numbers below, the sun on the underside of her right breast with the word YES, and the moon on the left with the word NO.

Billy lit the candles and placed them on the piano. He turned off the green-shaded banker's lamp and watched Rachel lift herself onto the blanketed piano, where she stretched out on her back among the candles. She released the glass teardrop from the choker and placed it in Billy's hand.

"This is the planchette," she said. "Oil me up so it can glide."

Billy rubbed a thin glaze of olive oil over her pale skin from her hips to her breasts. He set the silver filigree framed teardrop on her, just above her navel, point upward toward her face. It was coming back to him now, how this was done on a normal board. Some people called them 'witchboards,' he recalled. His arms broke out in gooseflesh as he placed his fingertips on the base of the instrument and Rachel placed hers on the sides where it narrowed to a point.

She said, "The motion can be intentional at first to get it started. Guide it in a circle around the center like this. Just relax, and when you're ready, ask a question. If she's here, it will start to move by itself and we just hold on lightly."

The planchette traced an orbit around her belly, gliding easily on the thin film of golden oil. The church was dead quiet. In time, the circle widened, and the letters and numbers were magnified by the glass eye as it passed over them.

Billy cleared his throat and said, "Olivia Heron. I want to talk with you. Are you here?"

The planchette shot out of the circular pattern in a straight line to Rachel's right breast, stopping with the silver point aimed at the stylized sun face and the word YES.

"Did you play the organ in this church when you were alive?"

The planchette slid back a few inches along the path it had traveled, then returned to YES.

He still wanted to test this with something Rachel couldn't know. "What notes did you play for me on the piano?"

The planchette guided their hands to the letter D, then moved along the arch of letters, dwelling on each one long enough to emphasize it before glossing over others to pause at the next, spelling out D-E-A-D. Billy reduced the pressure of his own fingers on the planchette as it moved, trying not to influence it, and almost losing touch entirely under the speed of travel. A frisson of excitement tingled through him as the glass eye settled again on the final D.

"Are the stories true? Were you a witch?"

The planchette returned to an aimless revolution around the center of the tattoo.

"Were you accused of witchcraft and murdered for it?"

The planchette shot forward to point at YES again, this time jabbing its silver point into the underside of Rachel's breast. She breathed a short cry that Billy couldn't differentiate—pain, pleasure, surprise, or all three?

"Why did you want me to follow the tracks? Why did you lead me to that place in the woods?"

The lens moved over the letters: TREE.

"The tree by the pool in the clearing? Did they hang you from that tree?"

NO.

"I don't understand. What about the tree?"

ASHES.

"Ashes. Did they burn you?"

YES.

"Tell me about the creature I met in the clearing. The face I saw in the pool. Who is he?"

MY LORD.

"Is he the Devil?"

OLDER.

"What does he want?"

TO PLAY.

"Is he good or evil?"

The planchette glided to the cleft between Rachel's breasts, the space between sun and moon.

"The pictures I found in this church tonight; did you bring them here? Do you know my friends from... the other side?"

The planchette circled before drifting over to the moon on Rachel's left breast and the word NO.

In a quieter voice, directed at Rachel, Billy said, "I don't know if I'm asking the right questions. Does it matter how you phrase them?"

She didn't answer. He looked up at her face in the candlelight. Her eyes were closed, lids fluttering lightly as if she were in REM sleep. The gentle undulation of the tattoo with her breathing had grown deep and slow but her fingers still touched the planchette, her hands still hovered above her flesh.

Billy asked, "The man who works with me here, the one named Rail, do you serve him?"

In answer, a revolution away from and back to NO.

"Did you ever know him before we came here?"

Another revolution ending at NO.

"Thank you," Billy said, relaxing the set of his shoulders, lifting his fingers from the planchette and expelling a quivering exhalation. "That's what I needed to know."

Rachel's hand seized his wrist in a grip so powerful his circulation was instantly cut off, his hand going numb as fear flooded him. Her eyes shot open, no longer hers, wild and intense, feral and feline. She spoke in a voice that was also not her own, the timbre of an entirely different set of vocal chords, the words accented with a dialect he couldn't quite place.

"He followed me to the sacred grove. John Van Buren followed me there, though he had a wife, he watched me always, and he did see my prayers and offerings to the ancient one."

Billy felt chilled to the bone, as if his thundering heart was pumping all of the blood right out of him onto the piano and the floor.

"When I would not lay with him, he claimed I was a sorceress, that I had afflicted him with demons. 'Twas slander and libel, and some knew it. No witch had been hanged since the law of the Crown held sway. But they feared me and hated more than they feared. Hags and their cruel masters. They hanged me and burned my body to ash."

Rachel's nails bit into Billy's wrist, and he struggled to breathe through a throat constricted with fear.

"No consecrated ground for my flesh. No burial at all. They feared that I would blight the crops if I touched the earth. So they fashioned a globe of glass, a witchball, and sealed my ashes within, never to mingle with earth or wind, never again to lie with the Lord of Beasts, never to rest in rain, dirt and dew."

"What do you want from me?" Billy whispered.

"I hunger for life, for sensation. I scavenge where it spills out its heat. I have feasted this night where the one who treads the serpent path lays the joker in a shallow grave, but it avails me not. I yearn to ride the wind, to kiss the earth, to tremble in the reed pipe. And you, kindred soul have come to free me from the hollow tree where I am bound. You must release me!"

And having issued her command, the price of her council, Olivia Heron released Rachel, who in turn released Billy. There was a crashing, dissonant chord from the piano, and the candles went out as if quenched by the power of that sound, their smoke trails rippling in its wake.

* * *

Echo

When the fever broke, she could see the stars through a window. Orion's belt. How long must she have wandered for the moon to be dark? The last thing she could remember was trudging through the creek at the edge of the forest, her skirts muddied and torn, and stumbling into the churchyard where Sarah was waiting for her lesson.

"You're back, ma'am. Oh, I'm so glad you're back. Can you

hear my voice?"

And Sarah was here with her now. A damp cloth touched her head. "I can, child. I can hear you, dear. How long have I been gone?"

"Most of a week, ma'am. I've stayed with you. I begged my parents to let me nurse you, and they did, they let me."

"It was kind of them. You're a good girl, from a good family." She reached out to the space beside the bed, feeling blindly about with her fingers. "Is my…."

"Your accordion, ma'am? Yes, it's here. It's fine. I found it in the woods after I found you roaming. In a delirium you were."

She sat up too fast and her vision swarmed. Memory rushed in and shocked her into lucidity. She took Sarah's hand in her lap. She needed to see the girl's face when she asked. "Did you see anything else in the woods when you found my instrument?"

"No, ma'am. What do you mean? Did you lose something?"

"The forest can be a dangerous place in the winter, dear, when the wolves are about. You didn't see any beasts, did you?"

"No, ma'am."

"And what of me? Have I been talking in my fever?"

Sara looked down at the white wool blanket and bunched it under her fingers.

"You can tell me. I won't be ashamed if I said strange things to you, only I'll be sorry if I frightened or offended you. Sometimes a sickness is like dreaming and we can't control ourselves. It was like that when my husband was taken by the typhoid. Did I frighten you, dear?"

"Mayhap, ma'am. But I wouldn't let anyone come near when you were in such a state. Not even the doctor they fetched from Kingston. I told them you were modest, that I needed to cool you down with ice before I could clothe you to be seen. Only I didn't want them to see… what you did. Or hear your words."

"And the doctor listened to you, did he?"

"He did. I think it was only because I refused to leave your side. He would have seen you naked, but not while I was present, you see."

"And what did I say that you didn't want them to hear?"

"The words were so strange, ma'am. I'm sorry, but they were

in no tongue I never heard before. Monstrous speech, all twisted and dark, and I was so scared they would think it was incantations." Sarah's words accelerated as she told the secret, her voice rising in pitch. Tears spilled from her long lashes onto the blanket as she finished. "You don't know incantations, do you, ma'am?"

Olivia cradled the girl's head in her hand and stroked her long hair. "No, dear, I've never learned any."

"I'm so glad you're back to yourself. I was so afraid for you."

Still holding the back of Sarah's head in her palm, Olivia looked into her eyes and asked, "And what did I do, Sarah? What did my body do while my speech ran away?"

Sarah closed her eyes, squeezing fresh tears out onto her freckled cheeks. She shook her head slowly in denial.

"Tell me, Sara. You must tell me."

"You'll want to confess it and you can't. They can't know."

"Tell me and we shall never speak of it again, I promise."

Whispering fiercely, rushing to get it all out in a single breath, she said, "You were like a bitch in heat. It was horrible, straddling the bedpost or the broomstick or anything you could reach."

"Oh! Forgive me."

"I thought to tie you to the bed, but I'm not strong enough. So I locked the door to keep you in."

"Thank you, Sara. Thank you. You have done me a great kindness, and I am in your debt. I am so sorry you witnessed it."

"When the doctor did see you, he said it was a very strange fever. He never saw its like before and all we could do was give you water and wait for it to pass."

"I should be thankful he didn't try to bleed me."

"I wouldn't have let him. My mum says that it doesn't help and they should know better. But this was a city doctor, so maybe he knew."

"You should go to your mother now, Sara, and tell her I won't be needing nursing anymore. You can sleep in your own home tonight."

"Are you sure you're well enough?"

"Yes, dear. You can visit me tomorrow."

* * *

When the girl had gone, Olivia looked at the stars again, reading the time of night by their positions. The village would be sleeping. No one would see her pass under the dark moon in her black cloak.

She had to go back.

She needed to hear that strange and beautiful music again. The sound of it had been a balm for her sorrows, had been all honey of the sun and milk of the stars in her bones, foam of the blue ocean in her blood, and never mind how grotesque the player, how dark the stench of his presence.

She remembered. Walking the Indian paths, spinning and dancing with her accordion and following the sound of her own echoing melodies deeper into the wood. And then, what she had taken to be an echo unfolded, revealing a counter melody, teasing her with sound and silence, encouraging her accompaniment, leading her deeper into the shadows until she came at length to a sun dappled glade where the mountain creek swirled in pools and eddies at the base of a rowan tree, where mushrooms and wild berries abounded, and bees meandered amid the floating pollen.

There was a face in the shadow of the tree, human only in the most rudimentary sense. The sight of it had flooded her with panic and she fled to the sound of hooves splashing in the water and thundering over the rocks.

Somehow she had escaped, but the music was still with her. Haunting in its beauty.

Her father had been a storyteller as well as a fiddler, but she knew now that one of his tales was flawed. The old sailor had cried a lie when he passed the Palodes in the days when Tiberius reigned over the Aegean. The great god Pan was *not* dead. He had crossed the ocean at the helm of some strange vessel. He had come to the New World and fashioned fresh pipes from the reeds of the Hudson River.

TWENTY

Billy Moon was singing with a gun to his head. The song was "Black Curtain," and the gun was held by Rachel, who was pressing the muzzle of it against the back of Billy's head while he knelt in front of her like a condemned man in a Chinese prison, a microphone on a low stand before him. Jake was watching the meters, thinking that the reels were turning too slowly because the end of this take could not come soon enough. Jake was thinking that this had all gone too far, had crossed a line, was utterly fucked up. Jake was also thinking that the vocal sounded awesome.

> *Are you sick with fear? Then you are not alone*
> *The end is near, I can feel it in my bones*
> *Whispering in my ear 'til the big black curtain falls*
> *The end is near, I can feel it in my balls*

Billy repeated the lines over and over through what would be the fade-out. Jake only had to keep an eye on the needle and a finger on a fader, but he felt like he was driving an eighteen-wheeler through an icy mountain pass. When the beat finally broke down at the end, his palms were slick with sweat.

Rail said, "That's the one. Put a star on it." Then, into the intercom, "Bravo, Billy. Another inspired performance. Isn't it amazing the difference it makes, just knowing it's there? Knowing it's loaded?"

"Yeah. So you got what you need? I can go now?"

"You may go."

Through the glass, Rachel looked sweaty and horny and on the verge of tears, running her hands over Billy's chest, the Ruger now lying atop a wooden stool like just another instrument: a harmonica or a microphone. Billy kissed her, but then gently removed her hands. Jake knew Billy was going to pick up his acoustic guitar like he did every afternoon now and take off for a walk in the woods. Alone. She didn't look too happy about it.

They were in the final days of the project, and it was all about the vocals now, but there were only so many consecutive hours they could expect Billy to perform without diminishing returns, so they had established a routine: mornings were spent tracking, followed by a break for Billy in the afternoon when Jake and Rail would sift through the day's catch, making charts on the dry erase board and marking up lyric sheets with three colors of highlighter. Once the best takes were identified, they would cut and paste a seamless, stellar performance. After dinner, they would play the edits for Billy and then move on to gathering raw material for the next song.

Keeping meticulous notes was crucial now, so Jake didn't know if it was a blessing or a curse that Gribbens had simply stopped showing up for work. He couldn't really blame the guy; after all, he *had* been shot at in the studio, and witnessing Kevin Brickhouse's death was bound to catch up with him sooner or later. Considering the pressures, Jake wasn't even sure if Eddie would fire Ron for going AWOL. An assistant wasn't strictly necessary at this stage, although there were times when Jake wished he could just ask Gribbens what some bit of notation on a track sheet actually meant.

Rail was pushing hard for the deadline, and tension was reduced on only one front during those long days: Billy seemed to have surrendered fully to the producer. He showed up and sang each morning, then vanished into the winter woods. Jake couldn't help wondering if he was out there jamming to the impossible sounds of the pan flute every afternoon as the light waned. Rail showed no interest in what Billy might be writing out there, because whatever it was, it wasn't going on *this* album. Anything new was too late, and anything acoustic didn't fit Rail's vision. Sometimes Jake would stare at the row of blue knobs labeled L ᴾᴬᴺ R, and wonder what Billy's vision was.

Over lunch, while Billy was on his walk, Jake summoned the

nerve to ask Rail a loaded question. In the breezy tone of trivia, Jake said, "You ever hear about the ghost who supposedly lives here?"

Rail glanced up at the loft where Rachel was watching TV. "Of course," he said, "that's why I chose this studio."

"How do you mean?"

"To inspire Billy's dark muse."

"So you believe in it? The ghost?"

Rail said, "Let me tell you something about producing. All that matters is what the artist believes. I believe Billy Moon does his best work when he's fucked in the head. Some people come to a remote studio like this for a safety zone, but we're here for quite the opposite." Rail bit a cherry tomato in half in a way that somehow conveyed that the conversation was over.

As Christmas week dawned, Jake found himself avoiding the apartment. He kept a few things in the church refrigerator and went to work earlier in the morning, the housekeeping staff still cleaning around him as he made his breakfast. At night he would linger after Rail had retired to the house on the hill, obsessing over edits and telling himself it was natural to want his first project as principal engineer to be blemish-free.

God only knew what star mixer Rail would call on to finish the record, and whoever it was would be scrutinizing his work. He should take the time now to make sure he was delivering the best tracks possible, to double-check that the documentation was in order. After all, he didn't have anything to go home to. Not even a dog to feed.

Two days before Christmas, Eddie popped in to check on the clients and to apologize for the absence of the cleaning staff. "December is a pretty dead month for us. Here's my home number. I'm right across town if you need anything."

Rail asked if J.T. would still be available to cook for them.

Eddie scratched his ear and said, "Well, gee, not on Christmas, I'm sure. He has a family. But I'll call him and see if he could do Christmas Eve for you. Bring you some trays you can heat up when the restaurants are closed."

"That would be grand," Rail said.

Turning to Jake, Eddie asked, "Still no sign of Gribbens?"

"No. He hasn't called you?"

"Nope. His brother has an apartment in the city. He's probably

down there drowning his sorrows or something. Christ. Call Brian if
you really need help, okay?"

"Sure thing."

* * *

At four o'clock on December twenty-fourth, J.T. arrived in a
Santa hat. Jake helped him carry the trays and Sterno burners into the
kitchen. It was a perfect spread: carved turkey with gravy and garlic
mashed potatoes, coleslaw, cranberry sauce, stuffing, steamed veggies,
and the best biscuits Jake could ever recall eating.

Rachel turned heads when she descended the stairs from the
loft in a simple black dress, her hair newly cut and dyed black.
Without the goth makeup and blood red mane, she almost looked like
a girl you could bring home to your mother for Christmas Eve dinner.

After J.T. left, Rail went into the kitchenette and returned
bearing a tray laden with four crystal goblets of dark-red wine. His
resemblance to a waiter standing at attention was almost enough to
make Jake laugh, but then the flawless beauty of the crystal caught his
eye. He wondered if Trevor Rail traveled everywhere with them in a
foam-lined metal case.

Rail set the tray down on the white linen tablecloth covering
the farmhouse table. He handed out the goblets, then held his own
aloft. Jake found it unsettling to watch Trevor Rail raise a sparkling
chalice of red wine before a backdrop of stained glass. The moment
must have felt pregnant with poetry for all in attendance because they
laughed easily when he simply said, "To coming in under deadline."

There was scant conversation during the meal, and somehow
the silence made them feel like a real family for a little while. But Jake
didn't trust any of it. To him, it felt too much like the calm before a
storm.

Afterward, Rachel cleaned up. Jake offered to help, but she
shooed him away, so he took the chance to make his exit while Billy
was outside having a smoke under the stars. Jake stood beside him on
the front steps for a moment before asking, "You're not gonna offer me
one?"

"I noticed you stopped smoking after your girl took off," Billy said. "Most people, it'd be the other way around."

"I didn't tell you she left."

"Man, it's written all over you."

"Well, she didn't like me smoking."

"Yeah, it didn't suit you, anyway. I hope her leaving didn't have anything to do with me showing up at your place."

Jake considered telling him that hell yes, it had a little something to do with that, but refrained. After all, the guy was breaking out in a rare case of empathy. He just said, "It might have sped things up a little, but she would have gone anyway."

Billy flinched slightly, or was that just smoke in his eyes? Then something new and sweet occurred to Jake, and he smiled. He asked, "That why you're smoking outdoors now? Because you noticed I stopped?"

Billy shoveled some snow aside with the instep of his boot and said, "Nah, I just like a little fresh air with my cancer these days."

They exchanged a smile.

Billy swayed slightly and said, "Actually, the air's not helping like I thought it would. I'm feeling a little light on my feet. That wine must be good, 'cause I can hold my liquor."

Jake frowned and put a hand out to steady Billy's shoulder as the singer sat down on the church steps. "You've been getting a lot of fresh air lately," Jake said. "How's that going?"

Billy fixed his eyes on the center of Jake's chest and bobbed his head up and down. "Good," he said, "It's going good. *Really* fucking good. I sit there and listen, the flute gives me the melody and I find the chords. I'm getting a lot of songs."

"No kidding."

"Yeah. I'm never gonna let Rail touch them."

"I guess that's good… Billy?"

Billy's faraway stare floated from Jakes chest to his eyes.

"If Rail's the Devil," Jake said, "who's the piper at the pool?"

"I dunno. I think he might be my soul," Billy said with a laugh.

"I don't get it."

"Me neither. But I thought I'd lost my soul, and now, out there in the woods, it's like I'm finding it again. Like, check it out: I can't find my pills, right? Don't know where I put 'em. And it doesn't even fuckin' matter. That should be a *crisis* for me, but I'm doing alright.

Because I found my soul." Billy laughed again.

"I'm happy for you, Billy."

"Thanks, Jake. I talked to the ghost, too. Olivia? She says the thing in the woods isn't the Devil. I think it's Pan—you know the old Greek god?"

"Yeah, I know," Jake said, thinking that Billy was wading farther into the deep end with each step, talking not only to the Devil now, but to a ghost and a god as well. If only his own experience hadn't touched on these possibilities, it would have been a lot easier to dismiss the man as a burnout.

"Maybe Pan was her muse, and now he's mine."

"If it's helping you to look at it that way, and not making you paranoid, then it's probably an okay interpretation of what you're going through."

"Do you think?"

"I do."

"That makes me feel better about it. You're really the only person I can talk to about this. Rachel helped me get in contact with Olivia, but she doesn't remember anything. She was in a trance at the time, and I don't think I trust her enough to tell her what I'm doing out there in the forest."

"Keeping your cards close. That might be wise. You're in a vulnerable place." He slapped his car keys against his thigh to indicate that he was going.

Billy looked up at him and said, "So, Jake. Do you think you could record my new songs?"

Jake laughed and looked at the pine boughs above.

"When Trevor's not around. Just me and my guitar."

"In the woods?"

"No, in the studio."

"When?"

"How about you come back tonight after he leaves? It's still early."

"So much for a night off."

Billy looked down.

"No, it's cool. I don't have anything else going on. I'll come back in an hour or so."

"Thanks."

Jake thought Billy looked pretty stoned. Maybe he was. So what? As long as Billy didn't expect him to go back into those woods in the dark....

At home Jake opened a beer and sat down on a couch that felt far less familiar than the one in the control room. He tried to watch TV. Most of an hour had passed when he looked down at the bottle in his hand. It was still full. He drank some. He remembered breaking up with Lori Vandercross in High School. Every song on the radio at the time had magnified and articulated his suffering.

Now, sitting in the dark apartment in the aftermath of losing the girl he had believed he would marry, letting the photons from their cheap TV wash over him for no other purpose than to keep the silence out, he found he was grateful for the lack of emotional triggers in the flat, dry hip-hop beats and ego trip rhymes ricocheting around the room.

A hot blonde VJ in a Santa hat appeared amid swirling graphics. Jake didn't know what she was talking about. He flipped the channel, landing on a car commercial. Early morning golden sun, winding California coastal road, chiming anthem-rock guitar lines designed to evoke a yearning for wide-open spaces, or more likely a yearning for the sleek black car that was cruising through them. Jake felt a drop of moisture hanging from his nose and was surprised to find that he was crying.

* * *

Snow swirled in the headlights of the Pontiac on the secret dirt road to the studios. The accumulation silenced the already quiet winter woods. For a fleeting second, Jake saw a spotted deer standing at the side of the road when his high beams turned the animal's eyes into violet-tinted mirrors. He startled, pumped the breaks, and fishtailed the unwieldy vehicle.

He sat there with his heart hammering until the deer bounded across the road and into the woods. Having lost traction and momentum in the dead stop, he backed the car up to flatter ground and got a running start on the steep hill up to the church. As he cleared the top, he saw Trevor Rail's BMW still parked under the tallest evergreen, right where it had been when he left.

Jake considered turning around, but decided that would be just chickenshit. Rail might have seen his headlights by now or heard his engine working hard up the hill. He would want to know why Jake was here. Best to walk right in and give an excuse for coming back. He could say he wanted to grab a rough mix cassette of the edits he'd been obsessing over.

Maybe Rail would leave while he was dubbing a copy. But the church looked dark. The stained glass cast a weak, dirty glow onto the snow. It reminded him of the yellow light of dying batteries in a flashlight, struggling and failing to erase the shadows of the guardian pines. Jake was thinking, *That light can't hold a candle to the moonlight*, when it struck him that it *was* candle light.

He turned off the headlights thirty yards or so from the church and parked behind the shed where Buff kept a snowplow, a chainsaw, and some shovels. Hiding the car only increased his anxiety. If Rail found it tucked out of sight like that, no excuse about rough mixes would do. But hiding suddenly felt right.

He thought again about whether or not his headlights had hit the church windows. Probably not. And the snow under his tires would have masked the sound of his approach far better than the usual gravel. Maybe Rail *didn't* know he was here. He opened the car door and immediately realized that he didn't have to worry about being heard. Bass pulsed out of the church loud enough to remind him of the dance clubs in Miami. If he could hear it from here, it had to be deafening in there.

He cut a wide approach to the building keeping his footprints in the shadows of the trees. When he had halved the distance between the shed and the church, he recognized the song. It was "I Know It's There."

TWENTY-ONE

Billy thought he saw a flash of lightning behind the stained glass. Maybe it was in his head. He was not enjoying the game, but he thought it might get better. He felt buzzed and luxurious in his skin. Trevor Rail's voice was small and far away, as if it came to him through the talk back mic in headphones, but he wasn't wearing headphones. In fact, Rail must have been shouting to be heard at all over the blasting pulse of the music. Billy knew he had heard this song before, but he couldn't place the title. It made him horny. Who *was* this anyway? It sounded so familiar. He tried to focus.

A heavy rope swung before his eyes like a hypnotist's chain. But where was the watch? *I Like to Watch*, he thought. That was one of *his* songs. Oh, right! *This* was one of his songs, too. One of the new ones that he didn't care about anymore. Not since he started writing with Pan in the forest.

The rope was tied in an elaborate knot around a pair of wrists. A pair of hands poked out of the coarse bouquet. One of the fingers was wearing his platinum ring, but it looked too big for the finger. Shaggy black hair brushed the collar of a leather jacket. *That's mine, too.* Between the hem of the jacket and a bunched up pair of faded black jeans, a pale ass was exposed in the candlelight. He had the vertiginous sensation of having been pulled out of his body, viewing himself from behind and above. But that wasn't quite right. There was something familiar about the body beyond his hair and clothes.

"Rachel?" he murmured.

"She's not here, Billy!" Rail shouted in his little headphone voice.

Rail stepped between Billy and his doppelgänger, holding another length of rope, which also hung down from the ceiling. He pulled on it with both hands and Billy watched the bound figure before him rise. Rail handed Billy the rope and said, "Hold this tight!"

Billy did as he was told, watching fascinated as Rail picked up a tube of lubricant in his right hand and squirted a glob of it into his latex gloved left hand. Then he reached down and caressed the cleft of buttocks framed between jacket and jeans. Billy noticed his own charcoal-gray boxers stretched between his doppelgänger's thighs. He was surprised to feel the jeans he was wearing tightening around an erection at the sight. He grasped the rope tighter. The rough threads dug into his palms.

Rail smiled at him—the man's teeth looked like a stone wall polished by a sandstorm. "Come on, Billy," he said, "Come on and fuck yourself. Merry Christmas! It's what you've always wanted. Fuck yourself, Billy. Do it."

Billy tugged his jeans free of the button with one hand, the other still holding the rope.

* * *

Jake had found a view of the big room through the kitchenette window—one of the few that weren't stained. It was enough of a view to see that Rail was spending his night off from the job of record producer exploring a sideline as a porno director. Jake couldn't see a camera in the room, but neither did he see Rail's gun, so apparently this evening's festivities were the sport of consenting adults. Billy had probably forgotten all about the acoustic session. He *had* seemed high when he'd asked about it.

Jake felt uncomfortably like a voyeur for watching whatever this weird shit was they had gotten up to after more wine and probably some of Rachel's pot. He was about to go back to his car and head home before the still falling snow made that difficult when he saw Rail tie the other end of the rope into a noose and slip it over Billy's head.

Billy didn't resist. Perhaps he had experimented with this technique before. Even Jake had heard of it, but it was notorious for tragic mishaps. In Billy's present condition, it could not be okay to let him do this. What the hell was Rail thinking? Was he there to spot Billy, or was he trying to kill him?

Jake started for the front door. But as soon as the thought of intervening formed in his mind, so did the image of Rail holding him at gunpoint and tying him up as well. Why couldn't all those candles just set off the fire alarm? That would at least get Eddie up here.

Jake circled the building and considered climbing the tall pine tree nearest the second-story bathroom window. But that was crazy. The branches up top were probably too thin, and he knew his athletic limits. He would only end up badly scratched and covered in sap before having to give up. And time would be wasted. Fortunately, when he tried the side door off the control room—the one Billy most often used to embark on his afternoon walks—he found it unlocked.

There were no candles burning in the control room, but the recessed lights had been dialed down to a yellow-brown haze. The red and green LEDs on the console and outboard gear sparkled like a Christmas tree. The glass doors to the big room were closed, but he could see Billy and Rachel through them when he peered between the speakers, hunched low over the console. He craned his neck until Rail came into view.

Rail was standing in front of Rachel with his latex gloved fists held together before him in imitation of her own bound hands. He was sweeping his hands toward the floor, presumably to demonstrate that she should do the same. But it wasn't working the way Rail intended. Rachel was too out of it to get the instructions, her eyes flickering between a squint of pain or pleasure and an upward rolling motion, her irises disappearing under mascara-smudged eyelids. She didn't look like she could focus on Rail at all.

In frustration, he grabbed her forearms and pulled them downward. High above them on the catwalk, the thick rope slid over the arm of a heavy boom stand weighted with sand bags. The stand acted as a pulley, and Billy was lifted up on his tiptoes by the noose around his neck. The expressions on their faces told Jake that this act of leverage brought Billy deeper into Rachel while simultaneously cutting off blood and oxygen to his brain.

Rail let go of Rachel's arms. They rapidly swung back up above her head as Billy came down again onto his heels. Rail held something too small to make out under Rachel's nose. He cracked it with his thumb and she jolted into a momentary state of alertness—eyes widening, nostrils flaring—and shook her head. Ammonium nitrate. Having restored her to consciousness, Rail demonstrated the mechanism to her again. This time, she took up the rhythm of her own volition.

Rail turned away from the S&M seesaw he had set in motion and walked toward the control room doors. Jake ducked under the console, scurrying as far back into its shadow as he could get. He pulled his knees to his chest just as the doors opened, flooding the space around him with the music from the speakers in the big room. Black slacks and snake skin boots moved into view less than a foot away from him. The music cut out abruptly.

Jake slowed his breathing in the now silent room. The boots stayed firmly planted for what felt like an aeon, during which Jake could vividly imagine Rail sniffing the air. Then he heard the unmistakable click-scratch of the Zippo flipping open and igniting. The pungent, bitter aroma of a cigarillo wafted down to him. He could picture Rail sucking smoke through his cupped fist in that odd, deviant way of his, while admiring the spectacle he had initiated.

A dirty yellow wave of smoke drifted under the console and lingered in the claustrophobic space. Jake's heart beat harder, driven by the certainty that Rail had come in here and muted the music because he had seen him. Was the hunter toying with his quarry, smoking him out of his hole? The involuntary urge to cough seized him. He covered his mouth and held his breath until his eyes watered. Then Rail's snakeskin boots pivoted and strode away.

When he heard the control room doors close, Jake allowed himself to breathe again, daring to believe that Rail was on the other side of them, returning to his game.

After a couple of minutes had passed, he crawled out from under the mixing desk and looked around. The control room was empty. He almost laughed when he thought of telling Rail with a straight face that he'd just been checking a few connections under the hood. Staying low, he scanned the field of buttons, pressed one, slid a fader up, and listened to the sounds of live air, creaking rope, and raspy respiration, picked up by one of the mics in the big room. Then he crouched back down and sat Indian-style under the console, listening.

Rail's voice came through the monitors. "Have you heard the story of Olivia Heron, Billy?"

"Mmm. The ghost."

"Do you know how she became a ghost?"

No reply. Only creaking rope.

"She was the church organist. One night a priest caught her playing lascivious music in the nude. Perhaps he requested a duet and she refused. Word got around town that she had engaged in congress with Satan in return for the gift of infernal song. Are you listening, Billy? Billy."

Jake winced at the sound of a loud slap. It was followed seconds later by the crack of a paper-wrapped glass capsule and labored breathing in fits and starts.

"You're okay, Billy. All of the blood is in your dick. Not much in your head. Feels good, doesn't it? Are you getting that full body buzz?

"As I was saying, Olivia Heron was accused of practicing witchcraft, and a very rare event occurred right here in this church as a consequence. The priest performed an exorcism. A *failed* exorcism. The rite lasted seven hours. When the sun cleared the horizon in the morning and it was determined the Devil had not loosed his grip on the girl, they ended it by hanging her. Right here in this room. And I know this because I was there. D'you take, my meaning, mate? I was right here when it happened."

Billy mumbled something. It might have been "liar."

Silence for a while, then the seesaw sound of rope creaking in rhythm. Jake wondered if Rail was assisting Rachel again.

"History repeats itself, Billy," Rail said. "But sometimes the echoes of history cancel each other out. Tonight, we complete a circle. Only, on this darkest night of the year, our ritual transforms the noose, the instrument of fear and hatred, into the stimulus for ecstatic union.

"This is it, Billy, the ultimate act of unabashed self-expression: fucking yourself in defiance of the very grip of death at your throat. Isn't it what you've always wanted? Isn't this what the stadiums full of adoring fans are a substitute for? The need to love yourself? *Such* hunger for others to love you, to fill that hole. And now, it's my gift to you. Embrace your darkest drive, Billy. Rock-and-roll always has. That's the glory of it.

Do you know what instrument Nero played while Rome burned? The chittara, a forerunner of the guitar. And they said he was the Antichrist. The same sound seduced you as a boy, the sound of six strings. Those timeless vibrations of shameless lust and aggression. Are you getting off on what I'm saying? *That's* it. Put your hips into it. The sound of *power*. The sound of *fire*. Harder! The sound of Holy Fucking Thunder. Now rock harder!"

The control room doors swung open. Jake froze. He watched Rail's boots come into view again, moving swiftly this time, motivated by his own rant. Jake felt sick at the thought of Rail noticing that the mic was on, noticing the controls he'd changed. Then the music came blasting on again at distortion-laced maximum volume. Rail left again, this time leaving the doors open in his wake.

Jake ventured a glance around the side of the console just in time to see the front doors of the building swinging shut on a flurry of swirling snow beyond the pumping, swinging spectacle that was Billy and Rachel.

Was Rail going to get something from his car?

He took a step into the big room, feeling terribly exposed. Now he could see that Rachel was standing on one of the milk crates they sometimes used to raise guitar amps off the floor. He thought of the gloves Rail had been wearing. Had the ringmaster left this high stakes freak show to run its course and look like an accident?

He scanned the room. On the table in the kitchenette, the Japanese dagger lay tangled in the silk scarf Rachel had once used to blindfold Billy. God only knew what other games had preceded this one. Jake seized the knife and ran to the interlocked couple with it. They took no notice of him. Rachel's eyes were closed and Billy's were turned upward and inward. The rhythm of their sex was now labored and drowsy. Billy weighed more than Rachel, but if she collapsed, if she fell off of that crate, he would hang.

Jake slid his left hand between Rachel's bound wrists, catching the rope with the web between thumb and forefinger. He pushed it up, raising her arms above her head, taking her weight off Billy's end. Holding her up like that with one hand, he sawed at the rope with the knife.

Highbeams flared in the windows—Rail pulling out onto the road. Thank God.

Three times the blade slipped. Sweat trickled from Jake's hair into his eyes. Coarse threads sprung from the rope in clusters, but sawing was taking too long. He drew the blade back beside his ear and placed his trust in its flawless geometry. He slashed, the rope severed, and the lovers fell.

Jake removed the noose from Bill's neck and checked them both for breathing. They were sprawled on the floor in a semiconscious state that might soon become sleep, but they were both alive. He draped a pair of packing blankets over their partially naked bodies before collapsing onto the couch. He looked at the ceiling, where the rope still dangled from the boom stand on the catwalk, pressed his palms to his eyes, and sighed with relief.

"Oh, man, she's right," he said to himself. "I do not get paid enough."

In a little while, he checked on them again. Feeling more confident that he didn't need to call an ambulance, he pulled the rope down, coiled it around his elbow like a microphone cable, and brought it out to his car, where he tossed it in the trunk just for the comfort of knowing it wouldn't be instrumental in any more mischief. Then he drove home in the snow, hoping it would continue to accumulate through the night and cover his tracks.

* * *

Billy woke up on the floor in the ashen light of dawn. Rachel was sleeping on the couch, wearing his clothes. He slipped the platinum ring off her finger and put it in his pocket. She didn't wake.

He ran his fingers through his stiff hair, then felt his throat. Touching the bruised skin caused enough pain to tell him everything he needed to know without a mirror. It wasn't a dream. He felt like he had a bad case of the flu. His head was cloudy, his tongue, cotton. He drew a glass of water from the kitchen sink and drank. It hurt to swallow. Then he fished in the pocket of the leather jacket Rachel was wearing and found his cigarettes. He lit one and pulled a drag. The result was twofold and entirely predictable: he had a coughing fit and his head cleared.

He pulled on his boots and an inadequate hooded sweatshirt. Outside, the virgin snow glowed golden in the creeping morning light. Individual crystals sparkled with rainbow colors as he turned his head, taking in the silent landscape. The powder crunched under his combat boots as he waded through a knee-high drift between the church and the woods. Under the cover of the trees, the accumulation was much less, just a few inches. It would be an easy walk to the pool. Not that it mattered. He would have trudged through chest-high drifts to meet his daemon on this Christmas morning.

Although their exchanges had been wordless, hours spent in a dialog of flute and guitar, he brought no instrument with him today. Today there would be no music. Today they had something to talk about. Billy Moon wanted to make a deal. By the time he was on the path he knew so well, his extremities felt colder than he thought they should in such a short time. Maybe it was fear contracting the blood from his limbs. He couldn't predict how the creature would react to his request.

As he approached the clearing, he was stopped in his tracks by an impossible sound—the voices of birds. Not crows, December's lingering scavengers, but the sweet, varied chirps and trills of the migrators who would not return until April. Billy couldn't tell one kind of bird from another but he knew enough to be unsettled by their chatter. He knew *these* birds had no business here on a winter's day. He kept walking, and a few paces on, a dragonfly crossed his path, soaring in a wide arc around a gnarled oak. It hovered at Billy's elbow for a brief inspection before continuing over the white ground, weaving between the dripping black branches of the trees.

A warm breeze that should have smelled only of wood smoke or nothing in this time and place lifted his hair, bearing the clean fragrances of peat and honeysuckle. Soon, a green mirage shimmered between the sparse trees.

The stand of naked birches through which he glimpsed the clearing soon revealed one or two among their number bearing clusters of leaves. Stepping between them, Billy found that trees closer to the glade were even more profusely aroused from hibernation. Oak, sycamore, even flowering dogwood were not merely budding, they were cloaked in rich garments of green, swaying in the balmy breeze. All Billy could think of to make sense of it was that it looked like the opposite of a bomb site. Every step closer to ground zero—which he knew to be the pool— brought him out of the dead winter terrain of skeletal black and gray, and deeper into the epicenter of a green explosion.

He pulled a limber branch aside and stepped into the clearing, eyes widening, breath quickening.

The creature sat on the mossy tree stump where Billy himself had so often perched these past two weeks. In that time, he had only caught fleeting glimpses of the enigmatic piper in the wood, fragments like those even Jake had seen. Now here the creature was, revealed at last: shaggy legs stemming from cracked cloven hooves, olive-toned muscles bronzed by the sun, ancient dirt detailing every line of the powerful hands, noble face draped with a curly black beard wherein ruby beads of wine or blood glinted like dying stars in the fraying fabric of uttermost night, eyes veiled by drooping lashes, hair a mane of frozen fire swept back between ridged horns, serpentine cock undulating in the shadow of the reed syrinx flute laid across his lap.

The pool, which on Billy's previous visits had always been black, now cast a limpid sheen on the trees, radiating shafts of green and gold light from its heart. The creature looked up from the hypnotic dance of light in the water, and as those lazy lidded eyes passed over him, Billy saw in them the same luminous hues of green and gold that danced in the pool.

His right knee started shaking. He knew performers, some of them very successful, who got weak in the knees with stage fright. Something about coming face to face with such a primordial creature in the flesh was triggering a similar response in him. As was his usual practice with fear, he bypassed it by stepping through it without giving himself time to think.

Billy said, "Are you Pan?"

The sound that arose from the creature's throat only resembled speech in the consonants that broke the drone into familiar shapes. The vowels were modulations of a waterfall after a heavy rain, October wind through the hollows of a lightning blasted tree, the sigh of a millstone dropped down an endless well. The creature smiled and said, "I am Pangenetor, the bornless one. Some call me Silenus or Faunus."

Billy said, "The melodies you've given me. Why did you play them for me?"

"To play is bliss."

"Is there another reason?"

"No!" The leaves on the trees trembled, casting off golden morning light like spinning coins. "How could there be more than the bliss of creation?"

"But I thought..." Billy felt his knee shaking again and forged onward, "I thought you wanted me to record them, so that the whole world could hear our music. I've been making false music all this time, for a cruel master."

"The Liar."

"Yes. And I thought..." Billy sighed and said, "I wanted to ask you... if I did what you wanted, would you help me be rid of him? But now I don't think I know what you want."

Pan laughed. The sound would have tickled a needle on a Richter scale. "I want nothing," he said. "I am."

Billy thought about that for a moment, and said, "But you want to play, right?"

"I play, I slay, I lay, as the urge arises. There is no want."

"I need you to help me kill the Liar. Will you help me?"

"Begetting and devouring are equal pleasures."

"Why haven't you killed me?"

"To play is bliss."

"I was going to tell you that I would destroy the false music and record your music, if you would help me."

"Do what you will. I have no use for frozen music."

"Will you help me kill him for the joy of it?"

Pan smiled. "For the joy of it, yes. He has masqueraded as a cheap perversion of what I am. Bring your master to your monster and we shall play."

Pan gazed into the pool for a moment with a look of faint amusement on his craggy face. He said, "There is something else you must bring."

TWENTY-TWO

When Billy arrived back at the church and climbed the stairs to the loft, he found Rachel watching TV and biting her nails.

"Rock-and-roll camp is over," he said to her and climbed into bed, still wearing his hoodie. He pulled the comforter over his head, curled into fetal position, and was soon engulfed in sleep.

When he woke, it was dark and Rachel was sleeping beside him. He sat up and blinked. Had he really burned up the whole day? How long had he slept? It was dark by four in the afternoon now, so it might not be *that* late. But he knew it was. He wouldn't find Rail and Jake downstairs still working, and that was good because he had awoken with absolute clarity about what he had to do.

Sleeping in the hoodie had glazed him with sweat. He tugged it off in a tangle with his T-shirt and threw the clothes on the floor. Wearing only his jeans, bruises and tattoos, he walked barefoot across the catwalk and saw the studio was dark and empty below. He went down the spiral staircase, opened the control room doors and stepped into what felt like a gem-flecked cave of red, green and amber lights.

The multi-track tape machine in the corner was more brightly lit than the rest of the room, emitting the yellow parchment glow of the VU meters, their needles all lying dormant. Billy went to it. He took one of the boxed master tapes from the shelf above the machine—he didn't care which, didn't even read the song titles listed on the spine. He removed the reel from its box and threaded it through the rollers and capstans as he had so often seen Jake or Ron do. Then with both hands, he punched in all of the RECORD READY buttons, four at a time until 24 red lights were lit. All tracks armed. He pressed PLAY and RECORD and watched the big wheels roll.

There were five master tapes. Billy had erased two and was

starting on the third when he heard the doors open behind him.

"What are you doing?" It was Rachel. "Are you recording something?"

"I'm recording nothing."

"What does that mean?"

"I'm recording twenty-four tracks of nothing."

Rachel picked up the tape box and read the song titles in Gribbens' neat hand. "You're *erasing* it? What's wrong with you? Stop. Stop it!"

Billy held a hand out to keep her away. She shot out her arm under his, too quick for him to stop her. She slapped blindly at the surface of the machine. Billy pushed her back and tried blocking her like a basketball player, hoping she wouldn't remember there was another STOP button on the remote control tier near Jake's chair. Finally, he stopped her flailing by seizing her shoulders, pressing her arms close to her body, and looking into her eyes.

"What do you care?" he said.

Still struggling, she said, "How can you even ask me that? That's your best work. You think I'll just stand by and let you destroy it?"

"It's not my best. You just want to be able to tell everyone you were here when I did it."

"Is that what you think I am? *My* performances are on there, too, you know. I got you off, so you could get into it. I'm your fucking muse, and I have as much right to stop you as Rail."

Billy released her at the sound of Rail's name. He uttered a sardonic laugh. "Oh, you don't want to be in league with him. He's a sick fuck. Don't you know that? This album isn't mine; it's his. It's his baby, and we're just his pets. I'm his trained canary." Billy's voice had risen, spittle flying as he ranted. He no longer needed to physically restrain Rachel; his intensity was enough to hold her at bay for the moment.

"He's been sucking me dry for years, sucking my soul out, and leaving a husk. Mutilating my music and feeding his fortune with my fame. How can you be on his side after what he did to us last night?"

"What *we* did, Billy. What *we* did last night."

Billy felt a growing revulsion for her. "He put something in that wine. He tried to kill me and make it look like an accident."

"Don't overreact. We're taking your creative process to extremes. Don't back down now."

He took his hands off her and stepped back in horror. She lunged for the buttons, and he sloppily threw his weight against her, knocking her to the floor with him. A chair rolled across the room and crashed into the wall. The tape reels continued their slow revolution. Rachel found her feet again. She launched herself from the floor, threw the double doors open, and ran to the wooden support beam where the fire alarm was mounted.

Billy couldn't figure out what she was doing until she had already done it. As he watched her pull the alarm, he felt the bottom drop out of his stomach. A siren rose from the vented metal box high in the steeple. It wailed across the silent woods.

* * *

Jake woke to the ringing of his phone. He plodded into the kitchen in the dark, and answered.

"Jake, it's Eddie."

"Yeah."

"The fire alarm went off at the church."

"Kay."

"Your client's not answering the phone up there."

"Um… I'm going. Okay, I'm going. I'll check it out."

"Thanks. I'd go myself, but you're a lot closer. If it's a false alarm, call the fire department right away and then call me."

"Got it."

"Go!"

There was no fire Jake could see when his car jumped out of the snow-laden trees at the top of the hill. The church was dark. He exhaled hard; he'd expected to see the place ablaze, considering how things had been going. He left the engine running, headlights focused on the front door, and ran through the misty beams and into the church.

The big room was empty. The siren blared overhead. In the murky light of the control room, Jake saw Billy standing at the tape machine. Several disturbing aspects of the scene struck him simultaneously. Red lights on the machine. Lots of them. All of them. Rachel strapped to his chair with what looked like an entire roll of duct tape. Racks of effects-processing gear overturned on the floor amid a litter of ashes and cigarette butts.

Billy said, "I know what I'm doing, Jake. Go home."

"Stop him," Rachel said. "You have to stop him! He already

erased some of the tapes."

"Jesus, Billy, is that true?"

"Two down, three to go."

Jake stabbed the STOP button on the remote tier. Nothing happened. The reels behind Billy kept rolling.

"I unplugged it," Billy said.

"You can't do this," Jake said.

"Sure I can. It's my dime, right? It all comes out of my advance."

"Billy, I know you're under a lot of stress. I know Rail's a psycho, I truly do. But you're right, you're burning money, man. A lot of it. You've been here for two months filling those reels. You *owe* them a record. Don't screw yourself."

"I'm done with my contract, whether anyone likes it or not, and it's none of your business anyway."

"None of my business? Then what *is* my business? I've spent every waking hour on those songs. If you do this, I may never work again. For fuck's sake, Billy. *Please.* Think about someone besides yourself for once."

Jake took a step forward.

Billy swept up a razor blade from the surface of the tape machine and waved it back and forth in the space between them. "Get back!" he barked.

Jake shifted his weight to the right and looked past Billy's right arm, then lunged to the left. The feint wasn't good enough. Billy brought the blade around, ripping Jake's right forearm open with a ragged gash that traveled from four inches above the wrist all the way to the elbow before the half-dull blade fell from his grip.

Blood sprayed the stainless steel face of the machine and splattered the meters. Jake fell to his knees and Rachel screamed. Billy stood back, eyes wide.

Jake held the bleeding arm against his stomach, soaking his T-shirt through with blood. With his good arm, he reached up over his head and clawed at the big square buttons. There was a loud mechanical clack, and the tape stopped rolling.

Billy's eyes blinked rapidly and ticked from side to side. He looked like a trapped animal. Then he touched his smooth bare chest where droplets of Jake's blood were running in little ribbons. It brought him back to his senses, and he ran to the bathroom to grab a heavy towel. He knelt beside Jake and stanched the wound.

Rachel said, "Jesus, Billy, is that thing even clean?"

"Yeah."

"Cut me out of this chair, so I can help."

Billy ignored her and kept pressure on the wound with both hands. Red roses bloomed on the plush white towel. Jake unclenched his teeth and spoke through white lips, "Call the fire department."

"What?"

"Tell them not to come, there's no fire. Button's labeled on the speed dial."

When Billy was sure Jake could keep the pressure on by himself, he got up and made the call. Then he knelt beside Jake again and said, "I'm sorry. I didn't mean for it to go down like this. I just lost it."

"Yeah, you did."

"Does it hurt a lot?"

"Like a motherfucker. But I don't think it's deep. There's a first-aid kit under the sink in the bathroom."

Billy ran for it.

Rachel said to Jake, "You probably need stitches, you know. You shouldn't have told him to call off the fire truck."

"I'll be okay."

Jake got to his feet and staggered into the big room, holding his arm in what had become a bright red bundle, dripping blood on the floor every three steps. He typed a code into the keypad on the support beam. The siren stopped abruptly, its echo circulating in the rafters a second longer. He sat down at the picnic table in the kitchenette. Billy came in and laid the first-aid kit on the table, sat astride the bench, and popped the latches on the little metal box.

Jake winced as he pulled the towel away from the wound. It was a good gash; there was no denying that. If the blade had been sharper, he might have been better off, but it was one that he had used a few times to splice tape. Billy got busy cleaning and dressing the cut with trembling hands and fierce concentration. Jake pondered the fact that magnetic tape was made mostly of rust particles. Would that mean he might need a tetanus shot? He guessed not.

Billy said, "You should have stayed put and told me how to kill the alarm."

"Let's just hope it didn't wake up Trevor at the Mountain House."

"For someone who was trying to stop me, you don't seem to want the cavalry to show up," Billy said, wrapping a tight band of medical tape around the already dimly stained gauze pads on Jake's arm.

Jake's voice was shallow when he said, "You don't have many friends. I want to at least know what the hell you're thinking before things get out of control."

Billy opened his mouth to say something, but the sound of an approaching car engine left his jaw simply hanging. He sprinted to the front door and locked it. He crept back to Jake and said, "We'll pretend I'm sleeping until he goes away."

"Rail? How do you know it's him? And who's gonna believe you slept through the fire alarm?"

Billy held his forefinger to his lips.

Jake turned the palms of his hands upward with a raised eyebrow: *what do you want to do?* It hurt to twist his arm that way and he winced. He whispered, "My car is parked out there. One of us has to answer the door. You should—"

There was a loud triple knock on the heavy door.

"Go and roll Rachel into the bathroom," Jake said, and then added uncomfortably, "Tape her mouth first. And get the reel off the machine fast."

The knock came again, harder.

"Throw it under the couch, if you have to. Go!"

Billy started to move, then froze at the sound of a key in the door. He stared at Jake, eyes wide. Jake waved Billy aside to where the door would block him and his blood-streaked upper body from view. The bolt went *CLOCK!* Jake reached the door and pulled it open five inches, stopping it with his foot and keeping his bandaged arm behind it. He stuck his face into the gap.

Eddie was standing there, hand on the handle, scowling at him, white hair jutting out at odd angles over his baggy eyes. He said, "What the fuck, Jake? You didn't call me."

"Sorry, Eddie. I called the fire department. There's no fire."

"I can see that. What's going on?"

"Uh… Billy and Rachel are getting a little wild, that's all. Private Christmas party, so to speak."

"Who's Rachel?"

"She's sort of his girlfriend."

"Why are you all sweaty? You look like shit, kiddo."

"Yeah. I, uh, rushed up here. I'm fine. Intense project. But no worries, they're not trashing the place or anything. Just horsing around.

Pulled the alarm by accident."   *

"Really? You sure they weren't burning anything? Those detectors will take a lot of bong boiling before they go off."

"Yeah, everything's fine, really. I should grab my bag and get out of here. They're not exactly decent."

"I see." Eddie couldn't help peering past Jake's head. "They keep goin' with you around?"

Jake shrugged and said, "I'm like the butler; they're used to me. You should go home and get some sleep, Eddie. I'm just going to move a few mics out of the way, so they don't get knocked over, then I'm outta here."

Eddie put his hand on the door (it was a big hand) and pushed it toward Jake slowly but firmly. Jake's boot slid two inches. Eddie said, "You're being a good soldier, Jake. All that stuff about confidentiality... I know; you heard it from me. But there *are* limits, believe it or not."

"Really? There are?" Jake said with perfect sincerity.

"Why don't you tell him to throw a robe on. I'll talk to him."

"No, it's cool. It's not like they'll be at this kind of thing again. Project's finished, actually. Rail wrapped early. I think it's their last night here."

"No kidding. Well, they're still paying for the full week they had booked."

Jake shrugged.

"I'll call Trevor in the morning," Eddie said, stepping back from the door and removing his keys.

"G'night, Eddie. Merry Christmas."

Eddie nodded and gave his best effort at a smile. It was weary, but it looked almost affectionate. "Merry Christmas, Jake."

Eddie walked back to his jeep, stopping to reach into Jake's car and turn off the still idling engine. "Save you some gas," he said with a wave. Jake closed the door and latched it.

"That was close," Billy said.

Jake turned to face him, his heart racing, the pain in his arm momentarily eclipsed by emotion. He said, "You know this is insane, right? Destroying your work, risking my job, attacking me... I can't believe I just told you to gag Rachel."

"That was a good idea, dude."

"Shut. Up."

"Man, the shit she's into, I'm sure it wasn't the first time."

"That doesn't make it okay!"

Billy put his hands up and stopped talking.

Jake took a moment to breathe, then said, "I just basically told my boss everything is okay and the project is done. Man, I am so far from right in the head." He took a good hard look at Billy and said, "What are you going to do?"

Billy sat down on the couch, craned his head back and looked at the ceiling. He said, "I'm gonna finish erasing the tapes. It'll take a while. Then I guess I'll let Rachel go. Seems she's on his side. She'll go right to him when I cut her loose and then the shit will hit the fan."

"That's your plan?"

"Yeah. Pretty much."

"Great plan. Totally self-destructive."

Billy nodded and couldn't keep from smiling.

Jake even chuckled. "Well then, I'm going home," he said. "It's clear I'm not talking you out of anything." He picked his jacket up and carefully slid his wounded arm into the sleeve.

Billy said, "Jake, that's not really all. There's one more thing I need to do tonight. But I can't do it alone."

"What's that?"

"You're right. I do need to deliver an album by the deadline."

"Billy, there's no way."

"A solo acoustic album. We'll still have a few hours before dawn. You want to produce it? Make a lot of money," Billy said with a grin.

Jake stared at Billy. Then he said, "Tune your guitar. I'll try not to bleed on the console."

Jake brewed coffee, lit candles and set up two mics. Billy erased the remaining tapes. It would be the kind of session that was about one thing only: capturing the truth of the moment. No click track, no edits, no overdubs. Just a songwriter and his guitar in the big wooden room. As the hands on the clock and the reels on the tape machine turned, Jake felt the conviction growing within him that whatever Billy had destroyed earlier that night, it was no great loss because *this* incandescent revelation the singer was pouring into his mics was the real thing. They worked until the salmon-tinged light of dawn appeared, smudged across the cloudy horizon. Soon after, Jake drove down the snow-packed country road with the new master tapes in the trunk of his car.

TWENTY-THREE

Billy went to the shed and found the little gas can Buff kept for the chainsaw. He used it to soak a couple of sponges he had taken from the housekeeping supply closet. Then he cut Rachel loose. She slapped him hard as soon as she could, tried to storm out without a word, and stumbled when her leg cramped. She punched his shoulder when he tried to help her stay on her feet. Then she rubbed her calf until it loosened up, holding the middle finger of her free hand aloft for him all the while. When she did leave, she slammed the door. Billy estimated it would take her at least a half hour to climb the hill to the Mountain House in the snow. That didn't give him much time to get ready for Trevor Rail.

* * *

The red sun in the southeast was a dim bloodstain on a white sheet when Billy pushed through the front door of the church. He carried a stack of heavy master tape boxes that came up to his chin. Watching the steps for ice, he plodded down to the ground, took as many steps toward the woods as he could manage with his freight, and spilled the boxes onto the snowy ground. He puffed out three misty breaths, bent over, opened the lid of one of the boxes, and removed the aluminum tape reel, holding it in both hands like a cake on a plate. He examined it, rotating it until he found the light blue strip of low tack adhesive tape that kept the reel from unwinding. He pulled it off and ran a few feet out, the thick brown ribbon dangling in the snow.

Even a single reel was heavy, and he was feeling weak from

lack of sleep. This was not going to be as easy as he had imagined. He looked around until his gaze settled on a low tree branch—smooth, strong, dead, and only a couple of inches in diameter. He went to the tree, snapped off the branch, and poked it through the hole in the reel making a kind of spindle that reminded him of World War II films he'd seen on the Four O'Clock Movie as a kid. Some foot soldier expert in demolitions would run from a dynamite-packed bridge with a spool of wire, letting it out as he dashed to meet his partner with the detonator pump.

Billy wrapped the loose end of the tape around the little tree in a crude knot. Then he took a ziplock freezer bag from his pocket— fumes overwhelmed him when he opened it—and removed the gasoline-soaked sponge. He placed the sponge on the tape reel, securing it to the metal flange with a piece of duct tape. Then he picked up the reel by both ends of the smooth stick and walking backwards, watched the reel spinning on its wooden axle, letting out gasoline-coated tape. When he felt confident it wouldn't snag and snap, he altered his grip so he could walk facing forward with the tape unwinding behind him.

He crossed the partially frozen creek, where it was necessary to throw the reel across and pick it up again—tiptoeing over the stepping stones without his arms free to balance him would have surely meant falling in. He left a few feet of tape twisting in the chuckling water and forged on into the woods. Over mossy boulders and fallen oaks, he plotted a meandering course to the little glade he knew so well.

The reel got lighter as he went deeper into the forest. Eventually he was able to jog. When it ran out, he threw the empty metal spool into a thicket and ran back to the church with the stick in hand to get another full reel and pick up where he'd left off, tying the tape ends together and trailing the brown ribbon deeper into the woods, emerging more winded each time until he was hacking up phlegm, spitting it into the snow and feeling mounting dread upon each return, a growing certainty that this time he would meet Trevor Rail on the path. He needed more time.

Yet every time he went back to the church and didn't encounter Rail, he felt not only relief, but growing puzzlement as well. He knew Rachel would be fetching him for revenge—she had gone off in that direction. And this stunt was taking entirely too long. Once she reached Rail's lodging and roused him, it would be a short trip down the hill in the Beemer. But there *were* other houses on the studio grounds, and until she found Rail's car she wouldn't know which one he was in. If Billy was lucky, she might be trudging up the wrong driveway right now. *Or, she might be noticing smoke from his chimney, which would be a real giveaway since none of the other cottages are occupied.*

Three master tapes were enough to make a trail all the way from the church to the clearing. When Billy reached that familiar place, it was winter there again and the little round pool was a sheet of black ice. His heart sank, but there was nothing to be done. He had to keep moving on faith that the creature really did exist outside of his imagination, and would appear when needed, and that somehow this showdown between the devils on his shoulders would give him a way out. There was no other path to take.

When he got back to the church for the third time, he tossed the remaining tape boxes down the shallow ravine toward the creek and kicked snow and dead leaves over them. He smoothed over the disturbed track with more snow. Even though all of these tapes were now erased, Rail wouldn't know that. It would only waste time if Rail thought he could salvage something.

Billy stood still for a moment and listened. Was that the sound of a car engine on the air? He climbed the church steps. There was just one more thing he needed.

* * *

Trevor Rail pumped the brakes, cranked on the wheel, then gunned the gas, jetting away from the trees he had almost crashed into, and back onto the snow-covered dirt road. This was more like skiing than driving. The car wasn't made for it. Well, at least he didn't have to listen to that little tart screaming. He had driven away to the sound of her hollering, knowing better than to bring her along, sensing that her usefulness was spent. He shot out of the trees at the bottom of the hill, aimed the car at the church and skidded to a stop just short of hitting it.

Climbing from the leather seat, he reached into the deep pocket of his trench coat and wrapped his fingers around the grip of the Ruger revolver.

The chaos of boot prints near the church took on some coherence when he saw the tracks leading toward the edge of the woods. They led him to a tree where a length of magnetic tape was tied like a ribbon. His nostrils flared at the sight of the tape trail winding away through the woods. Rachel had got him moving when she said that Billy erased some of the tapes, but the extent of his losses was still unclear. Did Billy know how to wipe the tapes clean? Had he pressed all the right buttons? Did Rachel know what she'd seen? But this—seeing one of those tapes stretched and knotted and dragged through mud—was too much. The hours he had slaved over these tracks. Did the little shit think this was some kind of game?

Rail held the gun up and fired a single shot at the sky. Crows took wing. He bellowed at the top of his lungs, "Biiillaaay! Come out! Come out here right now and I may show some mercy."

There was no answer from the church or the forest. Falling pinecones and melting icicles patted against the ground. That was all. He leapt across the creek and bounded into the trees, following the tracks.

* * *

Sitting on his tree stump, Billy heard the shot crackle across the sky, but not the ultimatum that followed it. Now it would be soon. He walked to the edge of the pool and tested one of the overhanging branches of the rowan tree to see if it was strong enough to take his weight. It was. Holding onto the branch above his head with both hands, he swung his feet out over the pool and stomped on the black ice with his boots. It didn't even fracture. He regretted not bringing the axe from the tool shed.

He returned to the tree stump where his guitar case lay on the wet ground, popped the latches and lifted the lid, revealing the wine red Les Paul he had favored from the age of sixteen. He'd found it on the used rack, already bearing some of the character-building dings and scratches that it would acquire over the years. It had been waiting for him like a pound puppy at the music shop in his hometown.

In the years that had passed since, he had subjected the guitar to two world tours and many more treks across America. Now it was a relic, an old warhorse, well beyond what you could call 'broken in,' yet it remained his favorite. He owned guitars that were better by technical standards (and many that were far more expensive than what he'd paid for this one back when a kid could still get a real Gibson with the savings of a hard-working summer) but this one still held a tune and screamed and wept and roared like no other. This one had his blood and sweat in the wood. This one had the years and the songs in its wiring.

And somehow Pan had known about it, had told him to bring it here today, even though he had only ever brought his acoustic to the pool in the past. Was that further evidence that the creature existed in some dark part of his own mind? Had the psychedelic years fractured him, rendering a laughably familiar archetype autonomous? If that was all that was happening here, there was no sane course of action.

The only way forward was to continue operating under the assumption that Pan, god or devil, phantom of his psyche or beast in the flesh, knew what he was doing. The goat man had told him to lead Rail to this place and had told him to bring the wine-red guitar. Could that have been just so he could use the heavy mahogany instrument to crack the sheet of ice? Why not just tell him to bring an axe? Why didn't the creature thaw the ice himself, if he had any powers? It made no sense.

Sure, players referred to guitars as axes , but what the hell kind of practical sense did that make when a gun-toting madman was on your trail? Was Pan misreading his mind and drawing unfortunate metaphorical conclusions about what would serve him? Maybe, but he had a strong suspicion that the sublime and terrible god would not give a shit about what served Billy Moon's personal interests, because maybe Billy was himself just an instrument. He hoped he was an instrument the goat man was fond of.

Forcing himself to stop thinking—it would only slow him down now and possibly paralyze him with doubt—Billy took the guitar from its case and went back to the edge of the pool. He held it by the neck, close to the body—no need to swing it like a real axe as Townsend or Cobain had done for theatrics. He raised the heavy guitar and dropped the butt end of it on the ice, driving the strap peg like a spike. Hairline cracks radiated outward from the point of impact. He raised the guitar and brought it down again. This time the ice shattered into pieces, and black water splashed up onto the red wood.

Billy didn't know what good it would do, but it felt right. It felt utterly necessary. He reflected that this was the same strategy he had employed for most of his life—doing what *felt* right—and it had only led him to his present predicament. On the heels of this observation, another voice inside him, inarticulate and deeply buried, spoke up in contradiction: something about ambition and calculation being his prior guide, something about how following his feelings was a recent development and he shouldn't flatter himself with a romantic and selective memory. He shut it down, walked to the tree stump, sat down on it, and set about tuning the guitar, mostly to distract himself from those inner voices.

The familiar feeling of the guitar neck in his hand soothed him a little. When it was back in tune, he strummed a couple of chords. Without an amp, it was barely audible in the open air. The urge to put it down and flee the site was intense. What exactly was he doing sitting in the middle of a snowy wood with an electric guitar, waiting for a sociopath to come and kill him?

Twigs snapped in the underbrush.

Billy looked up and saw Trevor Rail in a black trench coat and muck-covered boots marching out of the naked trees, gun in hand, eyes ablaze. An unexpected wave of calm washed over Billy. The waiting was over. He took a cigarette from the velvet pick compartment of the guitar case, lit it and took a drag. His calm deepened.

"Are these the master tapes, or is this just some dickless stunt?" Rail asked.

Billy blew smoke in his direction by way of reply.

"Are these the masters? Answer me!" Rail yelled.

Billy just looked at him.

Rail did a little pirouette with his hands held aloft, the stainless steel gun barrel shining on high, and his trench coat fanning out at the bottom. He laughed at the sky and said, "Of course. Of course they are."

Billy thought, *A drama queen to the bitter end.* Then he said, "Don't worry, Trevor. The weather can't hurt them."

"Why, pray tell, is that?"

"'Cause I already erased most of them. Only, I didn't have time to finish. This one here at the end might still have 'Language of Love' on it. That's the hit single, right?" Billy drew on the cigarette, then reached down and touched its glowing orange tip to the tape. It ignited immediately, shriveling in a line of flame that ran through the trees like a mythical salamander, disappearing in an instant as the fuel was consumed.

Rail aimed the gun at Billy's heart. He said, "You're insane, Billy. I've always known that. So why can't you be crazy enough to kill yourself? You're so fucking close. Why do I have to do it for you?"

Billy only shook his head and tossed the butt into the snow. Balancing the guitar on his knee, he pulled the platinum ring off his finger, held it up to his eye for a second to look at Rail's puzzled face through it, then flicked it off of his thumb like a coin into a wishing well. It spun through the air in a little arc, catching the light, and vanished with a *plunk* into the pool, lost between the chunks of floating ice.

It took a few seconds for the incomprehension on Rail's face to morph into rage. Even after all of the rebellion, he still did not expect Billy to be so bold as to think he could break their contract that easily.

Rail slipped out of his coat, letting it fall to the ground around him so that he appeared to be standing in his own black pool. Still holding the gun, he tugged up the sleeve of his red silk shirt to bare his left arm. The gesture was aggressive, determined, radiant with grim resolve. He walked to the pool slowly, each step a threat, each step a testament to the seriousness of the violation.

He knelt beside the water and looked at Billy. He said, "I thought I could work with you. I thought I could make you great, but you don't have it in you. I *enjoyed* scaring the hell out of your father the night he died at his shop. I thought just maybe you'd get a good song out of it. But no. Because you don't give a fuck about anyone after all. Well, you're married to the music, Billy, and you're going to die with that ring on your hand. You're going to wear it in your coffin and it will hang on your finger-bone when the flesh has rotted off."

Rail reached into the water. Something shifted in his face when his hand kept going deeper, past the point where he had expected to find the bottom of a shallow puddle lined with dead leaves. He reached in deeper, submerging his shirt to the shoulder. Billy marveled at the man's determination when the freezing cold water reached his armpit but Rail seemed not to register such a trifling discomfort. His jaw was set, his eyes locked on Billy. His other hand pressed the gun against the ground for leverage.

Suddenly Rail's body jerked, seized from below the surface of the pool with enough force to slap his chest and face into the water. When his head struck the surface, he squeezed the gun, firing a shot at Billy. He bobbed up from the water, wet strands of hair plastered across his brow like a web work of black roots through which his eyes beamed pure terror.

He was wrenched forward again, harder this time and fell face-first into the pool, submerged up to the waist, his legs kicking and scrambling at the muddy ground, trying to dig in, to find purchase, to anchor his body. He dropped the gun and scratched at the ground, took hold of a thick root. Pulling on it, he wrested his upper body from the water. As he did so, the root ripped out of the frozen ground but did not snap. He muscled into it. Slowly his face withdrew from the dark liquid followed by a grotesque mirror image: the face of the horned god, locked with him in a bloody kiss.

Pan emerged from below, third eye blazing electric blue, ripe lips drawn back revealing yellow fangs that were pierced through Rail's bottom lip, peeling it away from the man's gums. Pan's tongue writhed in the space between them, catching the stream of blood that flowed from Rail's mouth.

Rail screamed through torn lips—a high, distorted shriek braided of equal parts pain and panic. He let go of the root, and pounded his hands against the ground. He found the gun, squeezed the grip, shoved the barrel against the creature's head—only inches from his own—and pulled the trigger. His arm recoiled with kickback. A spray of gray matter, bone fragments and blood-clotted fur erupted from the other side of the creature's head. The force of the shot tore the fangs from Rail's lip, shredding it to ribbons. Thick blood poured from his ragged mouth, gushing over his chin.

Pan, however, did not bleed from the bullet hole. He merely reached into the cavity with an earth-encrusted claw and plucked a piece of brain tissue from the smoldering wound as if he were clearing wax from his ear. He flicked it away, let out a seismic peal of laughter, then licked the blood from Rail's chin with his thick, purple-veined tongue, reaching behind the man's head as he did so and raking his claws through the dense black hair like a ravenous lover.

Rail's scream hit a new pitch, fraying his vocal cords with the last reserves of air from the bottom of his lungs. Pan shifted his weight, pulling his prey back down into the water. But before Rail's face touched the surface again, he put the gun to his own head and fired it. Blood spattered the gnarled trunk of the ancient rowan tree.

As Trevor Rail's limp body collapsed with a splash into the shallow pool, Pan morphed into a twisting cloud of black smoke, which hovered in the air for a moment, and then scattered on the wind.

Billy Moon stirred from his awestruck paralysis. He looked down at the Les Paul in his lap and the .357 slug that had broken his D string and bored into the dense mahogany between the two pickups.

He laid the guitar in its case and buckled the latches. He stared at the blood spray on the tree at the edge of the pool. Following the gray trunk up toward the sky, he caught a glimpse of sunlight flaring out from a hollow where the bark bulged as if a bees' nest had altered the growth in that place. He went to it, stepping around the body of Trevor Rail, and saw that the hole in the tree contained a blown-glass sphere on a nest of dead leaves and feathers. He reached in and took it in his hand, felt the weight of the thick, bubbled glass—the witchball, in which the ashes of Olivia Heron swirled and settled like flakes in a snow globe.

Billy had never cared for sports as a child, but that hadn't stopped his father from making a dogged effort to teach him how to throw a ball. Spying a stand of tall, thick oaks not far off, he said, "This one's for you, Dad." He wound up and let the ball fly with all the speed and power he could muster. It shattered against the rough bark with a loud crack, dust coating the tree at the point of impact and billowing out in a little cloud. The ashes drifted toward the ground, then were lifted on an updraft of gentle wind. The forest sighed.

TWENTY-FOUR

The police questioned Billy for just under nine hours. Long enough to give him a wealth of opportunities to contradict his original story. Long enough even to riff on the good cop/bad cop routines he'd seen so many times on TV. But ultimately, detectives Stark and Cronk needed only the first fifteen minutes to determine two things: one, Billy Moon was not right in the head and two, he was lying or omitting something in his account of how Trevor Rail had accidentally blown his own head off trying to kill a bear that had wandered over and attacked him while he was waving his favorite gun around to illustrate some creative differences he was having with his artist in the middle of the woods at ten in the morning.

When word got around the coffee maker that the dirtbag in Interrogation 2 was Billy Moon, yes *the* Billy Moon, someone must have made a phone call because by noon Echo Lake, normally a sleepy town between Christmas and New Year's Day, was a traffic jam of news vans, camera men and talking heads. And it wasn't just the local Catskill stations. Due to the town's proximity to New York City and the fact that it was a slow week for news, all of the networks, plus CNN and Fox, had a presence on the scene.

By the time Los Angeles rolled out of bed, the speculation frenzy was in full swing. Danielle Del Vecchio spilled her coffee on the floor when she flipped on the little TV in her kitchen and heard that Billy Moon had kidnapped a teen-aged girl (who was going to do an exclusive with Larry King the following night), tried to burn down a legendary recording studio, and was now being held for questioning in the shooting death of his producer.

The phone rang. It was Don Lamar, president of Gravitas Records.

"Danielle. Holy... Shit. Danielle. What the... Fucking *fuck*, Danielle? What the hell is happening in New York? And why are you here? If he needed a baby sitter, you should have been there."

"So I could get popped in the woods for Christmas, too?"

"Maybe you could have prevented this, made sure he was properly medicated or something."

"You give an artist room to create. Let's see, who told me that? Oh, right, *you*. Don't try to make this my fault. We don't even know what happened."

"*Happened?* He went batshit crazy is what happened."

"Well, you know, if I was locked up in a cabin in the snow with Trevor Rail, I might have a breakdown, too. I'm going out there on the first flight as soon as I can get a couple of lawyers up from New York to keep him from making this worse."

"This could be worse?"

"Yes, Donnie, it could be worse. He could incriminate himself, if he hasn't already. Do you even give a shit about Billy, or is he just your cash cow?"

"Of course, I care for Billy. Hey, are you sending those Jews who ran it up my ass on his tour negotiations? *That'd* be good. Billy'd be a free man and the State of New York would be bankrupt by this time tomorrow."

"Hey, watch your mouth; you're talking to a Jew. I'm getting him the best criminal lawyers you can afford."

"Oh, is that right? Then you better shut your Rolodex and open the *Yellow Pages* because I'm hearing on TV that 'sources close to Rachel Shadbourne are claiming that Billy *erased the master tapes*.' Who the fuck is Rachel Shadbourne?"

"I don't know. Don't believe everything you hear on TV."

"If it's true, Danielle, I'll hire those two circumcised pricks of yours to pump Billy from both ends, I swear to God."

She thumbed the talk button, cutting him off in mid rant, then immediately pressed it again and started calling friends and associates back East while getting dressed. Forty minutes later she had arranged legal counsel to sit with Billy at the police station until he was charged or released. If he was released, they knew which hotel to sit with him at until she arrived.

* * *

Billy stuck to his story about the bear. He repeated it like the chorus of a hit song to anyone who wanted to hear it. And he sang the same tune to anyone who wanted to know what else he had in his repertoire: to the police, to his lawyers, and, after midnight, while partaking of the mini-bar in her room, to Danielle. He was shaken by what he had seen and was harboring some deep doubts about the very lax laws reality had been abiding by in his general vicinity lately, but he still knew for sure that talking to detectives about devils, ghosts and pagan gods might get him an insanity plea but it wouldn't preserve his freedom. He would avoid prison only to end up in a mental hospital.

His lawyers spent the day reminding the police that they didn't have any evidence against him. Little by little forensic results came in that concurred. The gun was registered to Rail and bore only his prints. There were no traces of weapon discharge on Billy's hands, and the angle suggested self-infliction. It didn't help Billy's case that they'd found no bear tracks in the area, no bear scat, and no sightings by the rangers now combing the woods, but it was evident that some kind of animal had chewed up the man's face.

It might have been a scavenger that showed up post-mortem while Moon was calling the police from the studio. In any case, the lawyers were already suggesting that their client could have invented the bear as a diplomatic solution to the problem of his longtime friend and professional partner killing himself. Perhaps he was in denial and really believed he had seen a bear. He was, after all, sleep deprived from the grueling sessions.

Detectives Stark and Cronk released Billy Moon at a quarter past eight that night on the condition that he would remain in Ulster County for the next three days. Cronk told his partner he had a gut feeling they would be officially arresting Moon at the Holiday Inn before the first twenty-four hours was up, after the lab geeks had more time to chew on the data.

But the next day came and went, and so did the one after that, with no breakthroughs in the case. The geeks all seemed fascinated by the utter freakishness of their findings when they explained that trajectories and powder burns all painted a picture consistent with the victim shooting himself. There were those damned bite marks on his lower lip that didn't match any known species of bear, but neither did they match the dental mold Moon let them take during his nine-hour interview. He was free to go. Cause of Death: accidental self-inflicted gunshot wound to the head. That much became fact, the rest remained mystery.

* * *

Billy flew home to San Francisco. He left his gear to be packed and shipped by Jake and the runners, with the sole exception of the red Les Paul, which he'd bought a seat for and carried on the plane. Until the day he flew home, it had rested in its case beside the control room couch where he had set it down before calling the police. Billy wasn't quite sure he knew why he had taken an electric guitar with him into the woods that day. Because the Devil made him do it? That excuse was starting to feel a little worn out. Because the spirit of the wood, buried in his poet's heart, disguised as a horned god by his tired mind, had deigned to save his life?

Maybe.

He had, in rare moments, felt that some songs had a life of their own—that they were hatched whole in the ether, merely waiting for someone with a guitar and pen to catch them and set them down. There had been far too few of these in his career, until perhaps recently. Guys like Dylan seemed to have a better butterfly net.

Still, he knew what it felt like to catch one and to be sure that he had no claim to the title of creator. It felt like being a vehicle for some greater voice. So maybe the god of song worked in strange ways. Maybe he rewarded the scribe with a commuted sentence every now and then, on a whim. Maybe God was a hoary old goat who liked wine and women and something you could dance to. Some sane people believed stranger things.

Billy restrung the Les Paul and hung it on the wall of his writing room, glad he hadn't told the detectives about it. They would have wanted to dig the slug out. He wanted to keep it.

Jake hadn't been around the last time Billy went to the church to pick up his guitar and pack his suitcase, but Eddie gave Billy Jake's home number and they talked one more time before Billy flew home. As soon as he heard Jake's voice, Billy regretted that it was only a phone call and not face to face. He was calling from the airport while he waited at the gate.

He'd wanted to go to Jake's apartment but was afraid of drawing attention to the kid if there were still reporters lurking around. Jake's last name was still unknown to the media because Rachel had never bothered to learn it, and the paparazzi didn't need to know that Billy had an interest in the address. Nonetheless, after all they'd been through together, after drawing blood from the kid, this felt like a shitty way to say good-bye.

"How's your arm healing?" Billy asked.

"It's fine, just itches a little."

Billy didn't know what to say next, but he stayed focused on Jake's interests, even though he had a favor to ask. "I asked Danielle to go to bat for you and squeeze a higher engineering fee out of Gravitas. So you should be getting a fat check."

"Okay."

"They would have tried to shortchange you since it's your first time and they know you're hungry for the credit, but Danielle's good; she'll get you what you deserve. Besides, they don't want you talking to the media."

"I wouldn't do that anyway."

"Yeah, I know that, but they don't."

"Well, thanks. And there can't be a credit if there isn't a record, right?"

Billy laughed, sending a short burst of distortion through the line. "True," he said. "They're still a little sore about that."

"I imagine they would be. They have nothing to show for what they're paying me, and that's still nothing compared to what they paid Eddie."

"Yeah, well... They're looking into having Bob Ludwig master your rough mixes just so they can put something out while there's a buzz."

There was silence on the line for a beat. "Don't scare me, Billy. They're not good enough. That's why we call 'em *rough*."

"It never crossed my mind I'd need to destroy those too. Now Danielle has them. It's out of my hands."

"Billy, they can't put it out like that."

"Well, they might. I thought you should hear it from me. I kinda don't think they'll do it, but right now, they know they could sell almost anything with my name on it."

"*Almost* anything?"

"Anything dark and fucked up."

"So not the acoustic record at the back of my closet."

"I wanted to talk to you about that."

"I'm listening."

"I'd like you to keep sitting on that. Forget about it for a while. The company would shelve it anyway, but if they knew I recorded it on their dime, I could never release it on my own."

"You can't be sure they wouldn't put it out if they heard it."

"They'd shelve it just to spite me after what I did. Think about it. They wouldn't let me produce my own record, they made me work with Rail because they wanted something heavy and dark, something consistent with my image. That's the image they think they can market. Now more than ever."

"I guess so."

"Now that I'm a hot topic, they'll want more of the same. They wouldn't put the acoustic stuff out unless it was the last thing I ever recorded."

"If they decide not to release the roughs, do you think they'll send you right back into another studio in L.A. where they can keep an eye on you? Crank out something quick with another producer?"

"Probably try to."

"What'll you do?"

"I don't know, but I won't do that. I don't have it in me."

"Well whatever happens, take care of yourself, Billy. No one else will."

"You too, Jake. It was good getting to know you."

"Hey, Billy, can I ask you something?"

"Shoot."

"What would you do if you didn't have to worry about what other people want from you?"

"Hmm. Good question. I don't know, man. I'd be an asshole to complain about my lot. I got what I wanted and most people don't."

"That's why I'm asking. Is it still what you want? I don't know what I want anymore and I'm just getting started. It looks like the sacrifices in this business are big ones, and maybe the freedom isn't really freedom at all."

"I know what you mean. I can't even go to the supermarket or take a quiet walk in the park. I've seen the world, but I haven't really seen it. I've seen dressing rooms and airports. They all look pretty much the same. Maybe I'd go somewhere no one knows me. Someplace I've never been, and really see it, hear it, smell it. Get outside of myself. That's what I'd like to do: get outside of myself, get away from everything."

"Sounds escapist."

"Hey, you ask an honest question. This way of life look sane to you?"

"No."

"So maybe the urge to escape it is healthy."

"Could be."

"My uncle taught me my first three chords. He spent some time in India. Had some stories to tell. Maybe I'd go there or the Mediterranean islands or something. If I can ever get released from my contract."

"They were ready to drop you a few months ago. Now they won't let you go."

"Yeah. My biggest problem is I keep getting what I think I want."

After talking business, the conversation dried up. Billy tried a few stabs at inquiring about Jake's life outside of work, but they both knew he didn't have one. In the end, there was simply a hesitation on the part of both men to end the call. They felt like blood brothers now, soldiers bonded by a friendship forged in painful and confusing circumstances, now saddened that those circumstances were all they had in common. Both seemed to sense that when they hung up, it would be the last time they ever talked.

It was.

* * *

Jake showed up at the main building at ten in the morning the following Monday. Eddie was on the phone as usual. He looked Jake over as he wrapped up the call, then waved him in to the office and told him to have a seat. "What are you doing back so soon? I figured you had about two weeks' worth of sleep to catch up on."

"Actually, I wanted to give you two-weeks' notice."

Eddie grinned and said, "Jake, you handled yourself well in an ultra fucked-up situation. If you've had enough, you don't have to sit around inhaling solder fumes for two weeks. When two people die on your project, you're excused. I'll give a good reference to anyone who calls."

Jake looked out the window at the snowy woods.

Eddie said, "If you need the money, you can hang around and do busy work. Do you?"

"Not really."

"Well then catch the first Greyhound outta here."

Jake laughed. It was a joyless sound.

"Do you know what you're gonna do?"

"I'm not sure yet. Go back to Florida for starters."

"Call me before you skip town. We'll have a beer."

But Jake didn't call; he just loaded the Pontiac with his scant possessions and dropped the apartment key in his landlord's mailbox with a check. He didn't have any idea what he was going to do next and didn't think telling Eddie that over a beer would make him feel like anything but a quitter. All he had to show for his brief moment of glory was a heap of student loans and two albums that couldn't be released.

Eddie was a true studio vet. The man had burned out years ago, and still he kept going. Surely he'd seen his share of overdoses and mind games. And even though he hadn't piloted a console in a long time, he still fed on the urgent energy of the place and seemed to loathe going home at the end of business hours. That Jake was opting out of a future that was Eddie's life seemed like a distance that couldn't be bridged, even for a drink. What would they talk about, sports?

When Brent the runner asked Jake why he was leaving the job, the best he could do to explain the move was to tell him, "You may find that records are kind of like hot dogs. You enjoy them a lot more before you know how they're made."

* * *

Back in Florida, Jake crashed on the couches of various friends for a few weeks. His old buddies were happy to see him and curious to hear his story, but respectful that he wasn't ready to tell it. He circled ads for apartments and went around looking at them in the afternoons. Even though his stint at Echo Lake had been relatively short-lived, it still took some time to get used to the absence of the encircling mountains on the horizon. It was also strange to not see a million stars at night.

The check from Gravitas found him, and he was able to rent a small apartment in Winter Park without having to worry that it might take a while to find work. The place was nice, with a mango tree and a little back yard. Maybe he would get a dog after all.

In the months that followed, Jake adjusted to civilian life. Sleeping at night, going out in the daytime, listening to the radio, and following the news. In June of that year, Shawn Fanning launched Napster at Northeastern University in Boston. It would be some time before Jake found out what that was all about, and by then the rug would have been pulled out from under the music industry before anyone knew it was even being tugged.

In less than a decade, artists would be giving music away for free instead of suing for copyrights, bands that used to fill stadiums on their own would be teaming up for double bills in smaller venues, and most of the big studios, including Echo Lake, would be shut down. In the end, Billy Moon would be among the last of the big rock stars.

Jake put off most of his unpacking, living out of boxes and digging for things as the need arose. It wasn't that he didn't have the time, he had all the time in the world, but he just didn't know if he was staying or only squatting until he figured out what was next. When he finally did make a focused effort to unpack, he found the journal that he and Ally had shared. That night he forgot to eat and stayed up late reading it.

After a short bout of restless sleep around dawn, he waited for the clock to reach a decent hour and then nervously dialed her parents' house. Her mother answered. When her tone remained warm even after he'd said his name, Jake found himself breathing easier. She put Ally on the phone.

"I'm back in town," he said.

"Really?"

"I'm living right back in Winter Park."

Silence.

"Could I see you some time?"

"Yes," she said so fast it overlapped with the end of the question.

* * *

Her beauty was amplified by absence. Especially when she smiled through her sadness. Sitting with her in a big wooden booth at an old favorite restaurant, he didn't care that he didn't know what to do with his life. There was this one thing he knew. Everything else was just details. He couldn't tell her that, not yet, so he talked about what he could remember from reading her journal entries.

She'd forgotten her own jokes from some of the earlier pages and hearing them now made her laugh and then cry a little. Then they both were crying and wiping their noses with the two paper napkins they'd been allotted, then swiping more napkins from a vacant table and holding hands. Neither one cared if they were making a scene.

* * *

Jake didn't cry again until two months later in September, watching the evening news. The lead story was about a victory for the tobacco industry in a state appeals court, next up a story on a recall of SUVs for a faulty fuel sensor. Jake was scarcely paying attention to the newscast in between chatting with Ally, who was chopping zucchini and summer squash in the kitchen. The majestic here-comes-a-commercial-break music climbed to a cadence under a panning shot of a small Coast Guard vessel below the Golden Gate Bridge, and Peter Jennings said, "When we return… rock singer Billy Moon is missing and presumed dead today, after a fall from the Golden Gate Bridge."

Jake sat bolt upright, flipped to the other networks and found synchronized commercials in progress, then flipped back to ABC where the inane sales pitches seemed to go on forever.

When the program resumed, a headshot of Billy filled the swirling graphics-framed square over the anchorman's shoulder. This was soon replaced by another face Jake recognized: Flint.

TWENTY-FIVE

It is the witching hour in San Francisco. The city is as close to sleep as it will come this night—the club hoppers have thinned out to the few with real endurance or chemical assistance, the working stiffs and early morning joggers have not yet risen. The bridge is quiet, traffic slowed to an intermittent drizzle of headlights across its pale maroon girders. A dense cloud of fog swirls in the cables like a tsunami hovering over the deck of a battleship.

A yellow convertible sports car cruises through the fog. Flint is driving. He will later tell the police that Billy Moon called from the back seat for him to pull over—he wants to take a piss off the most beautiful bridge in the world because you only live once. The bass player in the passenger seat will confirm this quote verbatim. "His exact words, dude." Was Mr. Moon drunk? the police will ask. Maybe. Yeah, probably a little drunk. They are driving him home after a session at an undisclosed Bay area studio where they have been writing and recording an album. The A&R guy has asked Billy's band mates to escort him.

There are no other cars on the bridge, and it does look beautiful lit up in the mist. Why not take a moment to enjoy the view? It's quiet up here, and it looks like Billy really does have to piss; he's bouncing up and down in the backseat, rocking the little car around. As soon as the car comes to a full stop, Billy jumps out and climbs the railing. His friends shout at him to get down. He holds a thick metal cable and leans out over the bay like a pirate in the rigging, moisture beading in his long black hair. A wave of fog sweeps over him and when it clears, he's gone.

They call his name. They tell him to quit fucking around. It's not funny. There is no reply. Flint calls 911. He passes a breathalyzer. He can't say if Billy fell or jumped.

Was he depressed lately? Sometimes, sure. But that's just Billy. Besides, he hated the record they were making.

Both of the musicians agree to drug tests. Remarkably, they come back clean. The police stop short of polygraphs because the two have no motive for pushing the singer, and their stories match perfectly in private interviews. The victim has a history of mental instability.

The body is never recovered.

EPILOGUE

The postcard appeared in Jake and Ally's mailbox one morning in early March, among the bills and equipment catalogs. Jake removed the rubber band from the bundle, plucked the one friendly looking item from the financial jetsam that had washed up on his little island this fine morning, and examined the image on the card. It was a photograph of a Himalayan mountain goat perched on a craggy cliff. Jake flipped it over. The postmark was smudged, but the stamp said NEPAL. The few lines of handwriting were in a slanting scrawl that reminded him of lyric sheets he had once handled.

Dear Jake,

The Greek isles were beautiful. Nepal is truly awesome. Next stop, India, where I plan to stay a while. Found your address at an internet café in Kathmandu. Hope you are well. You can put it out now. Buy a nice house. Burn this.

B

The End

CPSIA information can be obtained at www.ICGtesting.com
Printed in the USA
LVOW081321221012

303920LV00002B/1/P